LAST WORD

CARDINAL SINS BOOK 4

HEATHER LONG

BLAKE BLESSING

FOREWORD

Dear Reader,

We're here. I wish I had something pithier for you than we've made it, but here we are. The fourth and final book in the Cardinal Sins series is in your hot little hands right now. Clearly, if you have not read the first three books in this series, probably a good idea to go back to Kill Song and read that.

For everyone else? Let's continue.

Previously in Cardinal Sins, Cash worked with Fletcher, Rick, and newcomer (old contact) Horatio to track down Vienna. They managed to get to her just after she'd freed herself from captivity and torture by Sandra Jane. Exhausted, and wary of Cash being out of his cell, Vienna agreed to Horatio (who it turned out she also knew) to clean up the scene for her. While her lovers were happy to have her back, Cash was a volatile element in the cocktail of their relationship. He and Vienna clashed, but they eventually figured it out and because he wouldn't stop pushing her, they tracked down a location where they found… her father?

That's sort of a really small thumbnail of High Note, but it should give you enough to go on. A number of you have expressed appreciation for that recap, and if it helps, we absolutely don't mind doing it.

After three books of build-up, we are so stoked to share the twisted conclusion to the Cardinal Sins series. There were some twists and turns we didn't quite expect. There were also more than a few characters who popped up (or in some cases just strolled in).

We will warn you that as in previous books, this novel does contain graphic violence, depictions of human trafficking, sexual violence, as well as some scenes involving physical and psychological torture. This is very much a dark romance with emphasis on both the dark and the romance. We do try to inject some funny as well.

Please use caution and protect yourself.

Now for the short bit of business. This is a why choose/reverse harem which means the heroine is not going to have to choose at the end of the story.

Oh—and since this is a series, there will not necessarily be an HEA at the end of each book, but we do promise to sort out one by the end.

Probably.

Mostly.

Well, you know what? Just trust us!

xoxo

Blake & Heather

P.S. We love your reviews, your comments, your posts, your edits, and your TikToks. From Booktokers to Bookstagrammers to readers in our groups, you're all the best. Thank you for joining us on this adventure.

P.P.S. Give this to all your friends and make them read too. *winks*

PROLOGUE

CASH, AGE 23

I SMOOTHED a hand down my shirt to where it was tucked in my slacks as I climbed out of the car. Today was the day.

My first day as an official FBI agent.

I'd graduated college at the top of my class and after almost a year of rigorous testing and background checks, I had finally joined the Bureau. A sense of accomplishment settled on my shoulders as excitement filled my chest, knowing I'd soon be working my own cases.

If I'd expected any kind of praise from Pops, I would have been sorely disappointed. I almost snickered to myself. His nod when I was introduced to the team was good enough.

Us Morgan men weren't the emotional type anyway.

For my first day, Pops had snagged me to be his tagalong. And the team had agreed to allow him to help me get my feet wet as he checked in with some of his informants.

I was stoked. All my life I'd wanted to follow in Pops' footsteps. Work the unsolvable cases. Save people. But most importantly, uncover hidden puzzle pieces to see the bigger picture.

It was all about the puzzles and the patterns.

"Who are we meeting this time?" I asked as we left the parking lot of the park and moved deeper under the trees. This park was a decent size for a small midwest state. Big shade trees provided some semblance of privacy.

People were scattered throughout the park running with their dogs, watching their children play, or lounging on a blanket having a late lunch.

Pops pointed to two benches situated caddy corner to each other. I sat down on the end closest to the other one, avoiding the white bird shit on one of the slats. I would wager the informant would take the other bench and I wanted to be in the thick of things.

"Here," Pops said as he handed me a sub out of a sandwich bag. An Italian with extra seasoning and oil and vinegar. My mouth watered as I unwrapped it. Hopefully, he had some bottled waters in that bag to wash it down.

I had finished off half the sandwich when a man of medium-tall height distractedly walked our way. Dark hair, bright eyes, and decent if cheaper clothing all made the man less than remarkable. If you didn't see the intelligence shining from his sharp eyes…

From the way Pops' frame tightened on his approach, I knew this was our guy.

Except Pops grinned as the man took a seat next to me on the other bench.

Pops never smiled at anyone. I scratched my cheek as I studied my old man. He didn't like most people—period. Hell, I barely thought he liked me some days.

"Thad, it's great to see you."

The man nodded his greeting and pulled out his own homemade sandwich in a plastic baggie. "Morgan." He took a bite of his sandwich and slowly chewed. His gaze flicked over me then moved back to Pops. Everything this man did seemed deliberate. Methodical. "Why did you ask me here and who is this?"

"This is my son, Cash. It's his first day on the job." He cleared his throat, then continued onto more important things. "I was put on a case. Out in West Virginia, four boys were found in an abandoned house. They'd been kidnapped, but when they were recovered, they were the only ones in the house." Pops used one of the napkins from the bag to wipe crumbs from his mouth.

The other man paused in his eating as he watched Pops with a hard, unwavering stare. "I saw that on the news...You don't have any leads?"

"Well," Pops drawled. "That's what I wanted to talk to you about. What do you know about a man called the Curator?"

Thad's lips barely twitched before they flattened into a compressed line. "I've heard of him. He liked to collect children. Boys in particular, and offered services of providing an 'around the world' collection." His top lip lifted in distaste. "I also heard he won't be a problem anymore."

Pops sighed, rubbing the furrow between his eyes as he digested that information. "Anything else you'd like to volunteer?"

"Nope."

And the shit of it was, Pops just nodded. This wasn't the way informant relationships were supposed to go. When Pops explained it to me, he was very clear in the type of dialogue that happened.

This wasn't it.

"What about a man named Garrett Rutherford?" Thad asked.

"The stockbroker?" Pops' eyebrows shot up.

The informant nodded. Except it was more like Pops was the informant in this situation.

"He's wealthy, powerful, influential. All things you would expect of someone in that position…He's also rumored to be a little rough in his proclivities, but I've never seen any concrete evidence. Why?" Now the hesitance entered Pops' voice.

"No reason." Thad balled up the baggie and stuffed it in his pocket. He didn't need a napkin because no crumbs, condiments, or anything were on his face. The man seemed like a neat freak. "I need to run. I'll let you know the next time I'm in your city. We can do this again."

Thad didn't even say goodbye. He just got up and walked away.

"Pops…" I started, as I watched this conundrum mosey out of the park like he wasn't here to meet the FBI. "What the hell was that?"

"That was my best informant," he sighed. "We might as well get going." He stood, and when he saw I hadn't followed, his eyes drooped in defeat. He knew I wasn't going to leave without answers. "Let's walk and I'll fill you in."

While we headed toward the car, Pops kept his voice low.

"There's not a lot I can tell you about him. Only that he's a staunch believer in his moral code and he has his ear firmly planted in the criminal underground. He has no allegiances or loyalty to the monsters of the world. That's what makes him practically a unicorn. He doesn't share information in exchange for a deal or anything so superficial. For him, he hates the monsters as much as we do."

I'd never heard Pops describe the perps we tracked as monsters. But I couldn't argue it fit.

"That seemed like you were his informant. Not the other way around."

Pops chuckled under his breath. "Yeah, well, sometimes to stay in his good graces it works like that."

"Hmm." I could see that logic. Pops was, at the end of the day, one of the best agents in the field. I'd do well to follow his lead.

He'd never steered me wrong.

FLETCHER

"RICK," I called out to the big guy. He'd been in the kitchen working out a new recipe for the last hour. Worrying about her had become as natural as breathing. I would have teased him about it once upon a time. But it had only taken her not coming home once to teach me a harsh lesson I never wanted to repeat.

I needed her to walk through that door every bit as much as he did. Maybe how I handled it was different, but it didn't qualify as better or worse. When he'd done all the tasks he needed to do, Rick would stand at the window and stare out.

I'd offered to keep watch so he could do something else. That earned me a glimmer of a smile and a solemn nod. Fraisier cake was something he'd been reading up on. Fancy, French strawberry shortcake? Sign. Me. Up.

Pretty sure I'd started drooling the minute he mentioned it. Mouth watering, I'd parked myself in front of his favorite windows and worked on some research via my digital tablet in between watching for signs of headlights.

The sun was down. Nothing came up on my external cameras. The housing area had no external lights—well, we did, but they were all motion sensitive. I had both motion sensitive and regular monitoring cameras.

Better to have all of our bases covered. But I'd spotted the moving headlights before my cameras did. Excitement threaded through me. Cash going with her helped. That was what I'd told myself and Rick, but the surge of real happiness at their return wasn't something I would even pretend to ignore.

I rushed toward the kitchen with my empty coffee mug. Rick had made me a fresh pot when I took over watch and he'd let me have two whole mugs without a hint of scolding. Sure, they were half-decaf, but I'd had two huge mugs which equaled one full cup.

Caffeine was definitely my love language.

"It's not ready yet," Rick said with a frown, then he checked his phone. "She didn't message to say they were on their way back."

"She messages us when she's on a job, or a dangerous errand. Nothing about this was supposed to be dangerous." Yes, emphasis on *supposed*. Still…

"True," Rick conceded. "Cash was with her."

"See," I told him, with a clap to his shoulder. "This is working out for us. We should get the door."

"Agreed." The outer garage was already closing when Rick opened the door, I could just see past him. Vienna climbed out of the backseat—not the front.

That was—odd.

Cash exited the driver's seat and his expression was like granite. Utterly unreadable. It was the third person that got all of my attention though. Rick stilled, almost rigid, and I had to give him a not so gentle nudge to get him to move.

Then, I locked eyes with the most terrifying man I'd ever seen. It was bad enough when those dead eyes stared at me from the safe distance of a digital photograph.

The need to confess about those packs of gum I stole in kindergarten burned on the back of my tongue.

Thackery Drew.

Holy shit.

Thackery fucking Drew—her *daddy* was here.

Staring at me.

I'm. So. Dead.

He pulled to a momentary stop as he saw us quivering—I mean hovering in the doorway. Rick wasn't fast enough damn it, so I shoved him back to the corner and covered him with my body to get him out of the line of fire of *Daddy*.

How the hell was he here?

I mean, Cash said it was suspicious that she'd never seen the body, but come on. They left on an errand and came back with her dad like they'd picked up a puppy on the side of the road.

This stuff just didn't happen this way.

Once Thackery was over his initial shock, he traipsed by us and politely took off his shoes and tucked them under the bench like we always did.

I was glad to see he wasn't phased by strange men standing in his house.

Unless…Drew had told him about us.

I gulped.

God, I hoped not. That made me want to piss my pants even more to know I was on his radar as sleeping with his beloved daughter, more than him just spearing me with his identical tawny gaze.

He shuffled past us as Drew came in with Cash on her ass. She looked haggard. Pale, exhausted, and borderline distraught.

I got it. She had been mourning this idol of a father and now he was here? And she had to tell him she had three lovers, I couldn't imagine he took that very well.

Then again, I was still standing here, so maybe she didn't tell him that at all.

Did that mean we had to hide who we were to her? I didn't like that either.

Rick nudged my side and I glanced up. Hell, Cash and Drew had left us in the laundry room, with me sandwiching Rick in the corner like *I* was actually going to protect *him*.

Ha!

I preceded Rick into the kitchen as *Daddy* grabbed a water out of the fridge. He looked much worse than Cash and Drew on the cleanliness scale. He was slimmer than he'd been in the picture I'd seen. He was also dirty. His old clothes hung on his frame, but he still radiated a quiet aura of danger that had my ass cheeks trembling. The rest of me too.

I'd never experienced this level of intimidation before, and I'd been around some fucking powerful people in the Reed family.

"I'm going to take a shower," *Daddy* said, and the smooth timbre of his voice reverberated around the room.

Shit, I had to stop referring to him as Daddy. It would only take one slip up and I'd probably die. I can't imagine he'd enjoy that title from anyone but his baby girl, who he trained in his image.

"I'll walk with you." Drew moved with him as they left the room. Once they made it to the stairs, he let her go first, and after a brief hesitation she jogged up the stairs.

My heart stopped for two seconds, afraid he was going to come back in the kitchen and take care of us. But he didn't. He climbed the stairs after her.

Once a door closed, signaling they couldn't hear us, I turned to Cash.

He had some fucking explaining to do.

"What happened?" Rick beat me to the punch, his question equal parts concern and demand. More concern though than demand. I felt that in my bones. Drew looked like hell.

Fuck. Should one of us follow her?

Rick would be the natural choice for that, but *he* hadn't. My heart fisted so tight I worried it wouldn't be able to beat anymore. If Rick didn't follow her then shit was real. How much more real did it get than Thackery Drew, also known as the Judge, also known as Drew's previously presumed dead father, coming home?

We were so fucking dead.

So dead.

"We went back to a storage facility. Used a black light on the walls. Lots of information. Including info on Gregory Lescheva."

"I know that name," I said more to myself than to them, which was fine. Neither of them looked at me. Rick's attention was riveted on Cash, and Cash's gaze was firmly fixed on the direction of the stairs.

Yeah, we should totally go up there. You first, Mr. "Call me Cash." Yeah yeah. Not charitable, but then he was the one who brought her father back here.

"Lescheva is a consultant. I know him." Cash bit off each word like it was boot leather and he couldn't quite sink his teeth into it.

"Friend?" Rick asked.

Cash shook his head. "I'd have said yes—professional once upon a time."

"Not now." I followed that thought to its natural conclusion.

"No," Cash agreed. "Not now. The address on the wall is where we found him. Underground—in a cell—looking like that."

"He was a prisoner." Rick's hands curled into fists. "Her uncle…"

"Lied." Oh, the growl Cash said that word with echoed Rick's. Uncle Dipshit was gonna be Uncle Walking Fucking Deadman here soon.

"Why keep him a prisoner?" I asked, rubbing my jaw.

"What?" Cash cut his gaze to me and I lifted my shoulders.

"He's the Judge. Why keep him a prisoner? Why lie to her and tell her he's dead? Why—why do any of that?"

"Because he pissed off the wrong people," Cash suggested. "Turned down a job because of their ethical criteria for targets."

"Vienna does not do murder for hire," Rick said, his tone staunch in its defense.

"We know that, Big Guy," I assured him as I walked over to the fridge and pulled out a bottle of wine. It was for Drew. But right now? Yeah, I opened it and poured a big glass. Just one. But I needed something to settle down the rattling jangling nerves that were all shrieking red alert like a klaxon aboard a mythical starship.

I could totally go for one of those right now.

This was a terrible plan.

"So why keep him?" I repeated my earlier question with a quick look toward the stairs. No sign of Drew or—Mr. Drew.

Yeah, I didn't want to call him that either.

"Why hold the Judge? This is not a man who is gonna be friendly or easy to hold onto. Drew wasn't and that psycho whackjob only had her for a few days. How do you hold onto her father for a year?"

Silence poured into the kitchen. It was like salt on the open wound of worry. It wasn't helping my nerves or my concerns.

"Vienna," Rick said softly.

I jerked, pivoting in the hope of seeing her. But she wasn't there. It was still just us. "What, Big Guy?"

"He used Vienna," Cash said slowly, anger bleeding into his voice. Weirdly, it was the first time that fierce, cold tone didn't freak me out. He wasn't pissed at us. The chill in his eyes wasn't for us either. "Lescheva used some connection to her to keep her father in line."

That name again. How did I know that name? It was

gonna irritate the fuck out of me until I tracked it down. "Have we met him?"

"Don't know," Cash said, then he rolled his head from side to side. The vertebrae cracked. "But I've met her dad before."

Woah. I nearly spewed out the wine, as it was I inhaled some of it. Rick passed me a towel to mop my face and cover my mouth as I coughed.

Gaze fixed toward the stairs, Cash said, "He was an informant for my pops."

Oh, that couldn't be good.

RICK

I TUCKED my thumb under my chin as I looked at the spread in front of me. Braised duck legs, goat cheese grits with bourbon-glazed peaches.

I hadn't been planning on making the duck so soon, saving them for a special occasion. But Vienna was tense. The line of her shoulders was so rigid, she seemed like she was going to shatter at any given second. At least for the few moments I'd seen her.

She'd gone up with her dad and never came back down. I had the sneaking suspicion she was hiding out in her bedroom, collecting herself. That or waiting to ambush her dad before he came downstairs.

Both were out of character for her.

But what was she doing up there?

Regardless, I'd jumped right into dinner, preparing a nice meal in hopes to lessen some of the tension between everyone.

Fletcher had grabbed a second glass of wine and hid away in the study. He seemed upset too, but I needed to help Vienna, then I'd help Fletcher.

Cash grabbed a beer and leaned against the counter while I worked. He hadn't even touched the beer past the first sip or two. Instead, he'd been lost in his own thoughts while I went through prep.

The air electrified and I knew without looking that Vienna and her father were on their way back down, even if there was no sound. Just the movement of air gave them away.

I picked up the platter of duck, and nodded to the other dish. "Cash?"

He picked up the grits and peaches as well as a basket of fresh baked bread. Thackery and Vienna were rounding the bottom of the stairs as we left the kitchen.

I studied him out of my peripheral vision. Vienna's resemblance to him was uncanny. They had the same burnished blond hair, the same tawny eyes with such sharp intelligence, most people would probably have a hard time holding eye contact with either of them.

But with him, there was a thick wall of thorns around him, making the idea of approaching him for anything laughable. I loved that Vienna didn't inherit that from him. She got all his best qualities and managed to still be her own person.

The dining room was already set. I'd taken a few minutes to add an extra place setting while they were upstairs.

Vienna's lost expression as she followed on Thackery's heels tugged at my heart. I wanted to wrap her up in my arms and let her know that everything was going to be okay, but comfort wouldn't be welcome in any form right now. Not under the watchful gaze of her father.

As soon as she looked up and saw the platter in my hands her face brightened.

"Daddy, this is Rick. He's the one I told you about that saved me in an alley." Her lips twisted up for a fraction of a second before lifting in a too bright smile again. "He's a master in the kitchen. You wouldn't believe the meals he's created for us." Her voice rose as her hands fluttered over the back of her chair before she pulled it out.

Cash stepped up behind her with a hand on her hip, guiding her to her seat as he pushed in her chair. He didn't usually show such manners, but he seemed to understand, maybe better than Fletcher and me, how unsettled Vienna was.

I was glad he was trying, in his way, to soothe her.

The head of the table was usually my spot, but I took a side chair so Thackery could sit there. This was his house after all.

He seemed to understand we were deferring to him as he settled in the stiff, formal chair.

Fletcher came waltzing in with a glass filled to the brim as he moved to his seat. While everyone unfolded their napkins, I served the food to make it as pleasing to the eye as possible.

"Mr. Drew," I started, hoping a bit of polite conversation would dispel some of the tense air. "It's a pleasure to meet you. Vienna has only sung your praises, so I know how much it must mean to her to have you home."

Even if she hadn't told us specific stories in the beginning, the affection in her voice when she mentioned him and the profound grief when she discussed his loss told me all I needed to know. This man was important to her.

That made him important to me.

Without responding, he studied the food in front of him as though he wasn't certain of it. My culinary choices weren't for everyone, but our little family seemed to enjoy it.

"If that's a little too rich," I continued, mentally kicking myself. Cash said he'd been in a cell. We had no idea on what condition he'd been kept in beyond how gaunt he'd appeared upon arrival.

Gaunt and filthy.

The food might upset his stomach.

"Actually, it might be. I can fix you something a little simpler if you'd like. Toast. Eggs. Basic fare and probably not as tasty, but I wouldn't want to make you ill."

The man lifted his gaze from the plate to fix it on me. The thorny exterior seemed to intensify and the air shifted again. I didn't retreat from that measured stare though.

While there had been a warmth and curiosity to Vienna's eyes when she looked at me the same way—none of which appeared in her father's—I understood what he wanted to see.

Was I genuine?

I wouldn't shy away from him. Vienna was my whole world. Though room for Fletcher had been found and Cash had begun to make himself at home. I would make room for this bristly, unfriendly man because it would make her happy.

He didn't have to like me. I could accept that.

Yet, he offered no rejection or acceptance. In fact, he offered nothing at all. Instead, he cut a look at Vienna. "Are they staying here?"

"Yes," she said, lifting her chin and it was the first time a waver of uncertainty had filtered out of her voice. I frowned. That sound wasn't Vienna at all. She leaned forward. "Rick is an amazing cook, Daddy. He's right, you probably do need something a little blander. I'd say we should call one of the doct—"

"No." One word, cutting her off with a sharp shake of his head.

"I know, we don't know if we can trust them." She dropped her hands to her lap and sighed. "But you can trust Rick and Cash and Fletcher—"

"Can I?"

Cash hadn't taken a seat yet and it wasn't until Thackery Drew asked those two words that our former guest's posture registered with me. He had a hand planted firmly on the back of Vienna's chair and a second one on the back of Fletcher's.

Guarding them.

"Daddy—"

"Baby Girl, no. These men are your guests. If you want them here..." He pushed back his chair and rose. While his tone didn't change significantly in volume, the disappointment registered. "I seem to have been gone longer than I realized."

"Where the hell do you think you're going?" Cash demanded as the older man turned on his heel. The question crashed through the bubble of pressure squeezing the air out of the room. It lanced through it, rupturing the false sense of peace with a very real anger.

"Cash," Vienna murmured, it was almost a plea. She was on her feet, but Cash shifted all of his weight. He wasn't just backing her up anymore, he was getting between father and daughter.

Most of the time, he was too heavy-handed in his responses.

Most of the time.

The hurt in Vienna's eyes though, held me prisoner for all of a split second. Then I set the serving platter down to free up my hands.

"I'll leave you to play house," Thackery continued without a glance at Cash. It was as though he'd weighed, measured, and dismissed him. Or maybe he hadn't even bothered. He wasn't looking at me or Fletcher either as he left the table and went to the hall closet.

Inside was a panel I'd never seen and a small rack of keys.

"Daddy," Vienna attempted again, circling Cash and heading for her father. Fortunately, Cash didn't try to stop her but the riot of emotion vibrating off of him was damn near as thorny and uncomfortable as the wall around Thackery.

"I'll be fine," her father said, pausing as he pulled on a jacket to look down at her. "You have enough to deal with here. I'll use one of the other houses for now."

"You just got here..."

Crushed. His decision to leave crushed her. Jaw tightening, I tried to keep my glare in check. Still, I kept a wary eye on her father. This man had the power to hurt her.

Was hurting her...

From my periphery, I caught Fletcher tossing back all of the wine before he rose to his feet. His attention was firmly on Vienna. Good. He could get her out of here if Cash and I had to deal with Thackery.

"And you seem to have moved on quite well," Thackery continued. "This—" He gave a wave to the table. "This is not for me."

"It can be for you." Strength that had been missing threaded through Vienna's voice. "Having someone to come home to after a job is nice. Comforting. *Welcomed.*"

She stopped in front of him as he gripped the keys in a tight fist. It was the only sign he was bothered by our presence at all. Otherwise, his harsh words and unimpressed stare said he didn't approve but couldn't care less.

"Please don't leave, Daddy," she whispered.

I almost raised my hand to clutch my breaking heart. This, her sorrow at her father turning away from her, was not okay. This wasn't healthy. Didn't Thackery know how much she would need him here with her tonight, on his very first night back from the dead?

He must know.

From everything she'd said about him, it was clear he'd taught her how to survive, while relying solely on him. When you were someone else's only constant, there was no way you didn't know the power of your presence or lack thereof.

Thackery dropped his gaze and started to turn but Vienna caught his arm before dropping it as if the contact burned her skin. "Wait!"

Pausing, those golden brown eyes raised back to her.

"You haven't been formally introduced yet. At least say hello. Meet Fletcher."

Fletcher choked on his spit as he turned his head to the side and pounded his palm against his chest. "I'm okay. I'm quite alright," he wheezed. "I don't need to be introduced right this second."

Thackery speared him with a hard gaze as if he just took notice that Fletcher was an actual person and not a decoration in the room.

"Really, it's okay. We can chat tomorrow," Fletcher squeaked as he dropped his shoulders.

I raised my eyebrows at him. Was he really going to pretend like this would be any easier tomorrow?

"I don't think I need to meet the men in your life. I'll be in one of the—"

"Wait." I stepped away from the table. "Let me pack you a light meal so you won't go hungry." Barely making it three steps to the door, Thackery shook his head.

"Not necessary. I can source my own food."

Cash audibly ground his teeth, his face darkening with his mood. "Thackery, accept the fucking meal. There's no food in the other houses and it's late. You've also been in a cell for over a year. Show some gratitude for the kindness Rick is trying to show you."

My back straightened and I sucked in a slow, steadying breath. Cash was making a stand for our family when Vienna was hurting. I had no doubt any other time she would have been doing what Cash was, but for now, while she was out of sorts, Cash stepped up.

Thackery scoffed and his top lip curled. "Listen boy, gratitude and kindness are emotions that cloud judgment. Your father should have taught you that."

The fire whipping through Cash's eyes was as visible as the audible snap of his straightening spine. "Good idea. Let's talk about Pops." He crossed his arms.

Again, Thackery shook his head and walked through the kitchen.

Vienna didn't breathe as what color she had, drained from her face.

I didn't like this. I didn't like this at all.

Her father was supposed to be her anchor, her mentor. The one guiding light in her life.

What he *wasn't* supposed to be was the one who used his connection and bond with her to willfully cause hurt and distress.

Cash and I would need to do something about this to protect Vienna's heart.

VIENNA

I WAS in the gym when the sun came up, my fists flying at the speed bag. Rick offered to spar with me, but I just shook my head. I didn't trust myself not to react emotionally and hurt him. I didn't trust any of my responses.

Daddy was alive.

Then Daddy just walked out the door.

Was I supposed to be elated?

Devastated?

Confused?

Furious?

Nothing seemed right and yet everything felt accurate. I'd barely managed to eat my dinner and only the fact Rick had prepared it made me chew and swallow as much as I could. After, I went up to take a bath but I couldn't bring myself to sit in the tub. Instead, I'd gone through my notes.

Then, every single word Uncle David told me about Daddy's "death." Every noise from downstairs gave me pause as I waited for Daddy to come back. It was eighteen months earlier, and I was waiting for him all over again.

Fletcher came up to lure me down for a movie. He tried so hard to make me smile that I pasted one on for him. Even as we sat through the movie, nothing registered. At bedtime, I told the boys to sleep—I needed to think.

That involved a run. Cash followed me. He didn't pretend it was anything other than staying with me. He matched me pace for pace, even when I pushed myself to my own limits and the air burned in my lungs. There was comfort in the idea I couldn't lose him. Comfort in knowing he had my back.

I avoided running the whole of the subdivision. It wouldn't be hard to guess which house Daddy went to. As much as I wanted to talk to him, I had to be in a calmer state of mind. Daddy didn't argue. He never had. If I couldn't be reasonable, he wouldn't listen.

Instead, I followed the lonely road toward the interstate. No one was jumping us out here and even if they did—a part of me wished they would. I'd never truly craved violence before. Right now, though, I'd love to go trolling for some guy who wanted to hurt me just so I could hurt him back.

But I couldn't do that.

Not with Cash this close. I couldn't do it to him, because it would just piss him off and he'd kill them before they even got in a swing. I couldn't do it to Rick, because it would hurt him. I couldn't do it to Fletcher, because he'd already tasted enough fear.

So, I ran.

I ran until the muscles in my legs burned as much as my lungs. It was only when we were a block from home that I slowed to a walk. Hands on my hips, I ignored the stitch in my side. Cash said nothing. It wasn't until we reached the door that he put a hand on it to stop me from opening it, then tugged me around.

With his fingers beneath my chin, he tipped my head back but he said nothing. Asked me for nothing, just stared at me from the shadows. I was the one who moved to kiss him. A gentle brush of my lips to his, nothing heated or demanding.

A thank you I could show when I lacked the words to form on my lips.

Cradling my chin, he stroked his thumb over my pulse, then returned the same sweet kiss. It lacked all of the usual fire and heat. The biting edge was missing and it brought burning tears to my eyes. How long we stood there, the scent of his sweat in my nostrils and the fierce warmth of him sheltering around me, holding back the darkness, I had no idea. My breathing slowed to even and the stitch in my side was gone when I pulled away.

Inside, Rick glanced up from where he stood in the midst of a sparkling kitchen. Relief filtered through his eyes. I went to him and kissed him softly. "I need to shower." The words came out far rougher than I intended, but he just stroked my cheek, sweat be damned.

When I came back down, a freshly showered Cash slept on the sofa while Fletcher seemed crashed in the chair. Rick waited in the kitchen with coffee, and a light meal, as well as water. He didn't ask me anything, just sat there with me as I turned it all over in my head. Eventually, Fletcher joined us and Rick went to the living room after pressing a kiss to my head.

When dawn flushed pink on the horizon, I had no more answers than I'd had when Daddy left. But Daddy had always been an early riser. I hadn't fully processed my decision until I'd come back down in fresh clothes to find all three of them waiting for me.

"I need to talk to him," I said finally. "Alone."

It wasn't an order, but it also wasn't a request. I just needed them to trust me. Even if Daddy didn't…

God, that hurt.

I turned away from the guys so they wouldn't see my face. No, so I couldn't see theirs, or the pity.

I'd built Daddy up to them. He was important to me. The

one person in my life who taught me everything I knew. Who made me who I was today.

Then he comes back and when we should be celebrating, it was like he was a completely different person. Daddy wasn't ever the tactile type. I didn't expect him to hug me profusely or ask me about how hard it was when he'd never come back.

But his lack of interest in everything… In me…

The way he acted like I was the one different.

And I was, I had to admit that to myself. Not in a bad way, just evolved from who I was before. We did that. We adapted and evolved to get the job done. That wasn't unexpected.

Shit, I needed to go talk to him before I did something I regretted, like punching a hole in the wall. The last thing we needed right now was repairs, or to worry about leaving DNA in the walls.

No one tried to stop me when I headed toward the door. I was surprised that not even Cash tried to follow me, then again, I wasn't. They were respecting my need to work this out with Daddy. Unfortunately, they knew as well as I did that Daddy wouldn't talk to me with them present.

Of the small grouping of houses in this abandoned subdivision, there were only two that I could see Daddy staying in last night.

One on the farthest tip away from our house, and the one closest to the entrance so he'd know immediately if someone found their way out here. That house was also the one closest to the trail system leading away from here.

Daddy would have picked that one.

The old, gauzy curtains moved with just the smallest bit of air flow as I walked up the steps to the front door. A sure sign this was where he decided to camp out last night. He'd turned the air on.

I stopped at the door with my hand extended for the keypad.

I hesitated.

Before, I would have walked in. I wouldn't have felt like I was intruding to walk into a house Daddy was residing in. But now?

It felt like my presence wouldn't be welcome.

Sucking in a deep breath, I shook off the doubt and keyed in the unlock code. When it successfully beeped, I exhaled. At least Daddy hadn't reprogrammed it. That would have been a blaring slap in the face I wasn't sure I could have handled.

The doorknob was cool as I twisted it and pushed the door inward. I shut it and turned the lock, then moved deeper in the house. Daddy would already know I'd entered the house. He would have heard the keypad.

When he didn't appear, I resigned myself to the task of finding him.

He'd always enjoyed working in the study, enjoying the separation of work from the living spaces. There he was, behind the desk, reviewing something on the computer screen.

A pair of reading glasses perched on his nose as the luminescent light from the screen dispelled the shadows on his face from the night before. The curtains were drawn closed, as if he preferred the darkness now.

"Daddy, we need to talk." I braced my feet apart, crossing my arms. I'd never taken such a stance with him before. Nothing combative. I'd never needed to. Even when we disagreed, we were still always on the same page.

Not now though.

There was a mile of uncertainty between us.

Sometime in the last eighteen months we became strangers to each other. I hated it, but I hated that Daddy didn't seem to care more.

"There's nothing of importance we need to discuss." He didn't even glance at me.

"How about how you got in that cell in the first place?

Who put you there? Lescheva? Then we can move on to why you didn't escape. I saw the setup. I clocked three ways you could have broke free in the first five minutes, in poor lighting." Not to mention, what did this all have to do with Uncle David?

He shook his head. "That's nothing you need to worry about."

"I disagree. Whoever took you, we need to dispatch them. I've already been making inroads in cleaning up the Network. Don't you even want an update on what I've accomplished?"

It was so hard to breathe.

"I saw perfectly well what you accomplished last night."

That was it, all he said.

His new burner phone dinged on the desk next to the mousepad. He glanced over at it, and stood. "They're here," he murmured and moved around the desk, walking past me and to the front door.

This was wrong. It wasn't how it was supposed to be. I'd never felt like an outsider with my own father before.

Irritation scraped under my skin as I trailed after him. He moved with the faintest of limps. He definitely favored his left side. Yet the closer he came to the door, the more those signs melted away.

He'd said, "they're here," before he went to open the door. The question of who was here died unspoken on my tongue. Daddy didn't trust *others* with our location.

Bringing Rick here broke his rules. Back less than a day and now *Daddy* broke the rules? What was going on...

"Horatio," Daddy said, snapping me out of my internal musings. He clasped the accountant's hand briefly, then waved him inside as he said, "Dae. Thank you for coming."

Thank you for—

Horatio met my gaze briefly, the sympathy in his blue eyes was the last thing I expected to see. Honestly, I didn't want it.

The uneven ground beneath my feet had grown increasingly more unstable.

"Vienna," he said, giving me a smile, even as he narrowed the distance between us. Dressed in a casual polo shirt with a light sports jacket thrown on. Horatio looked like a man ready for golf, not a personal visit.

When he stepped into my line of sight, I tilted my head to glance past him to the tall, muscular Asian man who entered. With long white hair and a very distinctive jaw line, "Dae" was remarkable. The man was…unforgettable. A presence. Nothing about him blended in.

"I didn't realize you'd invited Lennon," the man said in a smooth, Australian accent. "If you want this cunt to do the work, you don't need me."

He flicked a look past Daddy toward me as well. Whereas a glimmer of sympathy marked Horatio's features, this man revealed nothing of his thoughts.

"The job requires both of you," Daddy said in a terse voice as he closed the door. "You don't have to like each other."

Only then did the newcomer give Horatio a dismissive look. For his part, the Vanisher merely smiled, though nothing in the twist of his lips touched his eyes. Dislike radiated from both of them, like tangible electricity in the air. Apparently, neither had been informed of the arrival of the other.

Brushing his fingers down my arm, Horatio nodded to the living room. "Why don't we sit…"

"We'll go back to my office," Daddy said, pointing both of them down the hall. "Go, I'll be right behind you."

Only, for the first time since I arrived, Daddy was looking at me and not anywhere else. Neither man followed Daddy's instructions. Horatio grimaced, but it was Dae who spoke, "It is a pleasure to finally make your acquaintance a reality, Vienna."

Surprise flickered through me.

"Thackery has often spoken of you—"

"Gentlemen, she is not a part of this conversation. Excuse yourselves." Daddy's cold tone held not one ounce of violence, but I knew that tone. From how they both reacted, they recognized it as well.

"Until next time then," Dae said with a nod to me.

"There won't be a next time, Casanova," Horatio snapped, giving me an almost sad nod in passing. "She doesn't know you and doesn't need to."

"But apparently you, she knows?" Dae challenged as the pair disappeared down the hall. Their voices faded as a door closed, leaving Daddy and I alone, finally.

"Daddy—"

"Vienna," he cut me off with a sharp shake of his head. "If I'd wanted your involvement in this, I would have involved you. I didn't."

"Clearly," I said. "That doesn't change the fact that eighteen months ago, Uncle David lied to me and told me you were dead."

Had he done *that* for Daddy?

His expression didn't change. He looked—older somehow. More chiseled. The lost weight was part of it, but there was a distance in him that I'd never seen before.

"What happened? Please—I've been trying to find who killed you. I've been chasing down Red—"

"Don't." One word. It snapped through the room like a crack in the ice that portended imminent disaster. "The job I did, the work I'm doing now? It's not your concern. Red Death? Forget the name. Go back to playing house with your new toys."

The last sentence sliced like razor wire.

None of this made sense.

"Daddy, did you tell Uncle David to tell me you died?"

He frowned. "Why would you ask me that?" Then he sighed, and all the weariness from the day before returned to him. Was I the problem here? Was I pushing him too hard? He was still recovering. "Sweet Girl, I don't have time for this right now. We'll discuss it later."

Would we? But he didn't wait for my response, just ventured back down the hall to his office. For the longest time, I just stood there.

Every permutation I tried to sort through didn't seem to lead me any closer to any answers. No, Daddy had the answers. He was currently in there confiding in two others. Others he'd invited to our home. Others he'd broken the rules for.

Was he angry because I'd done much the same? Or was this something else? The most important question, what did I do about it?

CASH

"YOU THINK it was a good idea to let her leave without one of us?" Fletcher asked as he moved to the front window, peeking out as if she'd actually look back and catch him.

She wouldn't. Not right now.

Distress was written all over her. The only thing Vienna was thinking about was that goddamn father of hers.

"I'd love to trail on her heels, but she needs to talk to her father on her own. But don't worry, if he fucks it up, we'll swoop in and fix it." I shrugged, relaxing my shoulders to hide how tense I was.

Since I recognized him, I hadn't been able to get the few encounters with him through the years out of my head. Had Pops known who he was? I would have said absolutely not.

Abso-fucking-lutely not.

But then I started thinking of how differently Pops treated Thad, or excuse me, Thackery.

The old bastard had never written a word about it in his journals if he had. I started laughing under my breath.

"Are you cracking?" Fletcher ducked his head to get a good look at my face.

"Sorry. I was thinking about Pops, and how genius he was if he knew Thackery's real identity. He never even got close to catching him. All his trails were useless when I took over the search. In fact," I scratched my brow thinking of the impressiveness of it all, "if he did know, he did a damn fine job leading the FBI away from him."

Fletcher blinked. But Rick didn't seem fazed by my words at all. After a quick flick of his gaze to me, he looked back toward the door Vienna walked out of a few minutes ago.

"She's going to be even more upset than she already was," he said quietly. "We should have gone with her to support her."

"The bright side, Big Guy, is maybe she'll be able to sleep after she gets a few things off her chest." Fletcher patted Rick on the back, but he didn't seem to believe his own words.

"She needs sleep," Rick agreed.

We all knew she hadn't slept at all last night. In an unspoken agreement, we'd rotated shifts to sit with her. I'd taken the first shift on her run, then Fletcher, then Rick.

Vienna had to crash sometime. I just hoped it was because she wanted to sleep instead of her body giving out on her. That was never good for the psyche.

"How about we wait on his porch so we're there as soon as she leaves?" Rick suggested.

"I like the way you think, but I don't think that would do Drew any favors. You saw *Daddy's* eyes, right? He has dead fucking eyes." Fletcher shivered. "I think it's better for Drew and us if we remain out of sight."

At least Fletcher had calmed the fuck down now that Thackery was gone. For the short time he'd been here with us, Fletcher had acted like a raging alcoholic with only two brain cells left. That wasn't unusual for him, but the cracked-out voice he'd been speaking with was.

He'd have to man up for Vienna's sake.

Clearing his throat, Fletcher tugged at his loose collar.

"Let's go back to you knowing Thackery. How did you not see him for the psychopath he was?"

I narrowed my gaze. Was he trying to offend me?

"Hey, listen—" he held up his hands—"All I'm trying to say is *Daddy* clearly gives off serial killer vibes. You're a good judge of character. You can read people. I've seen it with my own two eyes. So how did you not peg him for the bad guy?"

"He's not the bad guy," Rick piped in, finally bringing his attention to us. "I don't like the way he's treating Vienna right now, but he's not the bad guy. The people he killed were. Just like we're not the bad guys for taking out the child molesters and traffickers."

"Uh-huh…" Fletcher nodded without blinking. "I hear ya, I'm just saying, your hippy dippy happy radar has to be wonky when in his presence. Don't tell me I'm the only one who notices it." It wasn't a whine, but Fletcher wanted someone in his corner.

"Don't say that about her dad. She won't like it."

"Rick has a point," I agreed. "But to answer your question." I gave him a look that said I was being nice and he didn't necessarily deserve an answer. "Of course there was something off with him. But every informant is an informant for a reason. They usually have ties to the darker side of life, which means they aren't sparkling white when it comes to morals and crimes. They just haven't committed the crimes we're chasing, as far as we know."

"And look how that worked out for you. The mark was under your nose the entire time."

Rick popped Fletcher on the back of the head. "He's going to hurt you if you keep insulting him."

Fletcher grumbled and moved a few steps away from both of us.

I sighed. "Seriously? I don't have mind reading powers to know the exact crimes each person commits."

"Yeah, but look at that one informant, the blue-fucking-eyed fox. He at least doesn't give off crazy vibes. He could be a regular Joe off the street."

"Ratio," I growled. I still needed to catch up with him. He had the kind of secrets I didn't appreciate from my informants.

"Yeah, *Ratio*." Fletcher put so much emphasis on the guy's name that it cut a swath right across my irritation. "Let's talk about that psycho."

"Let's not," Rick said with a sharp shake of his head. "He helped us find her. He didn't have to. Correction..." With a pause, Rick pinned his attention on me and I raised my brows. "He helped *you* find her, when she needed someone to save her. I think he knew more than he told us."

"He didn't know she was being tortured." I rubbed my chin as I chewed on that thought. "He wouldn't have bothered calling me."

"Good." Rick folded his arms. I wasn't sure if he was self-soothing, barricading himself, or fighting some urge to punch one of us. The answer could be D, all of the above, but I didn't think so. He had taken some comfort in my certainty, but his attention was still wholly focused on Vienna. Not that I blamed him.

"You know," Fletcher said in a solemn voice that really didn't suit the guy. "The hardest part is how she looked after he left last night."

Oh. Yeah.

Rick sighed.

"She looked like you did Big Guy, when she didn't come home."

Now I sat forward and scrubbed my hand over my face. That look might haunt me. It had been worse than when we found her at Sandra Jane's. Worse than anything I'd ever seen in her eyes over the last few months.

Vulnerable.

Hurt.

The wound finding her father in that cell had inflicted on her had been gradually widening, tearing deeper into her. How much she recognized the injury and how much of it was just gouging into her, I had no idea. Until that moment, I had only seen her emotional maturity—lusted after it as much as I had her body and her brain. No, finding her father in that cell —a cell he could have easily busted out of in my opinion—no, that had rocked her backwards.

Fucking Thackery hadn't returned the impulsive hug she'd given him or done more than glance from her to me then back before he said, "You shouldn't be here."

No shit, *Thackery*. Your daughter shouldn't have had to come and get you after mourning you. If it had been Pops, I'd have probably slugged him. As it was, I was damn tempted. At least he hadn't shoved her away. Or shaken her off. She'd pulled herself together, given him the distance he seemed to crave. All of it was automatic.

All of it was behavior that spoke to the years of their relationship. So, he wasn't openly affectionate. I wasn't. None of us were Rick. He made it look easy. Even Fletcher had his ease with that. But Thackery only waited until she retreated before he issued the orders to leave.

I wanted to search the place.

No.

She tried to argue and he'd silenced her with a look. Then she'd taken over and filled in the rest of the emotional blanks. Of course, Daddy didn't want to stay there. They—not we— could come back later. It bothered me less to be cut out of that. She was trying to settle her father. A year plus in that dark cell? If it had been a year… Yeah, I'd probably be less than communicative too.

Still. Our Vienna was capable, brilliant, and strong.

"She's lost," Rick said, dragging me back to the present. "This is not a reunion she expected. His reaction is not what I expected."

"Well, no one expects the Spanish Inquisition..." Fletcher's joke landed with a weak flop and Rick gave him a puzzled look, but I had to admit a laugh escaped me. That had Fletcher's rounded eyes focusing on me suddenly. "You know, it's unsettling when you laugh at my jokes."

The corners of my mouth twitched and a second genuine laugh escaped. "I'd apologize, but I have a feeling we're both an acquired taste."

Fletcher's jaw dropped, but a beeping from his phone silenced whatever response he'd been about to offer. Jaw snapping shut, he pulled his phone out and then swiped across a few screens.

"Problem?" Rick asked when Fletcher's intensity ratcheted up a notch. One thing about Reed, he wore his heart on his sleeve and his wild cavalcade of emotions out there for anyone to see. Vienna's protectiveness regarding him made more and more sense to me every day.

Crazy little shit needed to be protected.

"We have company," he said in a purely business-like tone. "One of them is a friend of yours."

I was off the sofa before he even finished the first sentence. With Rick at my side, we converged on Fletcher to study the camera feeds. Cameras. Smart guy had put cameras up everywhere.

Fucking Ratio drove one car. But there was a second one behind him. The camera angles didn't give me much. Asian. I caught Asian. Then the cars vanished from one screen but popped up on another.

"Not coming *here*," Rick said, his voice a rumble of disapproval.

Oh, I was right there with you, Big Guy. But for now, I kept those words to myself. Where were they going?

"Thackery," Rick said softly. "He must have called them. Vienna would not give away this location."

"Agreed." Like the boys before her, Vienna hadn't allowed

me to learn the location until she was certain of me. In fact, the leap of faith it took her to trust me with their home base was probably the most profound display of commitment she could have made at the time. She'd given me her body before she gave me that.

Food for thought.

"So, the question is why does *he* want *them* here," I mused aloud, not that I really questioned it.

"Backup," Rick said, echoing the thought I'd already had.

"And on that note," I said, grim determination in my veins. "Vienna is there alone. Her father might not harm her, *physically*, but I don't know that other guy and Ratio still owes me an explanation."

"We're going?" Rick was onboard. No surprise there.

"Are you crazy?" Fletcher said. "Daddy doesn't want us here, a blind man can see that. The guy fucking terrifies me. Why are you so willing to confront him?"

"Because he doesn't scare me," I told him.

"That's insane. No way you looked into his eyes after you've had your dick in his daughter and not seen the promise of your death."

"She would never let him hurt us," Rick said, his tone firm and probably meant to be comforting. Fletcher broke off from staring at me to gape at him. "Trust Vienna."

"I trust *Drew*. It's *Daddy* I don't trust."

"Then stay behind me," I told him. "I'll deal with him if I have to." If it came to that, it would be *bad* for Vienna. So, I'd watch my step. "But nothing scares me. Nothing ever has. I'm certainly not going to start now. Not when she's about to be outnumbered, and possibly outgunned, and she is definitely far more vulnerable than she ever has been. You can stay here or you can go. Rick and I will keep you in one piece."

Rick nodded once.

"But we're going," Rick said, already striding for the door.

"Weapons, Rick," I told him and he hesitated. When he

glanced back at me, I kept my expression neutral. "We're not walking into that unarmed. It's not safe for her."

That decided him. He headed for the closet and the weapons locker she had stored there. I paused to meet Fletcher's gaze where he kept staring at me.

"What?"

"You don't feel *any* fear? Like—ever? Not the dentist? Not needles? Snakes? Heights? Getting your head blown off if you kick down the wrong door?"

"No. Fear has never been a problem for me. If you want to discuss this in one of Rick's therapy sessions, we can. For now, are you coming with us or staying here?" If he was by himself, he needed to be armed, and behind some sealed doors, until we returned.

Rick glanced back, waiting for his answer.

"Going," Fletcher said in a resigned voice. "I'm going. This is a terrible idea, but I'm going."

I nodded, then went to check my ammo and the weapons options. Since returning the night before, Vienna hadn't asked for my gun back. She'd let me keep it. I picked a second with an ankle holster on before I added a third to a holster on the back of my belt.

Fletcher wasn't going to take any, but Rick and I were immovable on this and the hacker finally conceded. He knew how to use firearms, no matter how much he didn't like them. Once we were ready, I was out the door.

"He doesn't feel any fear," Fletcher muttered to Rick, not seeming to care if I heard him. Which was fine. No secrets was better. "That explains so much, you know?"

I chuckled.

Huh, Reed was growing on me.

"He's laughing at my jokes, Big Guy. What do we do?"

"Go with it," Rick advised. "Protect Vienna."

Yep. That was the plan.

"WHAT THE HELL?" Daddy mumbled looking out the front window.

I turned as Ratio and Dae came jogging back down the short hallway.

Cash was leading both Rick and Fletcher across the yard with a serious as death expression on his face, even as his arms were relaxed at his sides. All it would take is one sign something was wrong and he'd have whatever hidden weapon in his hands ready to take out a threat. Rick was solemn, a slight furrow between his brows that could have been either worry or the sun.

Then Fletcher was a good five feet behind Rick casting jittery glances between this house, Cash's back, and our home. A trickle of amusement flashed through me at his clear uncomfortableness and it felt good. It was a welcome distraction from the shit storm inside of me.

"Who are they?" Dae growled as he crept close to my back to better see out the window.

I waited for Daddy to call him off. Growing up, and even as an adult, Daddy took my personal space very seriously. Unless I was working a job, no one was allowed in it. Ever.

When I glanced back, Daddy was watching me, a contemplative look on his face.

"Friends," Ratio said as if that was enough to explain everything. This time, Daddy scoffed.

I opened the door as Cash raised his hand, which seemed to be going for the doorknob instead of knocking.

Raising my eyebrows, I sent a silent reprimand. Bursting in on Daddy unannounced was never a good idea. He should know that.

He only quirked one brow, as if to say he didn't give a shit.

Cash crowded me, using a gentle hand on my stomach to push me back enough to allow all three men to enter. When I glanced up, his gaze was firmly, and coldly on Daddy.

I sighed.

We had enough problems, but Cash's strong protective streak could potentially make things harder on all of us.

Shutting the door once Fletcher very reluctantly stepped through, I turned and leaned against it. All the fire I'd initially possessed, had dwindled to something small and pathetic as I stood there while Daddy cut me out of his meeting. Now with everyone back in the same room, all the egos struggling for air, I was tired.

"Ratio, you owe me an explanation. A few actually," Cash said in a tone that brooked no arguments. It was good he hadn't started with Daddy, that wouldn't have gone over well. No one disrespected him, especially in his own house.

The accountant shot me another sympathetic look I absolutely loathed, then glanced between Daddy and Cash.

Interesting.

Cash must have thought so too, because he bristled when he must have realized how comfortable they were with each other. Or Daddy's lack of surprise at Cash knowing him.

I wasn't. Daddy and I had made an effort to know as much as we could about the Network and their acquaintances as well as their dealings, client list, services provided…

Not that I had known Ratio was his informant, but I wouldn't be surprised if Daddy had, especially after the way he'd hidden Ratio's identity from me.

Another insult in what I was finding was quite a long list, for both past and present.

"We have business to attend to. Vienna, I trust you can take your…men… back to the other house." It was a statement. Not even an order, because Daddy just assumed I'd listen.

Blood simmered under my skin, flirting with the boiling point.

"That might be the case, if you hadn't compromised this location for Vienna. Didn't you teach her that your location was sacred? Now, one day free, and you're giving out the address freely?" Cash argued on my behalf.

Daddy chuckled. "Freely? Who do you think sold this place to me? Dae found the real estate, and Ratio made the sale happen through a series of creative shell corporations."

I saw his lips move. I knew what he had said.

But all I heard was the blood pumping in my ears.

Uncle David helped get us this property. All our properties on some level. Right? Even when he hadn't known the locations. At least, that's what I thought. Uncle David was the one trusted confidant outside of me. That was the way it had always and would always be.

Except now Uncle David was suspect.

When had Daddy started building his own network and why had he excluded me?

Stares burned into my skin from the left, where Ratio and this Dae stood. From my right where Cash, Rick, and Fletcher were. I didn't dare look at them. There would be too much pity, too much sympathy. Just too fucking much of everything.

I kept my gaze locked on Daddy. Not blinking.

Oh hell, I couldn't blink or even look down, because then the hot tears filling my eyes would fall over and I couldn't let anyone see me cry.

No, *fuck* that.

Daddy would be disappointed. It would be written all over his severe frown that was already threatening. That wasn't important.

What mattered was not letting anyone—*anyone*—see my weakness.

Weaknesses could be exploited and I would never put myself in a position for Ratio or Dae to use emotion against me. Even knowing they were probably already drawing their own conclusions.

My chest strained and ached, and I realized I'd stopped breathing to try and make the tears stop.

Daddy pulled his gaze away from me, and moved to Cash. I recognized that expression. He was about to drop a bomb on Cash and Cash wasn't going to like it.

"How do you think Ratio came to be your informant?"

After the dinner and conversation I'd had with Horatio, I had begun to believe he might actually be on my side. A true ally of sorts. Then again, he was a man who occupied two identities within the Network. One, aka the Vanisher, terrified even the most hardened of hearts, but his other? The Accountant? Who didn't do business with him? People always worried about sharing their body dump sites. Yet, he didn't need to know that, he knew where the money was hidden.

We all needed our accounts.

Even me.

That thought scraped over my psyche like locked tires leaving rubber tread on asphalt. If I hadn't been looking directly at Horatio, I might have missed the faintest of droops to his eyebrows or the way his mouth turned down at

Daddy's revelation. That was not something he would have shared with Cash.

"Well," Cash said, elongating that single syllable like a person would as they pulled the slide back to chamber a round. "Takes an informant to send an informant, doesn't it, Thad? Does your daughter know that you worked with Pops?"

No.

I didn't.

Head rolling from side to side, I debated vomiting. I'd seen some horrible things in my time. Delivered more horrible things to people who deserved it. Horatio sent me another look, but I refused to look at that fucking sympathy again. But it was Dae who caught my gaze. He rubbed two fingers along the sides of his mouth to his chin, over and over. It was like he wanted to smooth down his non-existent mustache. Not even a speck of stubble interrupted the pure beauty of his features.

Aesthetically-speaking, I didn't think I'd ever seen a man as gorgeous as he was. The look in his eyes as he studied me wasn't lust or passion, but it was—something unsettling. A large back filled my view as Fletcher leaned back against the door next to me. He held out a hand and I glanced down at it then up at Rick.

Rick wasn't looking at me. No, he had all his attention on Horatio and Dae. His current position took them out of my line of sight.

"We don't have time for this." Daddy's humor had been short-lived. "Vienna…"

The snap of my name in his voice had my spine straightening. Taking Fletcher's hand, I threaded my fingers with his. The faintest tremor went through him. Fear. He'd walked into this situation with my father, a relative stranger, only to be here for me.

Protectiveness surged as I squeezed his hand and met

Daddy's gaze. Most of my life, at least since I'd gotten old enough to work with him, I'd never had a doubt about what Daddy was thinking or what he needed. He could communicate more in a single look than most people could with a full essay.

I understood exactly what he wanted.

Instead of *obeying*, I merely said, "Apparently, there is a great deal we don't know about each other. I, for one, would like some answers, particularly since it wasn't Dae or Horatio who came for you."

Straightening, I moved up a step to stand in the space between Rick and Cash, but I kept Fletcher behind me.

"I'm certain Horatio would have given me more data at dinner if he'd been aware of your location, particularly in the conditions we found you."

Instead of agreeing, Horatio's expression shuttered but Dae's eyes tightened. "Dinner?" He canted his head. "You had dinner with 'Horatio'?"

"Yes," I said, this time my smile wasn't forced. "Friendships should be nurtured."

"Since when are you and Horatio friends?" Daddy wasn't asking me.

Sliding his hands into his pockets, Horatio shook his head at me. "I thought you wanted to have a conversation, Thackery, not an interrogation. If you need a moment, I can walk Vienna back to her house."

"Nice try, Ratio," Cash said in a voice so bored it almost made me laugh.

Almost.

"You're not going anywhere with our girl."

Whatever ground I'd gained in those few moments evaporated as Daddy whipped his stare from Horatio to Cash. Where he hadn't reacted to Dae's nearness earlier, I could practically see the violent assessment in his gaze now.

Cash ran his fingers down my arm, just brushing the

shoulder then down my biceps. Yes, he knew exactly what he was doing. With Daddy at one angle while Horatio and Dae were at the other, I had to turn my head to keep track of all of them. Dae's stare no longer focused on Horatio but on Cash and me.

"Perhaps we should have a meal," Rick said finally. "I can make something simple. But the hostility present isn't good for Vienna and those who claim to care about her…"

Oh, Rick.

He made no pretense. "Particularly the man she has mourned, should take that into consideration. Clearly, there are issues we need to work out and targets that have to be dealt with, especially if they held you for so long."

"Take my daughter home and feed her. Try to keep her there this time, I'm sure you must have some uses," Daddy said, then he looked at Horatio and Dae. "We have business to attend." What ground I'd gained fell away as he turned his back on me.

"Daddy…"

He didn't turn to look at me but at least he paused. "Sweet Girl… now is not the time. Go away. I don't need you here."

The words were like sandpaper over an open wound. "That's good to know, from what I see, you've never *needed* me." Quite the opposite. For the first time since Horatio and "Dae" arrived, I recognized what they were.

My rivals.

I had always been his only partner—or so I thought. But he worked with these two and never read me in. Negotiated with them and they both knew about the subdivision. Knew and…

And Horatio used it to his advantage to "watch" me.

"Don't be emotional…" Daddy began, it wasn't a reprimand but a warning and I allowed myself only a bitter smile.

"I wouldn't dare. I know how you feel about such things."

Fletcher squeezed my hand, a reminder that I wasn't

alone. Not only wasn't I alone, my sweet little pincushion came marching in here with Cash and Rick to defend me against Daddy.

Rick hadn't taken his gaze from Horatio or Dae, but I swore I could feel him right there next to me. Cash? He let out a sound of disgust and stalked forward the short distance between him and Daddy.

"Okay, *Thad*," Cash said without an ounce of irony or anything resembling give in his hard voice. Not once in the last few months of interaction with him had I heard this tone.

For the first time since our rather unfortunate first meeting, I heard the Federal agent in his voice.

Worse, I heard a Federal agent on the edge.

"Let's be clear, you mean something to your daughter or I'd have already broken your jaw for speaking to her like that. But keep it up, breaking your legs wouldn't be a hardship and I'd take some pleasure in watching you try to escape whatever *network* of lies you've constructed when you can't actually walk away. Being a prisoner seems to be your thing."

Daddy struck faster than I'd ever seen him move, but the throat strike didn't land. First, Cash shifted his weight and moved, then used a retaliatory strike to send Daddy to the floor.

But he didn't hurt him. He just defended.

Daddy rebounded but I released Fletcher and swept between Daddy and Cash. Behind me, Cash swore, but Daddy's next blow froze a millimeter from my face. His eyes shuttered, closing me out.

No one in the room moved.

No one breathed.

Not even me.

I locked eyes with the man I loved more than anything else on this planet. A man I had missed like some part of my own soul had been torn out.

What I saw, for a brief second before he shut me out, was that man. But then, only a stranger looked back at me.

Whatever answers Daddy had, he wasn't going to tell me. He'd called others for that. Others he trusted.

Others that weren't me.

The heat from Cash at my back was a furnace. Daddy shifted his gaze and the speculation was back in it as he assessed the man in my space. When Cash settled his hand on my hip, I relaxed into the grip and then Daddy dropped his gaze back to me.

"Dae. Horatio. We're going to my office." He held my gaze unblinkingly. "Don't be out here when we're done."

"As you wish."

I turned, not giving him the satisfaction of walking away again. Fletcher already had the door open.

"Don't," Rick snapped in an authoritative tone. I caught the flash of movement. Cash hadn't moved when I did, but Fletcher glared at Horatio, who didn't seem remotely perturbed by Rick. If anything, concern radiated off him.

Concern and pity.

I wanted neither.

"You know where to find me," I told him as if we'd already made plans to meet. "Clearly."

Then, trusting Cash and Rick, I strode out the door with Fletcher. If Daddy didn't want me to work on this case with him, if he didn't want my help? Fine.

I could hate it and still take care of things.

Like Uncle David lying to me.

I could take care of him.

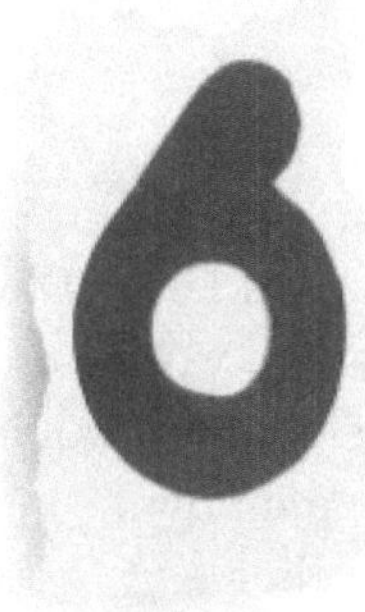

THERE WAS an extra weight to my steps as I marched across the yards and over the old street separating the houses. Grass crunched under my shoes and the noise echoed in my ears.

I didn't normally move this violently, but I couldn't stop myself. When I tried to lighten my feet, they quickened instead, until I sprinted the last several yards.

"Hey!" Fletcher yelled behind me.

At least Cash trailed me because his hand caught the door next to my head as I swung it open.

Fletcher grumbled and Rick murmured something I couldn't understand, didn't have the bandwidth to translate right then, as I rushed through the house to pack.

He didn't want me to be involved? Fine.

He had others working the job I should have been on? His prerogative.

That he had men he trusted more than me when he was everything to me? Now, *that* I had a problem with.

But that didn't change the fact that I had a mission I'd been working on the last eighteen months. I'd put in the work. Tracked down leads. Traced steps and ghost trails. I'd done everything I could to bring his killer to light...and justice.

Then I'd found him.

But not him.

Not the father I'd lost.

Irrational or not, I blamed Uncle David for that. For more than the obvious reasons. He was the one who had told me he was gone. And I'd trusted him. Put faith in him because Daddy had faith in him. And now...

Everything was unraveling and I couldn't get that day out of my head.

Cool sweat dripped down my spine as I stepped away from the line dance. I grinned as I scanned the crowd, retying the tails of my button-down under my breasts.

I had to admit, a hoedown wasn't the usual scene. Uncle David preferred the grungier types of locales. But he was the master chameleon, so in the end, nothing should have surprised me.

"Blue moon, please," I waved two fingers at the bartender, keeping my chin tucked as I continued to fiddle with my shirt. She nodded, and I turned away from the bar, leaning back on my elbows. The place was packed tonight. There was no chance she'd remember me under the dim neon lights. But I could never be too careful.

A man with tight Levi's, a short sleeved, yellow plaid shirt that had been washed too many times, appeared on the other side of the room. He was almost a head taller than everyone around him, and I had to shake my head.

Even with the ball cap pulled low and his severe frown carved in his face, he was drawing the eye of more than a few older ladies. One with too big bleach blonde hair fluffed it up as he stepped around her, and her face immediately fell when he didn't even look at her twice.

I chuckled.

Uncle David could pull women when he wanted to. And other times, he could repel anything human.

"Here you go, sweetheart," The bartender touched my elbow,

and left the beer sitting on the counter. I dropped a five and grabbed the cool bottle, pressing the damp glass against my cheek.

Grinning, I raised my gaze to Uncle David, but he didn't smile back. His face was set in a pained grimace, his lips so compressed, they disappeared.

"Girl, we need to talk." He nodded to the side where the barn doors were wide open.

I pushed away from the counter, leading the way, heading for the first isolated location I clocked. My heart already beat hard from the dances, but now, it was picking up with a nervous rhythm that had nothing to do with exertion.

Something was wrong.

The energy rolling off of him was palpable. Unusual.

There was only one reason I could think of that he would ask for a meeting instead of just calling me over a burner. They were secure, but some conversations couldn't be risked.

And others...

Every corner of the place was jammed with teetering people, sloshing their beers, gasping with laughter. We'd have to go outside. That might be better. Depending on what he had to tell me, I wouldn't have to mask myself so much.

A few men called out as I left the barn. I smiled back, but when they caught sight of Uncle David, they quieted and turned away.

Tonight, he was terrifying and they felt it.

A group of trees on the other side of the parking lot were cast in complete darkness. That would have to do. If anyone saw us, they'd think I was just a young girl testing the wilder side of life with a hardened older man.

Nothing out of the ordinary for the town hoedown.

The noise from the barn was still incredibly loud from this distance, but we were insulated by the trees. Uncle David released an audible breath as he took off his hat and scrubbed a hand over his head. He was great at adapting mannerisms of a specific demographic. It was why he was able to fit in so well no matter where we met.

And he'd taught me everything he knew.

"Ladybug…This is a visit I never thought I'd have to make…"

Ice water dumped down my back, shocking me into a reality I hadn't wanted to believe. But I didn't react. I didn't even twitch.

"The bastard was the toughest man I'd ever met. I was convinced he was going to outlive us all…" he trailed off, as if he wasn't sure what to say next.

"No," I croaked. The change in my voice could have been because I was parched from dancing.

A heavy pause settled between us. Uncle David made no move to come closer. "I'm afraid so. I got a message, asking me to meet him on the pier."

Back up. That was what Daddy used for any type of back up where Uncle David was concerned. It was never for true support, but usually when he needed resources, or information with no time to get it for himself.

He'd said the job wasn't a big one when I'd last seen him a few days earlier. I'd left for my own job and hadn't spoken to him since. That wasn't unusual. It was normal even.

"What did he need?"

"I never found out. When I got there. He…He was…" Uncle David cleared his throat and rubbed his neck.

"Where is he?" Life left my voice. The flat tone grating on my ears.

"Oh, Ladybug, no. I already took care of the body. You didn't need to see him that way." Uncle David's personality was softer than Daddy's. He was quicker to show his humor, his approval, and even his distaste. It was who he was, and maybe why his friendship worked so well with Daddy.

I'd never heard his sympathy.

I despised it.

"There's no…body?" I asked slowly.

"I took care of it so you wouldn't have to. Cremated just like he asked. I have the urn at my place, and I can bring it to you, but I didn't want to give it to you here."

Then why meet here?

Shaking my head, I turned and started walking away.

I—I couldn't continue this conversation. It meant everything changed. It meant I lost my best friend, mentor, and father.

Soon, I'd ask for all the details. It just wouldn't be today.

Because I was about to lose my shit, and I wouldn't let Uncle David see that. No one saw that side of me. Not even him.

"Ladybug!" He yelled softly, but I didn't turn around. I'd call him later, after I went through Daddy's files.

Right then, I needed space. Because his words wouldn't stop playing in my head.

I took care of the body. You didn't need to see him that way.

That meant that it wasn't natural. He'd needed assistance, so it wasn't an accident. It was murder. Daddy had been murdered.

Murdered.

The beep indicating the weapons locker was open sliced through the memory, leaving me in the bloody present.

"What's the target?" Cash asked from just behind me.

"I've got it. You guys don—"

"Drew, if you tell us to stay here and that we don't need to worry, I will take my life in my hands and bend you over my knee and spank your ass—and not even in a nice way. Since I like my various body parts where they are," Fletcher said in a rush of breath, "don't say it."

Silence punctuated the sentence leaving only the sounds of their breathing. Cash's breaths, deep and steady. Confidence filled every inhale and ease accompanied each exhale. Nothing fazed him.

Not Daddy.

Not Horatio—well, maybe Horatio. A faint smile pulled at my lips. He really didn't like my friendship with Horatio. As quickly as that smile arrived it vanished.

Did I even have a real friendship with the Vanisher?

Fletcher's breathing was a lot more erratic. If I put a hand on him, his heart would be pounding, there would be a bit of sweat on his brow, and his pupils would be narrowing to pin pricks. Passionate and reactive, my little pincushion wore his heart on his sleeve. Precious, dynamic, wildly impulsive, and so damn reliable it made me ache.

But Rick? My darling Rick? I could barely hear his breathing. It made me twist to find him standing only a couple of feet back. His posture straight, his gaze steady, and his eyes—they softened when I met his gaze.

Panic didn't even seem to register with him. Where Cash was all barely contained violence ready to be unleashed, and Fletcher was a wild tangle of electric emotions, Rick served as the calm in the center of the storm.

A grounded center.

"I will say it." I took the time to form the words as I glanced from intense cobalt to peaceful cerulean, and finally then to stunning turquoise. "You don't have to go with me. This has always been my mission. Maybe it's changed now, but so have other things…"

The threat to them could be more real. How much more did I not know? I couldn't let those threats get close to them. I couldn't let my world tear them apart.

Was it even my world anymore?

I shook my head. "I don't know what it means that Daddy is alive. I don't know what he wants with Horatio and Dae or why he's trusting them and not me."

My voice didn't break and those tears burning behind my eyes didn't escape their confinement. It took time to pack away all these emotions. The vulnerabilities I'd discovered with them.

Yet, not one of them looked away from me. Not when Rick let out a breath and his jaw tensed. Not when Fletcher's scowl deepened, and not when Cash clenched his fists until his knuckles went white.

The weight of all that focus on me should be uncomfortable. They were arrayed all around me in a semi-circle. Blocking all exits for me, but also anyone else's access.

"I don't know what any of it means. I only know that Uncle David lied to me."

Lied. To. Me.

A horrible lie.

A lie that…

"He told me Daddy was dead." No cracks. Compartmentalizing used to be simple. It was a task necessary to getting the work done.

The work—that was what mattered.

This—this didn't come so simply.

The work wasn't all that mattered.

Not anymore.

"He told me Daddy died. He told me Daddy called him for help. He told me everything I needed to know…"

"Except how he died," Cash said, Federal agent intact.

"I'm betting he didn't tell you where," Fletcher continued, rubbing his chin.

"I know he didn't let you say goodbye—because he couldn't," Rick added almost softly.

I nodded slowly. "He said he had his ashes."

Rick's expression shifted, but it was Cash's that drained of anything resembling warmth. There was a kind of rage in his eyes, I'd never seen before.

"What a fucking asshole," Fletcher swore in a tone far from the crazy bounce in his voice. "And he's your uncle? Uncle-uncle like related to *Daddy* or something? Or just 'uncle' cause that's what you call him?"

If they'd asked me even a day earlier, I'd have known the answer.

"I don't know."

"But you want to find out," Cash said.

Nodding, I checked the weapon I'd taken out then slid it into a holster before I pulled the shoulder holster on. Cash said nothing as he stepped forward and adjusted the fit, then fastened the snaps.

"We asking?" He met my gaze. "Or are we demanding?"

"You don't—"

The ferociousness of his kiss as he slammed his mouth down on mine ripped all the breath out of me. For a moment, the world spun and then I parted my lips. The bruising force eased, but only to something that gave as much as it demanded. His tongue swiped past my teeth to thrust against mine.

This wasn't a kiss, it was a brand and my whole body warmed to it. Cracks shifted under my skin, the compartments threatened to burst open and overturn, scattering what was left of my emotions all over the highway of my soul.

I bit him even as I shifted my weight and he chuckled against my mouth. "There's my dark saint. You bite me. You claw me. You fuck me up if you have to. But if you tell us this isn't our fight, it won't just be Fletcher's knee you go over, and I know I can take you down if I have to."

Pulling back an inch, I raised my brows. My lips were puffy and a bit sore. But I craved that sensation as much as I'd craved his kiss.

"Do you?" I challenged. "Really?"

"Oh yeah, because you, my dark saint, don't really want to hurt me. You want to protect me." Smugness suited him. It was there, glimmering around the edges of his quiet fury and determination. "If I didn't already fucking love you, seeing you stand up to your father for me would have done it. But don't you ever get between me and a hit again. I can take it."

"What if I don't want you to take it?" I fired back. Because I hadn't wanted Daddy to hurt him.

I didn't want him to hurt any of them.

"We'll protect him," Fletcher said. "Won't we, Big Guy? I mean, Rick will totally protect him and I will cheer him on."

It was ridiculous and perfect. I glanced past Cash to where Fletcher gazed at me with the exact same intensity.

"So, what is it, Drew? We spanking that ass red or we packing up our shit and going hunting? Cause you want something."

"We're going to get it," Rick said. "Together. All of us."

The last thing in the world I should say was yes. There were so many threats out there. So many things could hurt them. Cash cupped his hand around my throat, his fingers on my pulse.

They weren't a threat to me.

"I don't know how bad it's going to get," I admitted. Nothing could dissuade me from this course though. Not even them.

"Don't you worry about us, Drew," Fletcher said as he clapped Rick on the shoulder. "We got this." Then he held his hand out to me.

Cash let me go as I took it and then Fletcher kissed me with the same kind of ferocity Cash had, only there was an element of gentle passion in the way he chased my tongue and teased it.

Lifting his head, he whispered, "Together."

"Yes," Rick said, his tone firm and unyielding. "What do you need us to bring?"

I didn't deserve them. When I pulled from Fletcher to go to Rick, Fletcher let me go, trailing his fingers down my back and then I had my arms around Rick and he lifted me as he kissed me.

Heat pressed against my back, then Fletcher was there, sandwiching me between them. "Come on, Fed," Fletcher said. "Bring it in. We don't bite."

The sound of a hand slapping the back of Fletcher's head chased some of the darkness out of me, pushing it to the side, but then Cash was there, his lips pressed to the side of my head as Fletcher gave my ass a squeeze.

"Together," I conceded finally. I could leave without them. I could do it. I could get away. I knew all their weaknesses. I knew exactly how to hurt them.

I'd never do it.

I didn't want to hurt them, now or ever.

"Damn," Fletcher whispered. "Gonna have to work on that spanking idea later..."

Rick's muscles shifted and I felt the movement before his hand even landed against the back of Fletcher's head.

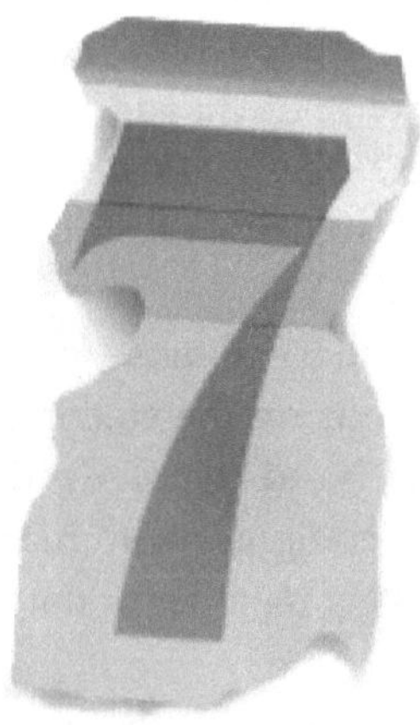

RICK

I GRIPPED the handle above the window in the backseat of the car. Today, we took a mid-sized sedan, bigger than what I'd traveled in with Vienna before. It seemed almost each house had a different set of resources, and whatever we needed, if it wasn't here, I was sure Vienna had it stashed somewhere else.

Right then, I was thankful for the extra space. As Vienna sped down various streets, she didn't watch her pacing or her corners. We took a particularly sharp turn and Fletcher ended up plastered against my side.

"Sorry, Big Guy," he groaned. "As much as I hate to admit this, I think we should add more core workouts to our regime. Rolling around in the back when Drew is feeling frisky is for the birds."

He separated himself from me, then twisted his lips to the side as he dropped his gaze. "I mean, there are fun ways to roll around in the backseat, this just ain't it."

Cash huffed out a quiet laugh as Fletcher fought to sit up straight just as we headed around a corner in the opposite direction. Fletcher was good for Cash. He brought out the more human side of our newest addition.

"What's the plan?" Cash grabbed onto his own handle, although it seemed like it was an absent-minded move instead of a necessity.

"We're going back to the address where we found Daddy." Vienna flexed her hands on the steering wheel as the speed picked up. "Because he said no, we didn't stay and look around. Whatever is going on, with him, with Uncle David, whether they're working together or not, that's our best bet of finding answers."

"That's not a good idea." Cash shook his head. "If he found out Thackery escaped, it could be a trap, he could be there right now searching for clues on how he got away, we should start back at the storage unit."

"No, we got as much as we could from the storage unit. Uncle David is currently my mission. We're going to the address where we found Daddy, then we're going after Uncle David. No negotiations." Ire whipped through Vienna's voice.

"That's not how we operate. Was it not you who just said we were in this together?"

"I didn't mean you could dic—"

"Hey, hey, now." Fletcher clung to the back of Vienna's headrest and pulled himself up to press his face against the side of her seat. "No one is trying to tell you what to do, right?" He shot Cash a very pointed look. Cash threw up his hands but didn't say anything. "We're having a conversation. A family conversation. Cash is just trying to say that he thinks it might be dangerous for us to go back to that place right now. I coul—"

"Fuck dangerous. If we don't move fast, any clues could be gone, because as Cash pointed out, Uncle David, or whoever was holding him captive, could know he's gone and be wiping away anything that would be useful to us." A vein in her neck stood out from her very apparent frustration.

Vienna *shouldn't* be feeling this way. This went against the very core of who she was. Since I'd met her, she was cool, composed, and methodical. Logical.

She was everything I had hoped to be growing up. That wasn't who I was, and it never would be, but I valued those pieces of Vienna. That she was acting so wildly out of her nature right now hurt on a level I hadn't felt before. I ached for her, and burned to make the issue go away.

Permanently.

"Who do I need to kill?" I rumbled.

She must have let off of the gas because the car slowed to a normal pace. Her striking tawny eyes met mine in the rearview mirror, and some of the unbridled hurt leaked out of her gaze.

Because that was what this was. She was hurt. Her father wasn't anything like she'd made him out to be, and it had taken everything I had not to break his jaw earlier.

When those terrible tears had entered her eyes, I wanted to stab a knife through his so he'd understand what he was doing to her. But I hadn't done that. It would not do any favors for Vienna right now.

I was also trying to give him the benefit of the doubt. After being in captivity for over a year, her father could be strug- gling himself. But I didn't give a fuck about Thackery, outside of general human compassion.

Vienna was my priority. So was Fletcher, and now Cash. When Thackery came back and started—then *continued*—to hurt her feelings by words or deeds, any compassion I had for him died.

I needed to talk to Cash. He should have a transitional period to allow for fuck ups. But not too much longer. Then Cash and I needed to step in. Fletcher could cheer us on while he distracted Vienna, just as he'd already offered.

A phantom smile drifted over her lips, her cheek lifting slightly. "Would you like to kill someone?" She asked, the soft, husky note in her voice warming my groin.

"At this particular moment, yes."

"Just not the person you actually want to kill," Fletcher mumbled.

"Depends," I told him and Vienna flicked her gaze back to me. At the barest lift of her eyebrow, I added, "The person I want to kill is the one you need dead."

Laughter, almost sharp and too bright against the open wound of her sadness, escaped her. "I adore you."

That sent a flood of real warmth through me. "I love you." It was that simple and so very complicated. The complications didn't faze me. Not when she was here, where I could protect.

"Thank you," she whispered and I nodded. Some things were personal, but I didn't care if Cash and Fletcher heard. They loved her in their own ways, as obsessed with her as I was. It was why we were all in this car.

"Okay, I'm feeling like I should be more in touch with my feelings so I can share in this mutual passion society—" Fletcher pursed his lips. "Not that I don't think you're the fucking best ever and worship the ground under your feet, Drew." The last was almost an aside, yet it amused me how Fletcher danced around his own feelings.

We'd have to work on making him more comfortable with expressing his needs.

Clearing his throat, Fletcher gave me a wry grin before he rested a gentle hand on Vienna's shoulder. Yes, I got that. The urge to touch her. To look at her. To just drink in her nearness.

Even when I wanted to kill whatever phantoms haunted her.

"But?" she prompted, keeping the car steady. The frenetic pace of her acceleration had scaled back and her knuckles weren't so white. Cash rested his free hand on her thigh. It made me want to reach up and touch her myself, but I settled for the way her gaze caressed me when she glanced at me in the mirror.

"But," Fletcher said. "I'm gonna ask the hard question—who the fuck is the other guy with Horatio? And what the hell are they doing there? I thought the one dude was just the accountant."

"Fucking Ratio." Cash's rumbled response held a lot of jealousy. He shouldn't worry so much. Vienna liked the accountant and he'd done us a favor, but she hadn't brought him back to our house.

No. She hadn't invited him at all.

She only brought home who she wanted to keep. He was a friend, nothing more. Cash would learn.

Fletcher had. Cash would.

"Horatio is the accountant. I knew he and Daddy had—" A shrug of her shoulders, the wound gaping a little as she sighed. "I knew he knew him. He knew about the last job he'd been on, knew he'd been running alone *without* Uncle David."

She tapped her fingers on the wheel.

"Did he tell you that at dinner?" Cash almost growled the last couple of words. Almost.

Maybe he was already figuring it out.

"Yes," she said, then glanced at Cash. "You don't have to hate him."

"I'll decide who I hate. Ratio has lied to me for a long time."

"You probably lied to him. We all have our secrets." The ease with which she said that was countered by the darkness sliding through her eyes again. "Clearly, Daddy has more than I realized."

"That still doesn't answer my question."

"Dae is someone Daddy knows," Vienna said with another shrug. "I've never met him before."

"What?" I asked before fully completing the thought. "He behaved very possessively for someone you've never met."

"Did he?" No, that wasn't an absentminded question, that was a musing one. "It didn't seem to bother Daddy when he was in my space."

"Nope, *Daddy* didn't seem to mind that at all." Fletcher scowled. "Not like he did when we got there." Then lower and almost under his breath, he added, "Dick."

Cash snorted. "He did not like us claiming you."

Too…

"Too bad," Vienna said, echoing my thought. "You're mine." There was nothing absent in that and it soothed some very primitive part of me to be claimed by her.

"Then you won't mind when I deal with Ratio," Cash said, but it held more of an element of question. He tested the waters.

"Yes, I will mind," she informed him. "For now, he is a possible ally. We will not alienate him."

"What about *Dae?*" Fletcher grumbled.

"I don't know about him."

"Then we leave him alone until we see what he does." Cash didn't even try to contain his dislike. "If you really want to go back to that house where we found your father," he continued. "I'm going in first."

"Will that make you feel better?" She glanced at him and some color returned to her face and her lips softened into a smile. "Taking charge and running point?"

"Keep it up, Dark Saint," he admitted with a grin. "And we'll be spanking that ass sooner rather than later."

At her chuckle, Fletcher brightened up. "Dibs! I said it first."

That pulled a genuine laugh from her and I shifted my gaze to the side mirror where I met Cash's gaze. He raised his eyebrows in silent question and I nodded.

Yes, we definitely needed to talk.

"Find out everything about the address," I told Fletcher who was already reaching for his laptop. Cash recited it without any of us needing to ask. "We need a plan for when we get there…"

Fletcher wasted no time in furiously typing over the keyboard. A myriad of expressions crossed his face as he clicked through screen after screen.

He'd started showing me some of his work, and I appreciated that. I wanted to be useful in any way I could. And if he was unavailable, I wanted Vienna to still have access to these resources without having to go to an outsider.

We were entering a small town, and Vienna's driving had slowed down. I caught the smile on my reflection in the window. Between the three of us, we'd managed to level Vienna out. She was still upset, rightfully so, but she was much calmer now.

We had done that.

Our family.

"What's Uncle David's full name?" Fletcher asked.

"David Lennox. I never knew his middle name." The strain in Vienna's voice came back, but not nearly as strong as before. It reminded me of a child telling secrets they knew they shouldn't.

"Thanks, Drew," Fletcher murmured as he kept typing.

Vienna seemed lost in thought as she navigated us back onto a major highway and we were leaving the small town behind.

We were only on the highway for ten, no more than fifteen, minutes and we were heading down the ramp and to the right. Rows and rows of midwestern cornfields surrounded us on either side. The house must have been close because Vienna soon had us on a dirt road that turned into just a path with two tire tracks.

"Uh oh," Fletcher groaned.

"What's wrong?" Vienna barked.

"First, I just lost internet access because we're in BFE. That's the first atrocity." He held up a finger. "Two, do you smell that? Because it just confirms what I found online."

Cash sniffed, then rolled down his window to get a better sense of what Fletcher was telling us.

I took in my own discreet sniff. Smoke.

Or what lingered of it. It was light enough that it was either very fresh or very old. Probably old, the way it lingered in the air.

"Fire," Vienna whispered. She didn't stop. Instead, she took us right by a property that still had a few vehicles in the yard. Whatever structure was there, only the charred frame remained, still smoking.

One man glanced at us, but they didn't stare for too long. And Vienna moved us down the road and out of sight. She pulled us under a tree and slammed her hand on the steering wheel once, twice, then a third time.

"Damn it! That was our only lead!"

"I really don't want to be the bearer of bad news, Drew, but from the looks of it, none of his accounts have been used in days. Since before you found *Daddy*." Fletcher shook his head, hitting the enter key repeatedly. "Still no fucking connection. We can never live out here. Not without some fiber optics or something tapped from a subdivision," he mumbled to himself.

Vienna screamed her frustration, hitting the wheel with both hands now. I wished I was in the front seat. I would pull her into my lap and kiss her frustration away.

Cash didn't let her down. He cupped the back of her neck and gently directed her face toward him so he could plant a punishing kiss on her lips. His jawline flexed as he deepened it.

When he pulled back just an inch, he stared into her eyes. "Hey, this is not the end. When one trail dies, you find another. When that one hits a dead end, we go another route.

We keep tapping our resources and looking at the information from as many angles as we need to. We'll find him, Vienna," Cash promised, darkness suffusing his voice, even as the sunlight danced over his profile. "We will. And there's one lead we haven't worked on yet."

Her chest heaved from her heavy breathing, caught in his spell. "What lead is that?" She asked in a soft sigh.

"Gregory Lescheva. My mentor. My pops' friend. He was on that wall."

Cash had mentioned him when we were trying to find Vienna. My gut clenched at the remembered terror I'd lived with for weeks, but I took in a long, controlled inhale. She was here now. And we would protect her.

"Gregory Lescheva..." Vienna touched her fingers to her lips. "Fletcher?"

"On it," Fletcher said as he opened a notes tab. "Cash, tell me everything you know about him..."

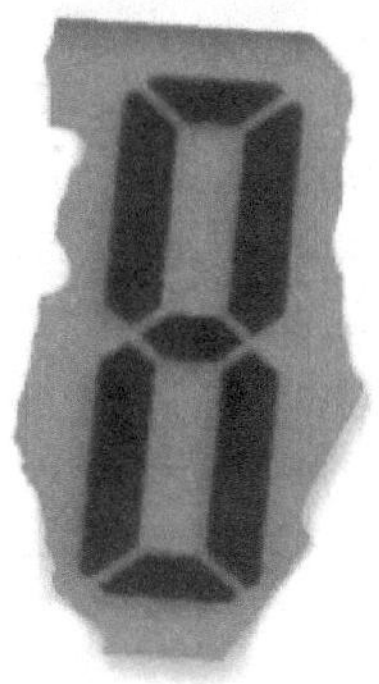

THE STILL SMOKING, but charred remains of the building where we'd found Daddy left an equally deep, burnt out crater in my soul. Getting him out of there had been important. No question existed within me on that subject. Daddy's condition hadn't been the best, even if there were multiple exits he could have used, he was definitely showing signs of malnutrition and torture.

So, why protect the person or persons behind it?

Cash's "friend" Lescheva? Uncle David? Some random stranger? We couldn't discount that. Not after Sandra Jane.

I'd called Uncle David.

Despite the wild disapproval radiating off of Rick *and* Cash, I'd called him. I had no idea what kind of message I would leave if the service picked up or even what I would say if *he* answered. At the moment, I wasn't running with a plan.

Not the best idea.

The clipped computer voice reciting the message hadn't changed. "Please leave a message, including time and return number."

Impersonal as hell. But then these were the kinds of things that could get subpoenaed.

"It's me," I said when it beeped. "Call when you can." Then I gave him a number for one of my burners. It was one we'd used before, so that was "normal." I kept my tone impersonal, polite, and business-like, all perfectly keeping within our previous interactions. Uncle David liked his games. He liked his disguises. He liked controlling when and how we met.

Then again... so did I.

Fletcher perched on the hood of the car, laptop balanced on his knees. Yet, he studied me and not the screen. Rick and Cash were right there. We'd stopped at a rest area off the highway. Other than a family that were climbing back into their minivan when we pulled in, we'd been alone. We parked some distance from the service buildings, beneath the shade of some trees that also shielded us from cars passing on the interstate.

None of them closed the distance between us. I couldn't really blame them, I was so on edge that I had to actually think to calm my breathing. Too many questions. Too many months. Too many lies.

Lies.

So many lies...

"Vienna," Cash said, "you don't have to decide anything right now. I know it feels like you need to, but sometimes the best thing to do is just step back."

"Is that the best thing?" I asked, frowning as I studied the tree line in the distance.

Rest stops were rather ubiquitous. The only thing that marked them as different was how recently the buildings had been constructed or refurbished and if their vending machines worked. The restrooms always smelled the same. Vaguely unpleasant with the hint of chemicals.

"Did you do that while chasing me?"

"Many times," Cash admitted and something in his voice pulled my attention back toward him. "Patience, Dark Saint. Distance. Deliberation. Even distraction if you need it. We have time. The clock running down on his killers stopped the moment we found him."

That was true.

"You know the five Ds?" Rick asked, sliding Cash a look.

"If one of them is don't be a dick, I think we've established that's not in my wheelhouse," Cash offered back. The playful banter pulled a real smile to my lips. The fact both men grinned touched something inside of me.

"Distance," I said softly. "Deflect. Distract. Determine." I blew out a breath. "Then, if necessary, death."

"You must be a real hit at parties," Fletcher said, the corners of his mouth twitching. The invitation to play right there.

"I don't know," I deadpanned. "I have done a few hits at parties though."

I wanted to play. I wanted to make them smile and laugh. I also wanted answers. Did I just want too much?

"You know, I bet you're hot at all the parties," Fletcher mused. "We need an excuse to put you in something sexy."

"She's always sexy," Rick corrected. "But I have seen her in a full gown and it's—amazing." His eyes flashed as he focused on me. I'd been all dressed up the night we took out Noel Warrick. It had also been the night we became lovers.

The memory warmed me and the energy it took to smile became negligible.

"Okay, the next sexy mission, I want to be the arm candy," Fletcher announced and I wasn't the only one chuckling. But Cash's laughter was fleeting as he fixed his gaze on me. The question was there in his eyes—what did I want to do? In Rick's, it was what did I need? In Fletcher's, it was what could he do?

I didn't deserve any of them.

But I would never let them go for as long as they wanted to be here, and I would never let anyone hurt them.

My resolve, like my heart, seemed to swell at that recognition. No. No one was allowed to hurt them.

"I need…" The hesitation wasn't deliberate, but the phrasing was not something I used often. I needed to work. I needed to do the job. I needed to complete the mission.

"You need?" Rick supplied, a hopeful light flickering in his eyes. His unwavering focus and support—honestly, their *presence*—had been what kept me going over the last forty-eight hours.

"I don't know what I need," I said slowly. "Not exactly. Just—I need you. I need all of you."

"You have us," Cash said, his tone not at all impatient despite the snap of the words. "Do you need us to take over for a while?"

To be in charge of me? I had let them all on some levels. Let them in… then given them that power. It had been heady in the release I found just letting them handle things. Did I need that?

"Yes." The single word escaped on a sigh. That was exactly what I needed.

"Fletcher, shut off the laptop, get in the back with Vienna and make her come. Rick—we need to find a good hotel. A secure one. Thoughts?"

My whole body rippled at the command and when I locked eyes with Fletcher, he had his laptop closed and a teasing grin on his face. "You heard the man," he said as he slid off the hood to stand. "Backseat, Drew. I've got my marching orders."

Even with the command, there was a single question in his eyes. Was this all right with me? I'd seen Fletcher at his most flirtatious, edging arrogance, and I'd seen him terrified but refusing to give up. I'd also been there as he faced his own demons and stayed with me, no matter how dark the path.

Some of the violent tension inside of me unlocked, warmth bleeding through the icy cracks in my soul. Yes. This was exactly what I wanted.

"We're going to a hotel?" was my only question as I passed the keys to Cash and headed to the backseat of the car. His hand moved, awareness rippled through me at the action. It was like the world slowed down to just us, narrowing and I could have moved but the open-handed slap he delivered to my ass sent scalding heat through my system.

"We're going where we decide to go, you get in the car and let Fletcher make you come. I want to hear you crying with it. We'll take care of everything else."

The command had my cunt clenching in absolute need. The torrent of emotions I'd been fighting to keep at bay threatened to crash over me. Fletcher passed his laptop to Rick, even as he moved toward me. When Fletcher held out his hands, I slid my palms over his. The gorgeous cerulean of his eyes held far too much sobriety.

"Let's go, Drew. I've got orders I can't wait to perform." The last he delivered with just the right amount of eyebrow wiggle and it chipped away at the pile of stones weighing on my heart. One tumbled free as he tugged me to him.

He slanted his head, blocking out the watery sunlight. Warm breath feathered my cheek an instant before his lips teased mine apart. The sweetness of the kiss was just a prelude, an appetizer for the demanding invasion as he swept his tongue across mine.

Toying with his piercing had me arching up to wrap my arms around him. When he tucked his hands against my ass and squeezed, I did as he beckoned and hitched my thighs to his hips.

The heavy weight of his engorged cock pushed against the front of his jeans. The low hum of contentment as I sucked on his tongue and the way he massaged my ass were all encouraging.

"Walk and kiss," Cash growled and that sent a hot pulse of lust through my system. The command in his voice seemed to vie with possessiveness.

Not pausing his devotion to our kiss, Fletcher moved. Every step bumped his erection against me. The clothes hid too much of the sensation though. At the door to the car, I fisted Fletcher's hair, freeing it from the band trapping it so it would spill over my hand.

"Yes, Drew?" he asked in a husky voice, the pupils of his eyes swollen but still rimmed in shimmering blue.

"Cash," I whispered, not taking my gaze off Fletcher. "Get my guns."

The corners of Fletcher's lips curved upward. "Do you have any idea how fucking hot it is when you get fierce and protective?"

"If it's half as hot as the three of you, then I'm glad."

Fletcher pivoted so he had his back to the door. My legs were still around him but he balanced my weight when I had to slide off my jacket, then my shoulder holster. Cash stroked his hands over me, nape, back, ass, thighs, and then to my ankles when I reluctantly let go of Fletcher's hips.

It was the most sensuous pat down ever. But he got all three guns and two knives. When he skated his hand under my shirt for the last one, I let out a shudder. The bra was undone and then he had my hair in his hand and my head tilted back.

Grinding against Fletcher while Cash devoured my mouth was a whole new level of delight. The sound of cars passing in the distance faded. The hot touch of Fletcher's fingers as he undid my pants had me groaning, but more when my pants were suddenly sweeping downward.

Bare-assed naked to the world, only I wasn't. The heat of all three of them surrounded me. Rick was there. Tugging off my shoes and then Fletcher lifted as the clothes were gone. Cash bit my lower lip before he released my mouth.

"Enjoy Fletcher, Dark Saint. I want to hear every fucking sound he brings out of you. Understood?" The last he delivered with a warning slap to my ass.

My cunt clenched in eagerness. "Yes, sir," I responded. "My little pincushion can fuck me however he wants. I won't be quiet about any of it."

Behind me, Rick chuckled and I twisted long enough to kiss him. Unlike Fletcher's wild passion or Cash's fierce possessiveness, Rick's kiss held only desperate devotion.

A sixth D, only for us. Then Fletcher slid into the backseat and I followed. It seemed an age since our last kiss and I savored the sharp demand of his tongue as he stroked my mouth.

"Living dangerously," I whispered as I straddled his lap. We were in the center. This position would not allow for seatbelts.

"They'll drive real careful-like," Fletcher assured me, pulling my shirt up. I was going to end up fully naked back here. Utterly vulnerable in a car on the highway, in the middle of the day.

I shrugged the shirt off without hesitation. Then Fletcher lifted me to lock his lips around a nipple. A groan rippled free and while my natural inclination was to quiet any sound, I didn't.

Releasing it was almost cathartic and it encouraged Fletcher to bite and suck in alternating pulses. It took me a minute to work my fingers under his shirt. "No more t-shirts," I groaned. "Only buttons."

"Gonna lose a lot of buttons," Fletcher admitted in a dark voice that just made my pussy spasm. "Worth it."

Then he dragged me back in for a kiss. My nipples against his hot skin and the piercings on his just lit me on fire. Some distant part of my brain processed that we were moving, but I didn't care. He roamed his hands over my back and then down to my hips. The shadows were chased away or maybe we outran them.

No chill or loneliness existed here. No lies.

No secrets.

Breath coming in sharp pants, Fletcher whispered against my mouth, "You can tell me anything, Drew. Tell us anything."

"I know," I answered in the same hungry voice. "I need you."

That confession spilled free as I got his pants undone and freed his cock so I could stroke it. Hot and heavy in my hand, he seemed to thrust against my grip even as I teased the piercing.

"I love your piercings," I admitted in between kisses. I wanted to nibble and play with all of them. "I love how it feels inside of me when you fuck me. I love how hot and cool the metal is… I love to feel every inch of you."

"Goddamn," Cash swore from the front seat.

"No comments from the front seat," Fletcher said, his eyes practically dancing. "Just enjoy the show."

"We are," Rick admitted. "Tell us more about what you like, Vienna."

"I like all of you," I confessed before nipping Fletcher's lower lip as he thrust up against my hand. I soothed the scrape with little kittenish licks. He groaned and then kissed a path along my jaw.

My core was soaked, and I teased his cock against my slit. The bump and brush of his piercing against my clit was better than a vibe. Especially with the hum of the car. Every imperfection in the road communicated itself.

A rumble escaped Fletcher as he reached my nipples again. This time, he had no patience in how he sucked and bit at them. Pain and pleasure pulled taut, leaving me wanting so much more. A mewling sound escaped me and it pulled his head up.

"I like being with all of you." The confessions spilled like tears I refused to shed. "I adore having you with me. I like that Cash and Rick are listening to us. That they want to hear us fucking. I like knowing that they are going to be hard as stone and wanting to fuck me as soon as we're done."

I swore his cock gave a little jerk against my palm. His breathing, like my own, came in harder little gasps.

"I love knowing that I'm about to sink down on you and there will be no barriers and that your cum will be hot inside me when they slide in next."

He clasped my nape and dragged me down for a kiss even as I positioned that beautiful, curved cock with the sweet piercing that rubbed a path upwards, leaving electric tingles in its wake.

"Hello, my darling pincushion," I whispered against his lips before he stole my breath again. His only answer was a groan before he thrust upward. Gripping my hip with one hand and my hair in the other, Fletcher moved me to the cadence *he* wanted and I craved.

Rotating my hips to increase the friction, I rode his every thrust. The stroking of his cock filling me lit me up and even as I shifted the angles, we were both gasping and groaning. There were no words needed for this, just the hard thrusts and the brutal kisses interspersed by the rub of his chest on mine.

When he put both hands on my hips, I braced mine on his shoulders. The increased pace, additional force, and angle had him nailing my sweet spot every single time. His every shudder seemed to echo my own.

More.

I wanted more, even as I savored every single one of his responses. More sounds escaped me, but they got lost in the way he kept swallowing my kisses. The orgasm sweeping through me a moment before his hips began to stutter was almost a shock.

His name escaped me on a shout as I spasmed around him. The warmth blooming inside of me as he came was exactly what I craved. His laughter was the second best thing. I sank into his kiss, teasing my fingers over his scalp. Shudders still bounced between us, but the feel of him inside of me was something I didn't think I would ever get enough of.

From any of them.

"How much time?" Fletcher asked after a long huff of breath. The edginess inside of me had been sanded away, though some tensions tried to creep back in.

"An hour," Cash fired back. "Make her come again."

"Pushy bastard," Fletcher said to me lazily. "Would you like me to make you come again, Drew? Or shall we do an Executive Fire Drill and get you a fresh hot cock to fill you up?"

Oh. I liked the sound of that. The sudden and rather abrupt changing of lanes told me Cash did too.

"The question," I murmured, "is how do we decide whose cock I get?" I gave him a lazy kiss and Fletcher laughed as his dick began to stir.

"Cash," Rick offered. "He's a terrible driver."

The absolute deadpan seriousness of that made me laugh for real and my pussy spasmed. Cash could be brutal and that sounded so good right now.

"Oh, she's hot for Cash all right," Fletcher murmured as he slid a hand between us and began to work my clit. "Just ride my fingers, Drew. We can get another one out of you before he finds a place to stop."

"Oh, yes." The command in Fletcher's voice was as hot as his touch. "Please."

At my moan, Cash pressed down on the accelerator. The force pressed me against Fletcher and then I fused our mouths together as I began to writhe against his fingers. My orgasm hit just as we came to a stop.

Fletcher didn't leave the back of the car, he just scooted

over and then I was climbing onto Cash's lap and slamming down onto his swollen dick.

Fuck.

Yes.

"Faster," I demanded. "I need Rick too."

I needed all of them.

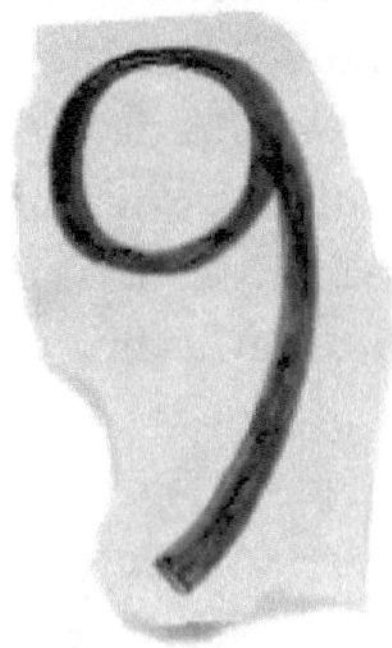

FLETCHER

HMM...

I studied the cameras. Tilted my head to the left, then studied them again. I reached out a finger and pushed the button to rotate through all the different angles I'd put up around the subdivision.

Granted, I didn't have *all* the rooms in that house under surveillance. But what I did have was very very quiet. No movement, no clutter looking like Daddy got up for a bathroom break and was coming right back.

The car in Garage Five was also missing.

I should tell Rick. No, Cash.

He could be the one to tell Drew that Daddy had gone missing. I certainly didn't want to be the bearer of that particular bad news. Where the hell would he have gone anyway?

I rewound the footage that looked directly at the house he was staying at. Thirty minutes after we left, the fucking blue-eyed fox and his little friend strutted out of the house.

Narrowing my gaze, I studied the other guy. Dae, I think his name was. He didn't have blue eyes. We were at least safe from him.

Both stopped at their cars and glanced toward our house. How did they even know which house was ours? They'd already been inside when we headed over there on a mission.

It wasn't my imagination. Drew hadn't told anyone about this place before us. Dae and fucking Ratio may have found the place for Daddy, but that didn't mean they would have known which place was *ours*.

I needed more cameras. And bugs.

That way, I could keep an eye on Daddy for Drew. But like, from a distance. An unseen distance that he would never figure out.

And if he did, I'd have enough time to shove Cash his way to take care of him.

Oh shit.

There was a way that I could potentially reel him back in…

It was a gamble. I didn't think Drew would be upset with me. And I did have faith in the little powerhouse. I mean, She took down Cash with one well-placed kick, and she seemed to have a history with Daddy.

I tapped two fingers against my lips as I snuck a look at the phone. Yup, I was doing it. All for the greater good. And if she happened to take *Daddy* down a peg or two…well, he deserved it for the pain he had caused, and was still causing, Drew.

If I got to watch the little powerhouse have a go at Daddy, bonus.

Pressing the button for the speakerphone, I turned the volume down. No need to alert the rest of the house. Rick was making dinner, Drew was checking her email, and Cash…was doing Cash things, but they were all busy.

"Hello?" She answered in her sugared tone.

"Mart, this is Fletcher, Drew's…" Shit, how did I describe myself? Boyfriend? Bleh. Man? Nope. Lover? I almost cracked myself up.

"Tweedledum?" she finished dryly.

I grinned. "Yes. I am one of Drew's minions."

"Where's Tweedledee and Asshole? Where's Vienna for that matter?"

Asshole must be Cash. I snorted.

"They're busy. I just wanted to call you and give you a heads up." I didn't wait for her response, plowing right into the money shot. "Thackery is back. Turns out, he's not dead. He was playing captive. Drew retrieved him a few days ago." It was a gamble using that particular phrasing, but fuck it.

"What?" She screeched.

I didn't say anything. Let her have time to absorb it. One, *I* wasn't the asshole. And from her reaction when Drew shared the news, she cared about Daddy. So on the plus side, I was doing a bit of good too.

"What do you mean he was playing captive?" Mart snarled.

I cleared my throat. I hadn't anticipated she'd ask me about it. *Rookie mistake, Reed.* "Drew found him in a holding cell, but apparently a poor one. She said there were at least five ways he could have escaped."

"She would know," she murmured. "Where is he *now*?"

———

Head canted, I stared at the video feeds after I hung up with Mart. I really hadn't had an answer for her question. Did *she* know about the subdivision? Horatio, the blue-eyed fox, and his dark-eyed buddy had, but Drew hadn't known that they knew. To be fair, I really probably should have considered what Mart's *next* action would be.

"Don't worry, Tweedle-Boy," she said in an almost soothing tone that did absolutely nothing to comfort me during my failure to respond. "I'll take care of it."

That sounded very much like a threat. Like a *threat*-threat.

Which, targeted at *Daddy*, I didn't mind so much. But it also sounded like an imminent threat. Lips pursed, I went to the cabinets where Rick and I had been organizing my gear. In general, I didn't want anyone touching my stuff, but Rick had some good ideas on making things accessible swiftly—also identifying when I needed something restocked.

The fact it let us work on some of his technical skills while also letting me call where things went was actually useful. For now, I checked the power strips in there, and then hesitated. Those power strips could be used as transmitters and information resources.

I'd done it a few times when I needed corporate info or info on what the family was doing. Power strips, outlets— they were great for harvesting information. Useful. Hidden in plain sight. Your targets willingly plugged themselves in.

That was when I did a full sweep of my office. I always took precautions. Old habits. But there was zero reason to think this house had been compromised. Drew said no one knew the locations. No doubt existed in me at her assurance. But now there was a blue-eyed fox who definitely knew, and his buddy too.

We'd taken her to a hotel the day before because she needed a break and she needed sleep. After we got there, Rick took her in the shower and her cries were more than enough to get me hard again. When she came out, she had me half down her throat before I was aware of what her intentions were. Another couple of rounds left me spaghetti and Cash got her into bed where he and Rick got her to sleep.

Coming home had been her choice at breakfast. But she had *slept* first. So here we were. I walked back to the screen and reviewed all the footage. I couldn't find where or if *Daddy* left. None of the approaches, however, showed his little pals coming to the house.

But what about before I had cameras up?

What about when *Daddy* lived here?

Panic and irritation vied for supremacy in my veins. Back to the cabinet, I pulled out a secondary digital tablet that I only used for sniffing out spyware. I had all the right cables. I'd need to scan every single outlet in the house. Then I was going to put out more cameras and add bugs to the new house.

I wanted to know what was going on there. With care, I left the office as *naturally* as possible. No need to cause alarm. Drew was in the living room, feet up on the sofa with her laptop open. It wasn't plugged into anything and her phone was next to her. When she glanced up at me, I winked and blew her a kiss.

Her smile devastated my senses and my cock immediately perked up. But we had to save that for later. I'd start upstairs. That made sense. Also where I could do this quietly. If I didn't find anything, no harm and no foul.

Drew already had enough to worry about. The sound of Rick in the kitchen followed me like a comforting soundtrack of our life. Big Guy was so damn good in the kitchen, he'd seduced me—like in the healthy, loving a full stomach with a gourmet appetite way—from the beginning really. He made the food, I ate the food. He controlled the caffeine, I kept my secret stashes.

It worked for us.

Trying for light footsteps, I headed for Drew's bedroom first. If I were a blue-eyed fox who wanted in her hen house— and I was and had definitely made myself at home—her bedroom was the place I'd want to keep eyes and ears on.

If they had, I hope they choked on all the orgasms we gave her. We should definitely work on making her louder. My cock stiffened right up, all in on this idea. With care, I started with the general plugs. One at a time. Then the power cords and bricks, finally the power strips.

So far so good.

Except…

The little alert on my tablet said there was a receiver in the room. I went over the power strip first. Nope. Not it.

The little brick that plugged into it.

That gave me a red dot.

Son.

Of.

A.

Bitch.

Incensed, I whirled around and nearly let out a very less than masculine scream at the sight of Cash leaning in the doorframe, arms crossed. "Why are you creeping around in here?"

I pressed a finger to my lips and he straightened immediately. When I held up the brick then turned the digital tablet around, his eyes went flat and his expression turned to stone.

One *might* be explained. It could be Drew's own bug to make sure *we* didn't fuck with her stuff. But Cash followed me like a shadow of vengeance as I went through the house.

Four more bugs later and this didn't seem like something she wouldn't have told us. Still wrestling with that part, my phone gave a little warning buzz that something had activated one of the motion sensitive cameras.

Who the hell could that be?

I opened the app on my phone just in time to catch a shiny, cherry red convertible pull into the subdivision. A woman with a mane of light blonde hair whipping in the wind behind her and a very expensive scarf headband gave me a clue as to who arrived.

Nope, I didn't even need to see her face to know that I'd done gone and fucked up. Suddenly, all of my life decisions over the last two hours seemed highly suspect.

I needed a do over.

"Someone here?" Rick poked his head into the study, the picture of calm and poise. If anything, he had a little pep to his step, probably hoping we were about to host a dinner party where he could wow everyone with his canapé game.

Did he not see I was freaking out over here?

"Oh, no one important. Just the little powerhouse I might have called earlier and let it accidentally on purpose slip out that Daddy made a comeback from the dead." Words vomited from my mouth. I knew it. There was just nothing I could do to stop it.

"Mart is here?"

"What the fuck is Mart doing here?" Cash stomped into the study. He must have been hovering in the hallway like a creeper to hear all that. I was purposely not loud to avoid Drew from hearing.

Although the bedroom door was shut. And we all knew that bedroom was insulated so a bomb going off wouldn't bother her.

Which was good. She needed a break. Thankfully, she hadn't retreated to the bedroom until *after* I got the bug out.

And hey! Bright side. She might be happy to see Mart. But…

"Maybe we should see how the next few minutes with Mart go before we alert Drew to her presence…" I winced.

Another ominous growl broke free of Cash's very muscled chest, and he stalked out of the room.

My phone dinged with another alert on the motion detector.

I swiped my thumb across the screen to turn it on.

Oh goody.

Daddy was back too. And he parked right behind Mart's car. Which wasn't parked in front of the house he had chosen, so I guess she didn't know everything?

That she knew where we were, and Drew likely wasn't aware she had this intel, was concerning.

But that was a future Fletcher problem.

I jogged lightly after Cash with Rick right behind me. We cleared the door, and I was so happy Rick didn't slam it.

If Present Fletcher would have told Past Fletcher what I'd be walking in on, I'd have never believed it. Daddy gave off such strong *I want to string your innards up and laugh* vibes, I would have thought anything would roll off his shoulders.

Hell, he'd been hurting Drew's feelings left and right and he didn't even blink. But right now, tiny Mart was shouting the house down, waving her arms in his face and he was standing there.

Sure, he was as stoic as ever, but the fact that he was taking it? That spoke volumes about the type of relationship they had. Mart was the fire to Daddy's ice, and it was a train wreck I couldn't look away from.

Against my better judgment, my feet moved me forward.

Then there was Mr. I Feel No Fear—yeah, I still couldn't comprehend that, but it made so much sense—stalking right for them.

Nope, just kidding. He stopped. He was probably enjoying this exchange too.

"I cannot believe you, Thackery Drew! A year! Over a year I haven't heard from you, and you left Vienna to fend for herself. For what? So you can *play captive*?"

His eyebrows shot up at the same time my stomach landed on my toes. Hopefully, the source of that particular verbiage would never reach Daddy's ears.

"What were you thinking? Seriously, sugar. Tell me exactly what you were thinking so I can determine the size of the bullet to shoot you in the ass with." She crossed her arms and pursed her glossy lips.

"Big Guy," I slapped Rick on the shoulder as he stopped next to me, which was ten feet behind Cash. "You might as well get the popcorn."

"Why?" Ah Rick, he was so innocent.

"Because there's about to be a show."

I'D DEBATED A NAP, that was what I told myself when I went up to my room. I didn't nap. Not unless I had a job. The day at the hotel had been a break I needed even if I hadn't realized it until we were there. Room service, a huge bathtub with jets, and all the care and consideration Rick, Fletcher, and even *Cash* could heap upon me.

Maybe the even Cash comment wasn't necessary, but he'd never struck me as someone who offered tenderness. That seemed to be something he left to Rick, but my bruised soul must have been showing because he was nothing but kind and tender with me. Even going so far as to sleep in the same bed with all of us, though he stuck Rick on the other side of Fletcher and curled up next to me so that Fletcher and I were in the middle.

Since returning to the subdivision, I'd been wrestling with myself. Wrestling with what to do next. Indecision was not a familiar place for me to spend a great deal of time. Life had always revolved around the mission. The jobs. Hunt the monsters. Study the monsters. Take the monsters down.

When Daddy died…

I pushed off the bed and smoothed the cover so it wouldn't bother Rick. Not that he would complain. The guys had all been giving me space since we got home. I appreciated it, but maybe I needed to ask what they thought. Get their input instead of just sourcing it all myself.

The idea of asking for help was unsettling enough, but then… it wasn't just me anymore. Daddy and I used to talk, or I thought we had. I'd been his partner. Now, I didn't know what to think except I never wanted the guys to feel like I was in this moment. I never wanted them to doubt their importance to me or my trust in them.

Cash had been vying for this since he walked into that scene at the docks. Maybe even longer. He wanted to be my partner. Rick and Fletcher—they already gave me so much, but they were willing to do more. Letting them take care of me had been what I needed. Maybe I was too close to all of this.

The downstairs was almost silent. The television was on, but muted. The kitchen was quiet. The oven was on and there were two pots on the stove, both were covered but the heat was off. I glanced into Fletcher's office, but they weren't there.

Movement on one of the screens pulled my attention. Cameras set up on the property. Fletcher had mentioned that he'd been putting some up before, but I'd half-forgotten about them. There had to be a few for the number of screens that alternated.

Then I found my guys. All three of them, outside.

Mart was here.

Oh, shit.

Mart was here and she was stabbing her finger at Daddy's chest. Pivoting, I headed for the front door. I didn't bother with shoes. The yoga pants were loose and the dark t-shirt would hide the lack of bra, but I didn't want to leave Mart out there facing Daddy's wrath alone.

"Are you quite finished?" Daddy asked as I cut around Fletcher and Rick where they stood watching, a safe distance behind Cash. Fletcher grimaced, his expression almost apologetic. I'd figure that out in a minute.

"Don't you take that tone with me, Thackery," Mart challenged him, her accent thickening. She only did that when she was well and truly angry. "You're lucky I haven't already shot you."

"I don't appreciate the interference right now, not after all these years." The comment and Daddy's flat tone made me nearly miss a step. It wasn't anger, it was—disappointment?

"You were never an *asshole* to her before." Mart thumped him, charging forward and Daddy backed up a step then steadied her when she went off balance at the hit. "I've never had a reason to question your choices before...do you have any idea how badly she's been hurting? How badly *I* have been hurting? Our dollbaby does not deserve this."

Our?

Since when did Mart ever lay claim to me? And when did she ever address Daddy in a *we* situation?

"She was never ours. I made sure you were well taken care of all these years in order to leave my daughter with me." Daddy shook his head, his choice of words belying a much stronger sense of emotions than his voice did.

Still.

"What do you mean leave me with you?" I barked as I closed the space between us with a few quick strides. Both Mart and Daddy startled at my question.

The warm color suffusing Mart's cheeks was all the confirmation I needed to know that Daddy had spoken nothing but the truth. As for what that truth was...

I was about to find out.

Daddy's gaze was both steady and heavy on my face as I studied him. He didn't appear to be flustered like Mart. Not surprising, since he very rarely showed any kind of strong emotion. Everything was methodical with him.

"What do you mean leave me with you?" I asked the

question with an exaggerated slowness, my voice vibrating with something I couldn't even name.

Staring at Daddy, the one person who meant the most to me through my entire life, and Mart, the one person I considered a friend, maybe to my own detriment, I was on the verge of chaos.

This was one more lie he'd told me. One more secret I wasn't allowed to know. Each one sat so heavy on my chest, I could barely breathe. How many more could I take?

How many more secrets could there be?

Learning what I had about Daddy the last few days, I was afraid to put a number to it.

I couldn't.

I refused to.

"Dollbaby," Mart whispered, a soft plea. "I—" She cut herself off, and clamped her mouth shut.

I didn't look at her. It didn't matter if she had kept a secret from me. I would expect nothing less. But Daddy, I begged him with my gaze to tell me the truth without making this a puzzle where I needed to hunt for all the pieces on my own.

If he forced it, I would. But it would irreparably break our relationship. I tried to put that in my expression too.

The second he opened his mouth, his choice of words would decide if we had a chance to work out our differences, given that he would share why he was so different *now*, or we'd go our separate ways.

Daddy blinked.

Fletcher and Rick moved to take up positions at my back. They each laid a calming hand on my body. Their touch allowed me to take in a deep, slow breath.

Cash stepped almost between Daddy and me. He didn't block my view, but he crossed his arms, braced his feet and faced Daddy.

Tears pricked my eyes.

They were showing they supported me. They would let

me handle this on my own, but they were silently telling me they were there for me, they were on my side.

Only, I never thought there would be a time I needed a side against Daddy.

"Mart was pregnant at nineteen. She wasn't ready to be a mother, so I compensated her to have you and leave you in my care." Daddy's words were measured, his gaze unblinking as if he were waiting to see how this news would land on my shoulders.

I held my breath for half a second as I let this new secret penetrate the fog of my brain.

Glancing at Mart, I took in her small stature, the tilt of her eyes, and even the shape of her chin. I resembled her. Why hadn't I seen this before?

"Damn it, Thackery!" Mart turned to Daddy as if she couldn't look at me. Or maybe she didn't want me to look at her. "This was my story to tell. The way you just spit the words out, you made it seem like I wanted nothing to do with her. Which was *not* the case."

Wasn't it? She hadn't been in my life in any meaningful capacity, not until recently. I'd met her as a preteen girl. Where had she been before that?

"We deal in facts, Mart. No amount of honeyed words will change the fact that you were her birth mother and left her with me to pursue your own goals."

"Why you—" She wound up her fist, and punched him right in the nose, just the way Daddy had taught her.

He cursed and cupped his face as blood leaked through his fingers.

"But wait..." Fletcher cut in. "You're the father, though, right?" When Daddy speared him with a withering glare, Fletcher's face leaked of all color.

"Leave Fletcher alone," I said, jerking Daddy's attention back to me. "He's got a right to ask the question. Considering the number of secrets you've kept and lies I've been told, verifying what I thought was absolute truth makes a great deal of sense."

I almost didn't recognize my own voice, and for the first time since Daddy came home, he wore a puzzled expression that seemed to put us on the same footing for once.

"I never lied about being your father," Daddy said, the chilling lack of emotion from our earlier interactions absent. Maybe it was the bloody nose adding a hint of stuffiness to his voice or maybe he really couldn't believe he had to tell me that.

I didn't know and, at the moment, I found myself hard-pressed to care. "Then what you said about your fling with my mother and her showing up pregnant was also true?" That was more or less what he'd just said.

"Dollbaby..." Mart said and I held up a hand. The wounded expression on her face cut at me but she went silent.

"I don't need an explanation from you," I told her and maybe I could have been kinder, but I just didn't have it in me. "You made a choice, I can respect that. You didn't owe me truth."

Then I looked at Daddy.

"You on the other hand..."

"Vienna," he said with a tired sigh, "if you want to discuss this with me, we can do this elsewhere and without an audience."

"We could," I agreed. "But we're not going to do that. You're asking me to respect and acknowledge our relationship—our partnership. You want me to trust you, blindly and without reservation."

"You find that so hard to believe?" Daddy demanded. Interesting. Daddy didn't demand anything. The world narrowed down to the space separating us. The few spare feet of concrete which might as well have been the Grand Canyon for the depthless abyss that had opened up between us.

"No, I don't find it hard to believe that you want me to

just blindly follow you. Except—I'm not blind, Daddy. I'm not an idiot. You died. I moved on. I focused on hunting your killers and finishing your work. Without question. But that devotion seems to be very one-sided and now I have a lot of questions."

The guys didn't move, Rick's hand on my lower back provided the stabilizing force I needed. Cash still maintained his position between me and Daddy, but he didn't block my view. None of them spoke. They were letting me handle this.

"Sweet girl," Daddy said, more frustration in those two syllables than I'd ever heard in his voice before. But instead of offering me answers, he just dragged a handkerchief out of his pocket and mopped at the blood on his face.

"Don't worry, Daddy," I said, offering him what comfort I had left in me. "I've learned a lot the last few months. I learned that I can survive without you, no matter how much it hurts."

His right eye twitched and his whole body went still. Mart actually turned her agonized gaze from Daddy to me.

"I learned that you did jobs without me always being aware, but I know you well enough to know how to figure out what those jobs were. I tracked them down—finished some—got answers from others. I know the Network is compromised. As it turns out, our enemies were probably even closer."

I was going to miss our home here.

But this sanctuary had been compromised a long time before I was even aware it had been.

Horatio and I might be able to strike a deal, but I didn't know Dae and I wouldn't trust the safety of my guys to speculation. We'd need to start over somewhere. That would take time and resources. I had enough.

Maybe.

Mart clearly wanted to say something to me but I wasn't sure I would ever be ready to hear it. She'd always been so kind to me, a friend before I understood what friendship was, and I rooted for her and Daddy. Awkward, I guessed. Daddy always said my mother made the right choice to leave me with him. He wanted me. She wasn't ready to be a mother.

I'd only been born because he asked and she agreed. So between them…

Right. I didn't know how to process that.

"But I don't have time for this," I said abruptly. "I have leads to track down and Uncle David to deal with—"

"Don't you dare," Daddy said, taking a step toward me. Cash straightened and Rick nudged me back one step with Fletcher sliding his arm around my middle. They were placing themselves between me and Daddy. "I mean it Vienna, you will *stay* out of this. Do I make myself clear?"

Daddy didn't seem all that moved by their positions and I couldn't say I was all that moved by his.

"Yes," I said. "You have. Now let me make myself clear… I am going to hunt him down. I am going to find out the answers to my questions. I will exact justice if it is required. You've been compromised, and maybe you have been all along. But for now? We—" And by we, I meant me and my guys, and I indicated as much with a little circle drawn in the air with regard to the four of us. "We are going to do this *our* way. You should get your nose looked at…Mart probably broke it."

With that, I turned on my heel but not fast enough to miss a flash of movement as Daddy surged forward and Cash struck. Daddy avoided the blow, but he didn't manage to see Rick's.

The punch caught him in the face and lifted him up off the ground and knocked him on his ass. A part of me wanted to go back to help him, but the rest of me resisted. Daddy made his choice.

I'd made mine.

Fletcher gave me a worried look but held out a hand to me.

My guys were with me.

"It probably is broken now," Rick said, his voice quite patient. "Don't ever talk to Vienna that way again, Mr. Drew. I don't want to have to kill you. You've already made her unhappy."

It was so Rick, I almost laughed as tears burned in my eyes. But they were with me within moments as Fletcher and I walked.

"Ma'am," Cash said, then he spit. "Thad." Then he was with us. "Keep going, Dark Saint. We're with you."

That was everything.

CASH

"WHAT DO you think about Vigilante Villains?"

I glanced at Fletcher in the rear-view mirror as we raced down the highway. I say raced, but we were barely doing five over the speed limit.

When you want to stay under the radar, you have to follow the easy rules to get away with breaking the big ones. Part of that was being a law-abiding citizen in almost all ways.

Almost. I smirked.

"Hm?" Vienna twisted in the passenger seat to glance back at Fletcher.

Rick had made a strong argument to drive, but in the end, I'd won. Vienna would have been driving except she wanted to triple check our research. She was also still processing the revelations she'd learned from Thad and Mart, although she wouldn't admit it.

"For our team name. All the greats have names. The Kinsmen like the mafia. The Avenger superheroes. Oh! We could be the Re-Vengers." A grin lit up his face.

"No." Rick shook his head.

Vienna pursed her lips like she was fighting a smile.

"That's quite a spectrum. A criminal organization to fictional superheroes."

"I've been thinking about it. We could get matching T-shirts—"

"Hell no," I said, also shaking my head. "No way in hell we're all going to match like some National Lampoon's vacation. Our jobs require a certain amount of anonymity. That would not allow blending in."

The smile broke free on Vienna's face and my chest squeezed. God damn, she was gorgeous. The perfect balance of beauty and strength. Skill and guts.

Like hell Thad would ruin that.

I moved my gaze back to the highway.

"Back to Vigilante Villains. You know, a nice cross between the two. Because while we do save lives, we technically break the law to do it. I like that one."

"No," we all chorused together. Fletcher's smile morphed into an immediate pout as he slumped back against the seat, mumbling something about how we suck all the fun out of life.

Without saying a word, Rick patted him on the shoulder.

"Re-vengers was used in another movie anyway," Fletcher mumbled, still sulking.

A year ago, hell, make that a month ago, if you'd told me this was the family I'd land myself in, I'd have laughed until I lost my breath. It would have been a ridiculous thought, nothing I'd have wanted for myself.

But it wasn't that bad.

"Fletcher, run through the file again." We were almost to the military academy, and we needed our heads in the game. It only took one slip and we could be exposed.

Between Vienna and I, and with Rick and Fletcher's growing skills, we were too seasoned to lose focus, but the moment we became too cocky was the minute we were caught or killed.

The irritation fell away from Fletcher as he tapped his keyboard and started reciting the details. This was his zone and he worked best when he was needed.

"Braden Sanderson, twenty years old. Son of Ronald Sanderson, self-made technology tycoon. Came from wealth, but grew it times ten. Car technology is his love, but he also dabbles in military intelligence, prosthetics, and cloud computing."

Rick whistled. "Every time you list his skillset I'm impressed."

"It's not hard to have so many specialties when you have billions to hire top of the line research teams, Big Guy," Fletcher said absently as he clicked on the keyboard some more.

"Good point," Rick mumbled.

The bright lights of an approaching car illuminated the inside of the cab, but the driver was too impatient with my responsible driving and sped past.

"While he keeps mostly to himself or confined to his one percent circle, he has been spotted with a few acquaintances over the years. One of which is…" he drummed his fingers on the back of my headrest.

I glared through the mirror.

He grinned and sat back. Yeah, this was a strange reality that I would fight and die for.

"You guessed it, shady Uncle David."

Glancing at Vienna, I turned on the right blinker. Her face was stoic, and she didn't comment to defend him, but she also didn't seem unbothered either.

My grip tightened on the steering wheel as I flexed my hands. Her fucking father was hurting her, then she had to come to terms with her Uncle David somehow being involved with her father's abduction, although we didn't know *how* just yet.

And now she had to deal with her birth mother living on the edges of her life without saying a damn word.

Her life was going to take a turn for the better. Soon. If I had to burn down the world to fix it for her, I would. With a smile and pep in my fucking step.

"Tonight's mission. Find out Ronald's favorite hideouts, ordered by preference." Fletcher snapped his laptop shut as we pulled up to a dimly lit gate.

I rolled down my window as the guard shuffled out of the guard station.

"ID and purpose of visit?" He grunted, rubbing his eyes. His mid-shift nap worked in our favor. He'd have a hard time remembering what we looked like, or what we drove.

When they were in hot water and couldn't remember, they tended to make shit up.

As for the cameras? Fletcher would take care of those. I flashed a plain servicing badge and dropped it. "Dermot's Plumbing. There was a break in the sewage line in the faculty hall. Pretty nasty, I hear."

He winced, jotted it down, and then waved us through.

As I rolled up the window, Fletcher blew out a breath in the backseat.

"Is it just me, or was that the worst guard ever? We have a car full of people, plain clothes, and he just let us in with no questions. How did you do it, man?"

"Confidence. You act like you're supposed to be here, and they'll believe it." I turned off the air to better hear our surroundings. We'd studied the map, and I knew the exact place we needed to park.

"This doesn't look like a military school," Rick said quietly as he gazed at the well lit estate.

"That's because it's for the wayward children of the rich and influential. It just wouldn't do for the public to catch wind that their children are tucked away in a strict military school to straighten them out. For all intents and purposes, this is an exclusive college." Vienna's voice was soft, but normal as I pulled into the lot at the far end of the school by lots used for field exercises.

No fourteen-mile ruck required for these snots. More like half a mile jaunt.

We climbed out of the car and shut our doors quietly. I grinned as we started through the sparse woods toward the school. The jobs were becoming my favorite part of our work. They energized me in much the same way as the hunt. Only now, there was no red tape to tie my hands.

When we started driving, Fletcher had provided full work ups on the staff. Two were alcoholics, most likely passed out cold by now based on our reports. One instructor was on an emergency leave, and the last was in the hospital with a nasty broken arm. Thanks to one of the kids.

"The student wing is just on the other side of this field." The light from Fletcher's screen highlighted the furrow in his brow. "The second entrance from the left is the door we need to go in. Here, let me check Braden's location. He successfully downloaded my game."

Twigs and pinecones crunched under our feet as we moved toward the school. We cleared the trees and I stopped, holding up a hand.

Muffled voices sounded like they were coming at us through a tunnel. "You all hear that?" I asked, glancing around. The field was set up with canvas tents ready for the brats.

"No," Vienna said, then covered her mouth. I couldn't tell if it was to hold in a laugh or hide a grimace.

I followed her gaze to a set of port-a-potties on the edge of the field. One of them was rocking.

"Nasty," Fletcher said through a gag. "I really hope that's not who I think it is."

"No," Vienna repeated. This time a choked giggled escaping while Rick just shook his head. I was with him. This place was a sprawling mansion for about a hundred co-ed students. There were better places to sneak off to.

"According to my app, he's just over there."

I shrugged. This just made our job easier. And quicker.

Leaving them behind, I started walking toward the rocking John. Barely perceptible footsteps trailed behind me. Rick and Fletcher were doubling down on their training and I noticed the improvement. We'd have to up their training even more soon.

"Oh, god, yes. Right there," a girl moaned.

Braden just grunted.

"We're sure this is him?" I twisted to Fletcher.

"Yup," he said hoarsely. "I'm sure."

Stepping forward, I pressed my hand and foot on the edge of the John, and yanked on the door, breaking the pathetic piece of plastic protecting their privacy.

"Wait!" Fletcher yelled, but it was too late. The stench of shit and ammonia washed over us and we got an eyeful of the girl half bent toward the wall with the guy drilling her from behind.

"What the fuck?" he shouted. The light pole cast just enough light on his face for me to recognize him. This was Braden.

"Ah shit," Fletcher belched as he twisted to puke right at his feet. I didn't watch him, I crossed my arms and waited for this fuck face to come out.

He didn't.

Sighing, I reached in and yanked his arm and his sad softening dick slipped out of her with a sickening squelch. How the hell had she been turned on in that rancid box?

Screaming, she scrambled to get her shorts up. At least she was mostly dressed.

"Shhh…" Vienna held up her hands in placating gestures as she helped the girl out of the port-a-potty.

Rick, who turned out to be very adept at sliding into whatever role we needed, took a few pictures of her coming out of the John, and a few of Braden still in my grip with his now limp dick dangling in the wind.

"For insurance." He nodded at me and Vienna as Fletcher finished losing his dinner.

"All right, Douchebag." I whipped him around to face me and shoved him against the side of the John. It teetered, and another wave of stench rolled over us as the contents of the port-a-potty sloshed around. "Lesson number one, don't fuck in a port-a-potty."

Then, so he'd know we weren't his friends, I gripped his shirt, raised him to his toes, and slammed my fist into his face.

The give of his nose against my knuckles sent a rush through my system. This was the satisfaction I'd missed when Thad had dodged my punch.

I opened my mouth to continue my lessons, but Rick beat me to it.

"Lesson number two, young lady," he said in a paternal tone as he sidled up next to Vienna, pointing his phone at her chest. "Don't let douchebags fuck you in a port-a-potty. It's unsanitary and you should have more self-respect than that."

Black streaks smeared across her face as she wiped her tears away and nodded wildly.

"Now, I have photo evidence of you and Braden at the port-a-potty. We won't use it. But it is leverage. Don't breathe a word of this to anyone, understood?"

"Y-yes," she whispered. Vienna released her, and she took off at a sprint toward the building. She used absolutely no stealth on her way back, but what the fuck ever. The security at this place was laughable at best. The girl would make it to her room with no problems.

"Listen, asshole," Braden tried to speak through his hands. "I don't know who you are but those pictures don't scare me. By morning, those pictures *and* you four will be history."

This kid needed a lesson in humility.

Grabbing him by the scruff, I frog marched him to where Fletcher had been standing and swiped his feet from under him. He landed with a hard grunt with his face right in Fletcher's puke.

With the port-a-potty, I couldn't even smell it.

Braden could, though.

"What the fuck, Cash!" Fletcher grabbed at his stomach as he stumbled to the bushes to dry heave.

The kid at my feet gagged as he rolled over to his back. "I didn't do anything to you!" he whined.

"Lesson number three, this is entirely too much talking." Vienna crouched down by Braden and pressed the sharp edge of the knife under his chin. "We know who you are, who your father is, and every single act that landed you in this dressed-up hell hole. If you'd like to keep those from reaching the public in a way that you'll never be able to outrun your past, you'll answer our questions." Her voice was cool, calm, and in control.

My desire for this dangerous woman went straight to my cock.

Braden twisted his head back, the cords in his neck popping out as he tried to twist his face from her view. Harsh breaths and whimpers fell from his lips as he experienced something he'd probably never felt in his life.

Fear.

I smirked. Fletcher still couldn't believe that little revelation I'd shared with him.

"We can't reach your father. He's at a very public event tonight, isn't he?" She paused, and when he gave one trembling nod of his head, she continued. "He's very good friends with a man named David Lennox. We believe he's at one of your father's properties. I need a list of addresses of where he might be. If we're satisfied with your answers, your secrets will remain under wraps a little longer."

He gave one weak struggle, probably just so he could tell himself he tried. Vienna shut it down quickly by grabbing his shoulders and slamming his head into the hard ground.

After that, he sang like a canary. Rick jotted down all the addresses, and when he was done, I gently moved Vienna aside. Then I landed a swift kick to his stomach.

Groaning he rolled onto his side, and into the cooling puke.

Fletcher retched in the bushes all over again.

"Lesson number four," I pointed at Fletcher's back. "Puke in the bushes."

Braden Sanderson didn't even hear me. He passed out like a coward.

"You think he'll follow the rules?" Rick stepped closer to stare down at him with a pensive gaze. I didn't doubt if we said no, that Rick would take care of the issue without blinking twice.

This kid was a class four asshat. We'd found substantial evidence that he was on his way to being one of the shady players in the game. But he was only twenty with no deeds that firmly placed him in that camp yet.

We could consider this our goodwill act in the hopes he'd straighten himself out. From what I saw tonight, the chances of that were improbable, but he was scared of Vienna. That was enough for him to keep his lips shut.

"Yes," I assured him and he nodded. That was all he needed.

As we walked away, Vienna organized a clean-up and Fletcher glared at me.

"You have to stop slamming peoples' faces into my throw up. It's gross."

"Stop puking and I will. It's DNA and it's a liability."

He clamped his mouth shut.

"Think of this as motivation to train yourself toward a stronger stomach. For the greater good," I said through a grin.

"Fair," he grumbled.

"Are we hitting these places tonight or waiting until tomorrow?" Rick asked.

RICK

THE INFORMATION PROVIDED by the Sanderson kid gave us a dozen different locations to investigate. We stopped for a night at an out of the way hotel, not the nicest of locations, but one I could clean to make sure we at least had a comfortable space.

There we planned out our route as Fletcher dug into each and every one of them. Cash and Vienna ranked the locations from least to most likely. Their criteria differed, but they each made compelling arguments, particularly when their three most likely were the same, just not in the same order.

"The problem," Vienna said before we called it a night so *she* would sleep, "is that we only get one, perhaps two attempts, before any internal security alarms warn the other residences."

"You're assuming Sanderson has that kind of system set up," Cash argued, but it wasn't a belligerent disagreement at all. It was thoughtful. "Sanderson and Lennox have a business relationship of some kind, does your uncle seem the kind to inspire loyalty or fear?"

The more I thought about that question, the more I grew to detest this member of Vienna's "hidden" family. I had not met her uncle at all. I'd only heard his voice on a call, but that didn't give me any insight into the man.

"Both," she admitted with a long sigh. "Uncle David likes

to control the narrative of any interactions. He always described it to me as a game, one I was very good at."

There was no missing the melancholy in that statement. To learn yet another person she clearly cared about might have preyed upon her emotions or, worse, that she'd misjudged them? It left an open wound that made me angry. A wound I wanted to repair and seek retribution for.

"Hey, Drew," Fletcher said, curling around her like some kind of touch-deprived octopus. "Here's the thing... family sucks."

I frowned but before I could say anything, Cash caught my eye and shook his head. He wanted Fletcher to finish, so I shrugged and waited it out. Fletcher had gotten very good with her, but I wasn't sure this was the right tact.

"My family? Totally loaded. More money than God, or so you would think. But they are cut-throat, lie to your face, and are generally out for themselves. To be honest... that was me for a long time."

Darkness slid through her eyes and she flicked a look at me. Darkness and concern. I nodded to her. We would protect Fletcher from everything *because* he was our family.

"But... " Fletcher added with a sigh. "I can let that decide who I am *or* I can decide for myself. We can't always pick the people we're related to, but we can choose the people we want in our lives."

The succinct summation of my own feelings on the subject *from* Fletcher, had Vienna turning into him and she hugged him back with the same ferocity he held her. That was what she needed—to protect and be protected.

When Cash nodded to the door after they were sleeping, I followed him out. We did have a lot to discuss.

That discussion was part of the reason why, when we had a body count at the second location, I asked Vienna to reach out to her friend—Horatio. We needed to clean the site and I could handle the environment. I wasn't quite sure about the bodies.

It was also an excellent excuse to test Horatio.

"Are you sure?" Vienna asked, though the question gave me pause. Because if she wasn't sure, Cash and I could change this plan right now.

"Yeah," Fletcher asked giving me a *look*. "We don't need any more blue-eyed foxes."

"You shouldn't call him that," Vienna said absently. "He's not a fox. Even if he is sly… still…" The hesitation was there.

"We need to talk to him, Dark Saint, away from Thad."

I wouldn't have been quite so blunt, but Cash was different. He reacted differently. While I also had questions for her "friend," I didn't have a prior relationship with the guy. Cash had more than one bone to pick with him.

"True," she said slowly, then looked at me. "I can handle the bodies."

"You can handle anything," I told her, a fact I believed implicitly. "But he has other methods, they might prove useful to us *and* Cash is right. We need to talk to him."

"Man," Fletcher said with a grunt. "I hate to say it but they're both right."

"So," Cash said in the driest tone possible. "Clearly if all three of us agree, it's a good idea."

A laugh bubbled out of Vienna. "I don't know that I would go that far, but… I'll call him."

To none of our surprise, except maybe Vienna, he answered her call immediately. The fact she was surprised served as another indictment against her father in my opinion.

It didn't even take him an hour to put on an appearance. Either he'd been in the area or he was following us.

He walked with a strange mix of timidity and sureness as he approached us. Today, he didn't look like an accountant, or a valued and probably deadly asset of the Judge. In a maroon long sleeve shirt and faded jeans, he was a regular Joe. Nothing special, especially not as he pushed up his large framed, amber glasses.

But as Vienna had taught me, nothing was as it seemed in our world.

Shoving his hands in his pockets, he surveyed the scene with a casual eye before moving his gaze to Vienna. Cash immediately bristled, and even Fletcher's eye twitched.

I waited as Vienna handled him herself.

"Ratio," she murmured softly in greeting as she stepped in front of us.

"Vienna," he returned with a small quirk of his lips.

Cash's top lip sneered, but he didn't make any moves to toss Vienna over his shoulder and cart her away. From the angry vibration in his body, the thought was there.

"We have a body clean up," she cleaned her hands on a wipe I'd handed her just a few moments ago. "One guard is inside the hunting cabin." She motioned behind us with a tip of her head. "He met an…unfortunate accident when he tried to shoot at Rick."

There was a warning in her voice. If Ratio tried to harm us, she'd dispose of him, friend of her father's or not.

My chest warmed. I'd never had anyone care about me the way she did.

Ratio inclined his head. Message received.

"While we have you here," Cash started lightly as he moved around Vienna. The sinuous movements reminded me of a lion prowling through the tall grass. The threat was clear in every line of his body. "I have a few questions for you, *friend*." He squeezed Ratio's shoulder hard enough there would be bruises.

"Oh? Is this an inquisition?" The dryness in his tone rasped against my skin.

"I don't know. Should it be? If you'd asked me a week ago, I'd have said no. Then I realized just how well you played me." Cash's voice bubbled with controlled anger. He was the dominant man in our group, enough so that he often butted heads with Vienna. He was also ten steps ahead of every player we'd encountered.

Part of me wondered if he was betrayed by Ratio's surprise deception, or if he was enraged that Thackery had outsmarted him for the moment.

It wouldn't last. Now that Vienna and Cash were onto him, Uncle David, and Ratio, we'd be ahead soon enough. Cash just didn't have the same level of faith as I did.

"I never played you. I played your game. There's a difference." Ratio shrugged, not even attempting to get out of his hold.

"You're splitting hairs," Cash ground out through his teeth.

Fletcher nodded and crossed his arms, happy to show his support. A smile was there and gone as Vienna glanced at him. He was the heart of us. We'd protect him always, and he knew that.

"You're smarter than that, Cash. You never told me all of your secrets, and I never told you all of mine. How many times did I give you information to help you close cases, create new informant connections, and lock away your targets? We have a two-way relationship and we both bene-fited. There's nothing to be upset about."

"Except for the fact that you had a relationship with Thad without Vienna's knowledge," Cash drawled. "You have been working behind the scenes and watching her without *her* knowledge. It doesn't give me a good feeling. In fact, it makes me question your motives and want to pick apart your every action."

Ratio laughed low and husky. Unbothered. "If you have nothing better to do, then be my guest. You won't find much." His smirk was too cocky for an unassuming accountant. But we'd already established there was much more to this "blue-eyed fox" than met the eye.

Audibly grinding his teeth, Cash dropped his hand and stepped back, studying Ratio through a narrow eyed gaze. No matter what he said, Cash would probably never trust him again. But taunting him and insinuating Cash's abilities were subpar, it was like he was happily waving a red flag in front of a bull.

"This is wasting time," Vienna interjected. "But I agree with Cash. If we're going to work together, we need to clear the air. The Network is compromised, and my options for services are limited. I want to believe that you're trustworthy, but…after the last few days, I need some assurances. If you require it from any of us, you have the right to question us. But this step is necessary."

Ratio's face softened as he gazed at her. "All right, Vienna," he said quietly. "Ask your questions."

"What is your exact relationship with my father, and what are you working on for him? Don't think about giving me the same vague bullshit answers you gave me over dinner. I need facts to know I can trust you."

The phrasing of the question wasn't lost on me, or Cash either. Fletcher curled his upper lip. If I weren't so focused on what Vienna needed from Ratio, I might have chuckled. Fletcher and Cash were both annoyed about that dinner still.

"I have known your father for several years," Ratio said slowly. He didn't question this admission in front of us. He didn't even try to ask for some privacy. "I met him when we were kids. Well, you were younger, but I knew about you to a certain extent."

Her expression didn't shift, but her chin lifted a fraction. I tried to put myself in Vienna's shoes. How would I feel hearing my father had hidden so much of his life? Especially when Ratio knew about Vienna.

I really didn't have words or experience for this.

"Initially, he saved my life, helped save my mother. It was a lucky happenstance that brought us into his path. I didn't know what he was or did for some time. But I did know I wanted to do what he did. I wanted to scratch off the ones who caused…harm to others."

Vienna frowned. "Did you decide to become an accountant first or was that after?"

Ratio chuckled as he spread his hands. "I needed to vanish into the Network, how better to keep an eye on it than to be the one everyone knows?"

"That's fair," she admitted and I had to agree with the hint of admiration. "But Daddy always knew?"

Another sigh as he clasped his hands together. "Your father is a cunning man. He thinks ahead, plans ahead, and when I asked for specific training—he understood why, I think even before I did."

"So, he trained you?" The element of pain in her voice had me taking a step forward, but I wasn't the only one who reacted to it.

Ratio closed the distance before Cash or Fletcher could stop him. I stilled, but Vienna didn't withdraw or react as though she were being threatened. So I waited.

"He provided guidance more than lessons. He told me what I needed to learn and where to learn it. I had the money, but I needed the contacts. He provided those and when I was ready…"

"Daddy brought you into the Network."

"Yes."

"Did he know?" She pursed her lips. "Did he know even then?"

"That there was something wrong?" The question was in and of itself an answer. "Yes, Vienna. I know you are angry because he kept this from you. More, you are wounded—"

That description had me shifting my weight. Yes, she was hurting and I did not approve of this *at all*. Ratio, if his demeanor was to be believed, did not care for it either. He closed the gap between them until he was toe to toe and eye to eye with her.

"I did not then, nor do I now, agree with how Thackery has handled much of this, but I have to respect his choices because he has played this game far longer than either of us."

"Don't align yourself with her," Cash drawled. "You are a part of the secret that was kept from her."

"Yes," Ratio agreed, not looking away from Vienna. "But you have *always* had my loyalty. Thackery was not keen on introducing you to just anyone. You know how often he kept you away from some elements in the Network itself. The only reason he ever introduced you to the accountant…"

"Was because I would need to make contact periodically to move funds." The sadness weighing down her words made me itch.

"Exactly. When Thackery went dark, that wasn't unusual. The length of time—that was."

Dark. He meant when he died.

"So you started to watch me." That wasn't a question. Clearly, they had already covered this ground.

"Yes. More because it was so unusual for Thackery to leave *you*. Even when he went dark with me or with Dae… you were never one he would leave to dangle."

Vienna lifted a hand to rub at the back of her neck. It was the first real physical sign she gave that betrayed her upset. It also made me want to end this conversation and move on. But Ratio was talking to her, giving her answers, so—we would have to endure for the moment.

"You didn't know." That wasn't a question. Vienna frowned. "You didn't know about whatever he was doing?"

One shake of his head. "No. I can guess some now and I suspected that the recruitment I received from Red Death triggered his choices…"

"Woah…" Cash went ramrod straight. "Your what?"

Ratio didn't glance at Cash, his focus remained fixed on Vienna. "What I told you at dinner was true. Red Death's actions may have precipitated Thackery's choices. I have no interest in participating in their activities or being recruited by whatever shadow network they have formed."

"It is a network." Tears drenched her tone on that last syllable and it took everything I possessed not to go to her.

"I believe so, but I didn't have confirmation before. Only suspicions. I informed your father because…because I trusted his judgment."

"You don't trust him anymore?" Her lips twisted even as she asked like the question itself was distasteful or left bitterness behind. Perhaps it did both.

"I can't answer that." Ratio sighed. "More to the point, I won't. What I am, is here if you require my assistance. I won't report any of this to Thackery. He made his choices—not all of which I agree with, and you called *me* for assistance."

"So we just trust you?" Cash asked, skepticism and disbelief a potent cocktail in his voice.

"I dunno, he wants to make Drew happy," Fletcher said with a grimace. "I trust his motivations even if I don't trust *him*."

I agreed with Fletcher on that, but the only one who could decide which fork in the road we took was Vienna. She stared at him for a moment, then glanced at Cash. For his part, the former federal agent compressed his lips. No, he wasn't happy about this.

"Why should she trust you?" Cash asked, shifting his attention to Ratio. It was the right question because it pulled the other man's focus from Vienna to him. Nothing in his body language suggested threat, only a kind of weariness that seemed to accompany sadness.

I understood that feeling too well. It had been there the day I found out my family died. A grief that soaked through my skin and into my bones. It had eaten away at everything, hollowing me out until the facility was the only place for me.

No… until the night in that alley when I saved her.

She, in turn, *saved* me.

"Why does she trust you?" The question might have seemed belligerent if Ratio hadn't voiced it with such genuine curiosity. "You're unpredictable in the field. You don't follow the rules. You set your own standards. You walked away from a career because you weren't a team player. You still aren't— no matter how you try to dress it otherwise."

Ratio flicked a look to Fletcher. "Why does she trust you? Your wealth has allowed you to paper over all your mistakes, bury it in blackmail, pay for fall guys, and when nothing else worked, buying off the victims your family left in its wake. You aren't a fighter, not in the traditional sense, and you wear your fear like a hair shirt."

Finally, he turned to me and gave Vienna his back. "You—"

I raised my brows.

"You, I understand. You worship the ground she walks on. You treat her as she should be treated and nothing else competes for your loyalty. Nothing and no one."

Accurate.

"You want more than you'll ever receive from her, but you've already accepted it." I understood Ratio in that moment. "You've accepted that you can have a place in her life, but it won't be the place you wanted it to be."

"Perhaps," the man said with a small shrug. "Her happiness matters to me."

As it did to me and he wanted me to believe him. Maybe I was the only one who could, because it was such a simple devotion at the end of the day, uncomplicated by history or other motivations. He was here because she asked him to come.

He would always come if she asked it.

Finally, he turned back to her and understanding seemed to settle in her eyes as she glanced at me. I nodded. Yes, I believed him.

When she looked at Fletcher, he wore a scowl like he couldn't believe it himself, but he nodded. That left Cash and he folded his arms, his expression mutinous. "I still don't like him."

Vienna's smile was an answer all in and of itself. "You don't have to."

"Good."

"Horatio," Vienna said. "Thank you for coming. I don't know how we will make this work in the future, but I do need your assistance now. We have limited resources and our list of allies has grown thin with so many issues in the Network."

"Tell me what you need," Ratio said. "If I can make it happen, I will."

"I need to teach Rick how to dispose of a body. He understands cleaning the scene, but we need to do it all and it's been a while for me."

That wasn't entirely true, but she aligned herself with me and it filled my chest with pride.

"Fine," Cash grumbled. "Make it three. Fletcher is gonna need to do something else though, cause I'm not cleaning up all the puke."

"Oh, thank fuck," Fletcher muttered and I had to hide my own grin when Ratio gave us all a look.

He stripped off his jacket and folded it over his arm before he began to unbutton his cuffs so he could roll up his shirt sleeves. "Show me what you have in the way of supplies. I'll teach you everything I know."

"Everything?" Cash shot him a look.

"Well, I'll teach him," he nodded to me and then said, "And I'll teach Vienna anything she wishes. You'll just have to try and keep up."

"I have a few things," I said before Cash responded to the taunt. "If you have a list of what I should have on hand, I'd appreciate that."

"We'll figure it out," Ratio told me as he followed me to our vehicle. "It's better to learn what you can do with what you have so you're always ready. We have a lot of options on body disposal, so staying flexible helps in most situations."

Interesting.

"First thing, unless it's useful, we always cover up the cause of death…"

As Ratio began to speak, I gave him my whole attention. I wasn't alone. Cash came to stand next to me as Vienna settled against my back, one hand pressed to my spine. Her trust filled me even as her need called to me. We would take care of this and I would learn everything the accountant offered to teach.

We would be Vienna's Network. The three of us—and when we needed him—the accountant too.

FLETCHER

"YOU DID GOOD TODAY." Cash clapped me on the back as I leaned against the kitchen island.

I scrunched up my face. "Yeah, I didn't puke, but that was probably only because I never went near the body disposal tutorial. Why can't Rick learn from a YouTube video like everybody else? That would be a better training method for him than in real life. You know, so he could restart the video as much as possible."

"First-hand experience is the best way to learn," Rick said quietly as he turned on the griddle and resumed velveting the pork. What the hell even was velveting and where was he constantly finding these cooking techniques?

I was with Rick probably ninety percent of the day. I hadn't seen him turn on the Cooking Channel once.

"Why are you looking at me as if I did something wrong?" Rick stopped coating the strips in sesame oil to face me.

"He's not looking at you as if you did something wrong, he's looking at you like you found the secret way into the cookie jar and he's jealous." Cash picked up a cubed piece of cheese and tossed it in his mouth.

I scoffed. I was a Reed. I wasn't jealous of *anyone*. The DNA just didn't allow it, even if I detested everything about my family. Well, most of them. I did have one cousin that was okay.

"What's going on?" Drew swept in and kissed me on the cheek before making her rounds to the other two. I grinned. This was definitely behavior I could get used to.

"We learned that first hand experience is the best, and Rick has mysterious ways of picking up cooking skills. I think he's an alien." I nodded to drive home my point.

Cash snorted and Rick rolled his eyes. Drew just grinned and boy did that bring those beautiful tawny eyes to life.

"He does have skills that are out of this world," she said cheekily as she grabbed his ass.

I couldn't help it. I cracked up, and Cash joined me. Rick, the lovesick puppy, just smiled and dropped a kiss to the top of her head as he resumed making the pork.

Was that a blush on his cheeks? Yup, a little ass grab from our girl had him flushed. Interesting, after all the ways we'd very much overcome any shyness with our sexcapades.

"What I want to know is—" I started but stopped immediately when the door to the garage opened. After two seconds, it shut quietly, then someone shuffled around in the laundry room.

Oh no.

That wasn't who I thought it was, was it?

But who the fuck else could it be?

Daddy walked through the doorway, just as imposing now as he was the last time I saw him. Although he'd gotten a haircut at some point. He paused and glanced at each of us. His gaze only warmed slightly when it touched Vienna. And when I say warmed, it was such a slight shift, I almost convinced myself it didn't happen.

"Vienna. A word?" His voice crackled like dry leaves in October. Hell, I was probably only referencing that month because he was worse than any Freddie Krueger nightmare I could dream up.

Daddy was definitely the monster in the closet waiting to get me. I shivered on how close that possibly was to reality. All it would take was him walking in on one of our more adventurous ways to pass the evening.

Then we'd all be toast. And not the fancy kind with compote that Rick liked.

"Daddy," she drawled, leaving her hand on Rick's shoulder as she adopted a cool composure. No smile for Daddy.

I would say he cared, but I wasn't in the habit of creating pain for myself. Pointing out that Daddy felt any kind of emotion was just asking for him to rain death on my head.

Although... I glanced at Cash, who pushed away from the counter and took two steps toward Daddy. Rick also had a stern look on his face as they each stared him down.

Rick and Cash could take him, at least as a pair.

"A word, please?"

"No, Daddy," Drew shook her head. "Whatever you have to say, you might as well say it here in front of them. I won't keep secrets from them."

Ouch. That was a jab. And from the way Daddy's head jolted back, he knew it.

"Fine." He moved farther into the room, but seemed content to leave the island between them. That was good.

Oh wait, he was closer to me.

I scooched back until my ass hit the back counter. Now Cash was closest. That was the way it was supposed to be. Our fiercest up front.

"I've been watching your house, waiting to see when you are going to come to your senses. Taking up with three men," Daddy shook his head, "that's not smart, Sweet Girl. I trained you better than this."

"I don't think you have any room to talk about who you let into your circle. We both know what you taught me is very different from how you operated." Drew dropped her hands and gripped the edge of the counter.

Just that small action had me gritting my teeth. I wouldn't object to Cash and Rick taking another swing right about now.

"That's very different, Vienna. I trained those boys. I know exactly who they are, what they do, and where it hurts most if I ever need to take action. What do you know about these boys? Nothing. I've done my own checking and I don't like what I found. This isn't the time for you to gamble with your trust." Daddy stepped forward, dipping his head to look Drew right in the eyes. "You and me, we might need help from time to time to do certain jobs, but we don't trust anyone *else*. Ever."

"What about Mart? Are you telling me you don't trust her? Even though you've protected her all these years?" Her voice started to shake but she raised her chin.

"That's exactly what I'm saying. We need to rely on others to a certain extent. I've taught you that. But that is where it ends. How much do you know about these men? Did you run background checks, did you engage someone from the Network to track their movements for a period of time to make sure they weren't double agents?" His gaze skated to Cash, then back to Drew. "Did you take precautions when bringing them here, so they're unable to bring others back?"

I winced at the disappointment in his tone. I'd never cared for my dad's approval, but Drew very much cared about his. The sympathy pangs at his tone singed my eyebrows.

Especially knowing she probably didn't do any of that with Rick. From what he'd said, he'd saved her in an alley and she brought him home that night. Then she had me erase him and build a whole new identity. So, on the one hand, we both knew *everything* about who he was *now*.

"I vetted them as much as I needed to. They aren't going anywhere. You might as well save your breath."

Daddy raised a brow. "Really? What about your Fed? He's a dangerous liability even if I let the other two slide. What are you going to do when he leaves DNA at a crime scene and then you have the entire Bureau coming down on your head?"

"We're careful, just like you and I were careful on all of our other jobs."

"Not good enough," Daddy shot back. "He's a liability."

"You know," Cash said in a lazy kind of tone that said he was anything but relaxed. "I find your definition of trust to be suspect."

Yes, go Cash. *You* tell him.

"Do you?" Daddy spared him a look that sent ice chilling down my spine.

"Daddy, leave Cash alone."

"Sweet Girl, I told you—"

"We don't trust anyone *else*. Ever." Cash said, still staring at him. "That's what you said. You told her you two don't trust anyone else. So why should she trust you when you clearly don't trust her?"

Drew didn't flinch. At least not outwardly, but her eyelids flickered and her chin lifted. It was such a subtle shift in her posture. Anger struck a harsh match inside of me, the crackle of flame fraying my patience. Or maybe it was just my hesitation. Because Cash was right. Daddy *didn't* seem to be trusting Drew and *that* hurt her.

"I trust her. You're worried that I'm going to screw up on some job and end up in a cell I could easily escape and let her think I'm dead for more than a year..." He trailed off and then snapped his fingers. "Wait, that was *you*."

"I think the Bureau has detailed records on everything about you," Daddy countered, seemingly unimpressed by the anger strolling through Cash's tone. Right now, I wasn't really sure which one terrified me more. No, that wasn't true.

It was definitely Daddy. Cash seemed to like me most of

the time. He wasn't even pretending to like Daddy. So, yeah, take that old man.

"Vienna means a lot more to me than just someone to order around and isolate. I don't mind if she trusts Rick and Fletcher. In fact, I fucking encourage it. There isn't anything they won't do for her and no one they won't take on."

Okay, definitely a hard yes on the first one, but I might have some limits on who I face down. Then again…I wasn't running from Daddy right now, no matter how much he terrified me.

"I encourage it because she deserves to have strength and support in her corner. She deserves to know she has someone watching her back just because they care, not because they want her to do as she's *told*."

He straightened to his full height and Daddy's expression shifted. Even the air in the kitchen seemed to charge, full of static like a storm rolling in off the cape.

"But, if the real problem is you're worried about my prints, well, that's not a problem at all."

Nothing prepared me for Cash's next steps. He took two strides forward. I half-expected him to just go over the island, knock aside all of Rick's wonderful dish preparations and make a huge mess as he throttled Daddy with his bare hands.

Yes, it might have been a little wish fulfillment for me, but this wasn't about me. Instead of taking that option to the bank, Cash slammed his hands down on the *hot as fuck* griddle. Shock bound me in place, like my legs had become leaden weights and I couldn't move or breathe.

A sizzling sound filled the air like bacon made when it began to cook in its own fat.

Only that wasn't bacon.

It was—

Gorge rose in my throat as nausea struck. I didn't vomit immediately. I didn't vomit when he slammed his hands down. I didn't puke when he lifted them up, every single fingertip reddened and blistered as his expression never changed.

Rick transformed though. Rage flickered in his expression as he shoved Cash toward the sink. "Ice," he ordered and I just moved. Not water. Ice. I opened the freezer and pulled the whole drawer of ice out of the ice maker.

"I can't believe you just did that to the griddle," Rick scolded. "I'm going to have to sanitize the whole thing."

"You're welcome," Cash told him in a dry tone. "You were talking about stripping it down to re-season a couple of days ago."

I couldn't look at Cash's fingers or breathe through my nose. Nope. I kept my breaths shallow and through my mouth as I took a spot next to Drew. She needed backup while they were busy. Maybe she was used to our nut job of a former Fed, because she didn't even flicker an eyelash as she met Daddy's stare and held it.

"It's time to go, Daddy. Rick is planning a family dinner and you've made your feelings clear."

"This is still my home, Sweet Girl." Yeah, I wasn't especially fond of that nickname. It didn't humanize him for some reason, it just made him seem all that much more terrifying.

"It was your home, you chose to leave it. You chose to take up in one of the other houses. You can stay there. This is *my* home and will be until the boys and I have finished moving out."

Oh, we were moving? Fuck yes, I should get started on packing.

"What?" Oh. Daddy wasn't happy with that announcement. "Where are you planning on moving?"

"That's not something you need to worry about, I've made my choices, Daddy. I trust a very small circle. The circle that trusts me." Honestly, in that moment, Drew mirrored her father so perfectly but where he was ice, she was fire. Where he was almost inhuman, she was far too human. "Where we go when we leave is not your concern."

I waited to see if she would say anything about the cameras. She hadn't even brought them up with *Horatio* during our last encounter. I really wanted to know who planted them, but I was also working on where they were uploading their data in burst transmissions.

So, if Drew wasn't trusting him with any info, then I was all right with that as well.

"Vienna," Daddy said at the end of a long sigh. "Sweet Girl..." Holy crap, he sounded less serial killer and more—right I didn't know what the word was, but warm worked in a creepy way, so I'd go with warmer than he had at any time in our not short enough acquaintance. "If you want to discuss this, let's go and discuss this. You and me."

"No, thank you," she said with a perfect veneer of politeness. "Like I said, we're about to have family dinner. So, I'll be staying here with my family. I'm sure you can find your way out."

She didn't budge, nor betray even an ounce of hesitation.

"She said good night, Daddy," I spat out into the fray when he didn't seem likely to move. Rick had already rejoined us and Cash didn't seem remotely perturbed for someone who'd just cooked their damn hands. "The door's that way," I continued. "Please let it kick you in the ass on the way out."

The weight of his stare slammed into me with the force of a swung ax. Maybe it was all the shallow breaths through my mouth, but I didn't throw up. I just held my ground. Drew held her ground for us, I could do this.

It helped that Rick suddenly loomed between us and Daddy—fuck I loved Rick so much—and said, "It's time to go, Mr. Drew. No one is asking."

No, we really weren't. The moment elongated, the tension stretched so thin and taut I swore I could *feel* the strings of it vibrating. Without another syllable, Daddy left. The muffled hush of the door closing echoed far louder than if he'd slammed it.

"He is so going to slit our throats while we sleep," I muttered.

"He won't," Drew said, threading her arms around me and I turned into the embrace, clasping her fiercely. "Don't worry, Pincushion. Daddy won't hurt you. I—*we* won't allow it."

I caught Cash's approving look and then Rick's. Despite the internal terror, I just tightened my grip on her. We wouldn't let Daddy hurt her either.

VIENNA

AFTER DINNER, we all helped with the clean-up. The guys tried to usher me out to relax with a glass of wine, but I didn't want to leave any of them. Daddy's visit had left an unsettling ripple in his wake. If I distanced myself, his distrust made sense on one level. He didn't know Rick or Fletcher. As for what he knew about Cash? I wasn't sure I could give any of that value because Daddy's relationship had been with Cash's father.

Yet, he'd sent Horatio to be Cash's informant. That relationship added another layer of complexity. After the third time Fletcher and Rick semi-collided near the sink, Rick pointed Fletcher over to me and I swore Cash snickered. With an adorable hangdog look on his face, Fletcher came over to lean against the counter where I'd perched.

Even if they wouldn't let me help clean, it didn't mean I couldn't be in here. I trailed my fingers over my little pincushion's head, across his scalp, then to his nape. I swore, he arched like a cat and some of the tension that hovered around him began to bleed off the edges.

"Should I apologize for what I said to your father, Drew?" The softness in the question tugged at me. Teasing my nails against his nape, I leaned forward and pressed a kiss to his shoulder.

"No, you shouldn't," I whispered before pressing a kiss to

his shoulder. A long sigh escaped him. "I don't understand Daddy, right now." Aware that both Cash and Rick had partially swiveled toward me as I began to speak, I raised my voice. They were very welcome to the discussion. Even if it was one I never thought to have. "I don't understand why he is making the choices he is—"

The hurt and the anger, they were all tangled up in this messy knotted ball inside of me. I couldn't seem to tease it free. Or worse, some threads loosened only to yank some other part tight if it didn't just break off altogether.

"He doesn't know you," I said slowly. "He doesn't *want* to get to know you." Those two threads dangled in plain view, but the snarl was further up. Where it connected to the rest, turning what had once been so very clear into something—I shook my head. "He doesn't trust my judgment."

That was where the knot proved too tight, impossible to tease free.

"Now I find myself asking if he ever truly did." I thought he had. I'd proven myself over and over. Daddy was protective. I understood his choice to follow me on my first jobs. The pride that filled me when I realized he'd allowed me to work without supervision had been heady. From then on, our relationship had shifted.

But had it? Really?

I continued to stroke my fingers over Fletcher's back, the contact seemed to relax him and it soothed me. "I don't like asking those questions," I admitted.

Cash focused on me, the intensity in his eyes held only one question. When Rick ordered him and his damaged hands away from the sink, he'd planted himself on the far side of the kitchen. The choice put him nearest the garage doors.

He was guarding us. The question in his eyes pulled at me. If I chose not to answer, he would just continue to ask. Maybe not in words, but in attitude and in glances. Stubborn, mercurial, and sometimes absolutely insane, Cash would dig his heels in and wait me out.

It was what he'd done while hunting us. What he'd done in the cell downstairs. What he'd done when they came for me. What he'd been doing ever since. Where Rick was steadfast and immutable, my absolute port in the storm. Cash was the storm, he would continue to lash at my defenses until I chose to open the door and let him in. Then my sweet Fletcher, for all his colorful blustering, he was the colorful fire that kept us all warm. Our heart. Infinitely more precious for how deeply he experienced every emotion.

"No," I answered Cash softly. "I'm not alright, but I also don't regret my choices. Even if Daddy were to offer me the most candid and understandable explanations...or never offered any, just that he'd been imprisoned for all that time without choosing to escape or..." I shook my head. "It doesn't matter. Daddy made choices. I've made choices. This —all of you—you're my life now for as long as you choose to be here with me."

"Oh shit," Fletcher muttered as Cash damn near charged across the room at us. The air crackled with lethality as he planted himself right in front of me, taking Fletcher's place. Only where Fletcher had leaned back and let me pet him, Cash invaded my space and occupied all of it. He wouldn't let me have a single drop of oxygen he didn't share.

"As long as we choose?" There was a dangerous note in his voice. He settled his damaged hands on either side of me. The cool marble probably felt good against his damn blistered skin. Fletcher said Cash didn't feel fear, but not feeling fear didn't mean not feeling pain.

I feathered my fingers against his cheek, the rasp of stubble prickled against my palm. "Yes, it will always be your choice to stay or go. I won't make you." That flew in the face of what I'd said to Rick all those months back. If he chose to come with me then, there was no way out. "I won't hold any of you against your will or try to force you to—"

Cash's mouth slammed own on mine. Heat rushed over me at the demand of his kiss, both a punishment and a reward. The bite of his teeth scraped over my lower lip before he followed the path with his tongue. He cupped my chin, tilting my head back as he pressed the full weight of his body against mine. As if determined to storm my senses, he snaked an arm around me. The solid weight of him and the ripple of muscle just added to the drunken invasion he promised with every breath, touch, and taste.

A groan escaped me as he dragged me closer. I didn't think I could get any closer with our clothes on. I fisted his hair with my free hand and then someone was lifting away my wine glass. Gratitude swam through the pleasure inherent in the ferociousness of Cash's kiss.

Focusing elsewhere was impossible under his sensual onslaught. "Hold onto me, Dark Saint," he ordered, though his lips barely left mine. "You can join us later, guys. After we settle a few things."

"Settling accounts with your dick," Fletcher called after us as Cash moved. He wasn't waiting for their response. "That's very American Gigolo of you, Cash!"

Laughter swarmed through me and I lifted my head long enough to search for Rick. He'd said nothing, but his expression was serene even if the look in his eyes was heated. I blew him a kiss and he inclined his head, a pleased smile on his face.

"Eyes on me, Dark Saint," Cash growled as he stalked up the stairs. Every movement ground me against his very erect cock. His jeans did absolutely nothing to disguise the thickness or his need.

"I don't have to see you to feel you," I told him, giving his hair a yank. "I don't have to see or feel you to *know* you're there."

"Good." He shoved open the door to his room, not mine, then slammed it shut with his foot. "But I want you to feel me even when I'm not there and taste me wherever you are. I want to burn myself on your soul the way you've imprinted yourself on mine."

"Cash…"

"No," he snapped as he set me down on the bed and then loomed over me. "I want you to *always* know *me*. Always know where I *am*. Always have me with you and in you—I…" His expression transformed to the most tortured I'd ever seen.

All of my humor dried up and I curled upward to hug him. Only he tried to push me back down. The tussle was just so natural, I locked my legs around his waist. With a twist, I yanked him off his feet and flipped him so he was on his back and I was above him. He tangled his fist in my shirt and dragged me back down.

"You don't get to think I'll choose anything or *anyone* else," he growled. "Do you understand me?"

"Not even a little," I whispered, tracing my fingers from his brow to his cheek. "Cash, you are intense, vibrant, passionate, and utterly out of control."

"Maybe, but I'm also yours." The rawness in his declaration robbed me of speech. "I've been yours forever. I used to say soulmates are bullshit. How can there be one perfect person for someone in the world? It's some new agey, romance novel crap. Then I found you. That day I walked into the warehouse before Fletcher gave me a concussion, I was already yours. You are *never* losing me. If someone fucking killed me, I'd be back as a goddamn ghost."

It was violent and abrasive and altogether him. "I love you," I told him simply. It lacked his savage eloquence. Their flavor sharp on my tongue like a shiny penny. These words were still so new and foreign spilling from my lips. His whole demeanor shifted. Heat flashed in his eyes and his grin was equal parts madness and possession.

"You love me," he repeated the phrase, like he needed to confirm it.

Dipping my head closer until our noses brushed, I whispered against his lips, "I love you." Kissing the corner of his mouth, I repeated it. When I reached the opposite corner, I said, "I love all of you."

Something I needed to tell *them* too.

"Fuck me, Dark Saint." The words were a rough rasp. "Please."

The plea ripped out of him on a pained note. "Don't beg," I told him. He would never need to beg. "I'm yours. Take me if you want me."

A wicked grin turned up his lips. "You *can* take me, can't you?"

"Hell yes, I can. Do your worst."

Throwing down the gauntlet was absolutely the right thing to do. Cash surged upwards, breaking my thigh lock and all but threw me down against the bed. Without a word, he stripped off my clothes, then his. For one long moment, he froze, his gaze speculative as he wrapped a hand around his cock. He sucked in a sharp breath, gritting his teeth. His hands had to hurt, but it didn't slow him down. His dick jutted out, fat, and sassy. The tip was damn near purple where it peeked out from under the hood of skin.

I licked my lips. If he was trying to turn me on with only the stroke of his gaze, he was doing it. My nipples beaded up tight and my pussy clenched. Liquid heat unfurled and I stretched out under his inspection. For the first time in my life, I truly understood why cats lounged in the sun. Sprawled out beneath Cash as he gripped his cock left me a puddle of pure need.

"I'm going to take my time later," he said, his tone firm and allowing for zero arguments. "I'm going to tease you right up to the edge over and over, then I'm going to invite the guys to do the same. You're going to come when we allow it and not a second before."

A shudder went through me at that delicious promise. "That's later?" I didn't need to manufacture any of the breathless anticipation. I was right there.

"Yeah," he said slowly. "That's *later.* Right now, though?"

He gripped my thighs and dragged me down the bed, forcing my hips up and without preamble, thrust the full weight of his cock into me. I was slick, and definitely open to the intrusion, but it rested right on the precipice between pleasure and pain. The thrusts were unrelenting as he set a furious pace without allowing me to grow used to his size or the sweet burn of the stretch.

Worry for his burnt fingers flew out of my head, pounded away by the slam of his cock. With my legs half up over his shoulders, I was bent in half, but I could help with this angle. I thrust my hips up to meet his and he let out a low growl.

"Just like that," he said. "Fucking feel me. Grip me with that pussy and take every goddamn inch."

Oh, I was more than happy to. The world narrowed to this room, this spot, this moment, and the wild pleasure coursing through me. He poured all his rage into his passion and then focused all of that sensual demand on me.

When he began to circle my clit with the knuckle of his hand, I bucked. The roughness of his skin and the barest hint of pressure was almost too much.

"Play with those breasts, Dark Saint. Pinch those nipples like it's me biting them."

I moved my hands at his command, and cupped my breasts. His eyes darkened as I rolled the nipples.

"Harder," he growled.

A balloon of heat expanded and threatened to roll me under when I pinched them as roughly as he might. It pulled a sharp chord within me and his hips began to stutter.

"Me," he chanted. "You're going to feel me."

"I do," I whispered, the words broken as I fought to keep pace with him. "I will."

"Mine," he said, followed by another string of words. He increased the pressure on my clit even as he deepened his strokes and the world splintered. I thrashed under the onslaught, but he was relentless. A sob tore from my throat. It was too damn much. Too much, and then he came with a harsh cry. His whole body shook as he covered me and I clung to him, cradling him against me as we rode out the tremors together.

"I love you," he whispered against my ear in a voice so dark it was almost indistinguishable from his own. "And I will never *choose* to leave you."

My limbs were almost too loose. It took real effort to rub my hand against his back and I pressed my lips to his shoulder. The hot taste of his skin flavored with a hint of salt from his sweat had me clamping down on him again. He rocked against me and I swore his cock twitched.

"Then you're mine," I told him. "Forever."

"Bout fucking time you accepted that," he grunted. "Now hush and let me enjoy the feeling of you drenched in my cum. Then we're doing this again."

A soft laugh escaped me. "Promises, promises."

Lifting his head, he grinned down at me. "You haven't seen anything yet."

I couldn't wait.

This was where I belonged. With them. Daddy would have to figure it out or he would have to get out of the way. I wasn't giving them up.

Not ever.

AS THE LAST one out of the house, I shut the door and locked it, wiping off the handle with the tail of my tank. Today was a rest day. We'd start with a light workout, then do some research for the pending jobs I had open. Another transport job came in too. That would need vetting before making a decision.

The job was at least from a colleague I was fairly familiar with. No bad deeds as far as I knew. We'd see after Fletcher did his thing.

I turned around just as Daddy appeared around the corner of the house.

"Vienna."

Fletcher jumped two feet in the air, and Cash caught his arm to make sure he didn't fall over.

"He's like the Bozo punch toy that just keeps coming back," Fletcher muttered to Cash. Rick shook his head, but turned to face us, squaring his shoulders and letting his hands hang loosely by his sides.

Cash was one ball of tension, watching Daddy with a lion's stare and a silent snarl.

Then there was my little pincushion, hiding just behind both of them. That was okay, they'd protect him.

They didn't know Daddy wouldn't actually hurt them. Daddy knew they were important to me and he'd never see me again if he tried to take them from me.

Not when they were here when he wasn't. For now, that was a line Daddy wouldn't cross.

"Yes, Daddy?" I sighed. I almost motioned for my men to head to the gym without me, but it would have been a waste. They wouldn't leave me alone until they knew what he wanted. Especially when Daddy was so set on turning me against them.

That would never happen, but I wouldn't take away their opportunity to defend themselves.

Fletcher's phone chimed and he cursed when he opened the screen. "What are *they* doing here?"

Cash and Rick crowded around him to see who cleared the gate. I had two guesses. Because he said *they*, I was confident I knew the identity of the two visitors arriving.

A slight pang reverberated through my chest. Daddy could work with whoever he wanted to. Things had clearly changed since he was back and we both needed to understand how things would continue to change.

"Dae and Ratio are here," Daddy answered as if they weren't watching them drive up on the cameras. If Daddy was offended that Fletcher had rigged our place with surveillance, he didn't mention it. Then again, he could have very well done the same while we were on our last job.

I didn't respond. I waited to see where he was going with this.

"There's a lead for a job I'm working, but I have something else I need to do. I want you to go with them." He nodded toward the other house where we could hear their car doors closing.

"No way. We don't trust them," Fletcher piped up.

"Unlike some, our trust doesn't change based on the situation. And unfortunately, I can't think of any situation where we'd trust your associates," Cash growled.

Holding up my hand to Cash, I turned to Daddy. What was his motivation? His game?

Daddy didn't play games, but he did manipulate to get his desired outcome. I'd just never assumed he'd try to manipulate me.

"What's the job?"

"You can't actually be thinking of leaving with them!" Fletcher burst out just to be shushed by Rick.

Pretending they weren't sharing our air, Daddy ignored them completely. "David has a silent investor who just landed in Texas to spend some time at his family ranch. I want to know everything he's been doing and who he's had contact with for the last month."

He paused, his gaze sweeping my face as his lips set in a firm line. Whatever he thought he saw, or wanted to, didn't happen, because his body didn't relax. There was no relief found.

So what had he been looking for?

"Quick job, in and out? Fletcher also gets the details to complete the sleeve on the investor."

"Now, wa—" Fletcher started but Rick smacked the back of his head.

"I have someone else working on the write up." Daddy shook his head.

"Not good enough. Now that Dion has been, disposed of, Fletcher is the only other hacker I will work with." It went without saying I only worked with Dion under very specific and sparse situations.

Daddy's tawny eyes flickered, then he slowly nodded. "I'll send him the details. Let's go." He pivoted on his heel, expecting me to follow, but I needed to explain myself first.

"The rule was, Drew, no jobs on your own." Fletcher's nostrils flared as he stared down at me.

"I agree with Fletcher. This is a bad idea. Remember the speech about us not trusting anyone else? That includes sending you off on jobs without at least one of us." Cash looked between Fletcher and Rick. "Without at least me or Rick."

"Thanks a lot, asshole." Fletcher scowled.

"Vienna can take care of herself. She did long before we met her." Quiet Rick always supported my decisions. That cost him. It was written in the way his fingers twitched at his sides. His unconditional faith in me warmed my chest just the same as Cash's overprotectiveness. Although, Cash's attitude often lit my temper too.

"Daddy is not the same man he was when he left a year ago. I want to know why, and if Dae and Ratio are as close to him as I suspect, they'll have some of the answers." I glanced back, catching sight of Daddy talking to the two men in question.

Dae cast a curious glance my way, while Ratio nodded solemnly. If nothing else, Ratio was neutral. I was certain he hadn't told Daddy how he'd helped us. He would be my best bet for answers.

"I need to do this. Daddy's never going to tell me why he came back a different man." Physically, he was a little slimmer, more pale, but otherwise, he was the same, strong man he'd always been.

Maybe it was just me who had changed while he was gone. I'd grown, met Rick, Fletcher, and Cash, and I couldn't ever imagine my life without them in it now. Without a doubt, I was stronger with them.

And with all the secrets coming out about how Daddy operated before he was taken prisoner…Maybe I was the one who changed, and I could finally see him for who he was.

"Shit, Drew. You really want to do this?" Fletcher pleaded with his eyes for me to reconsider. I cupped his cheek and went to my toes. "I will keep my phone on. I'll check in regularly. I'll also take the bracelet with the tracker. If at any point I miss a check in, or I'm not on the route to or from Texas, come find me."

He blew out a harsh breath as Rick's shoulders relaxed. They were still a little raw after I didn't come home the last time. I'd learned my lesson, and I'd do everything to help them through this.

At the same time, I couldn't live in a glass ball.

"I'll be watching the tracker," Cash said right before he threaded his fingers through my hair at my nape to tip my head back.

His kiss burned me from the inside out. As his tongue twined with mine, I felt it for the promise it was. There would be no opportunities for me to disappear without a trace. He'd always be there at my back, whether he was there physically or not.

"I know," I whispered when he pulled away. My left hand bunched in the side of his shirt, and I was reluctant to let him put so much distance between us. "For what it's worth. Ratio won't harm me."

"We know." Rick trailed his fingers down my arm and I moved into the circle of his arms. He swept me in a tight hug, his hands sliding down my back, then gripping my hips. "I'll miss you," he said quietly, brushing his nose against mine.

"I'll be back. I'll be cautious, and I know you three won't let anything happen to me." The cobalt blue snaring me in his gaze.

"Never," he agreed. Then he gently spun me into Fletcher's chest. Where Cash always tried to dominate our affection, and Rick was my gentle giant, Fletcher was the reckless spirit.

He pressed his cheek against the top of my head, and squeezed his arms around the tops of my shoulders. I relaxed into the hug, enjoying this moment of affection.

"Drew, you better bring your ass back here. If you leave me to deal with Daddy, I won't be pleased. There's a good chance I'll piss my pants, but I *won't be pleased*," Fletcher muttered sullenly.

A broken laugh bubbled up my throat. "It won't come to

that. But find everything on this investor that you can. I'll want to review it before we give any information to Daddy… If we give any information to him." Uncle David had a number of businesses he operated both for the Network, and to keep up appearances in society. But I'd never heard of him having an investor.

"I'd have to be in the same space as Daddy to give him the sleeve. We both know that's not going to happen."

I snorted.

"All right. Go on, so you can hurry back. I'll let these two give me a beating in the gym."

"Let?" Cash snickered.

"Yeah, yeah."

With one more look, that was more of a promise to come back, I turned and walked over to where Daddy was quietly filling Ratio and Dae in on something he didn't want the rest of us to hear.

I waited for the burn in my chest, but it didn't come. Or I should say, it wasn't nearly as sharp a pain as it would have been a few days ago. Or even yesterday.

Something cold settled over me as I ignored Ratio's and Dae's stares and kept my focus on Daddy. I wasn't sure if our relationship would ever be the same.

That was okay. It hurt, and it would always sting because of how close we were before. But now I had Rick, and Fletcher, and Cash. And they were all I needed.

"Vienna." Dae's soft voice purred as he inclined his head, a lock of silver white hair falling in his eyes.

"Vienna," Ratio echoed, a small smile playing at the edges of his lips.

"Boys," I nodded. "Daddy says you need assistance on the job."

Dae and Ratio exchanged a glance.

"We are always happy to have you along." Ratio measured his words as he cut his gaze at Daddy. When he turned back to me, he smiled. "I, for one, always enjoy your company."

"Interesting that she knows you so well, Ratio," Dae curled his top lip. "You still never said how you were introduced to Vienna."

"That's not important," Daddy interjected. "The important thing is that she can accompany you on this job. I appreciate you both willing to work together to help me find the answers I need. I'll have my burner if something goes wrong, but I know Vienna will be in good hands with you two."

Something akin to pride entered Daddy's voice and each man seemed to swell ten feet taller under his praise.

Grit scraped against the underside of my skin. These two men had spent a lot of time with Daddy, enough that his praise was important to them. All the deadened feelings I thought were behind me came rushing to the forefront.

"All right, you three. Get on the road. I'll check in periodically, and let me know if anything goes awry, although I suspect this will be smooth. Edgar Daryawesh never was very bright, and he's not a fighter from what I remember."

Daddy clapped each man on the back, gave me a measured stare, then left us in the driveway. That too was out of the ordinary for them, if their shocked expressions could be believed.

The front door clicked shut, leaving us standing in silence.

"Your…men didn't insist on coming?" Ratio asked as he moved toward the car. They had arrived in a black sedan. Nothing fancy, definitely nothing that would stick in anyone's mind.

"They wanted to, but they had other work they had to attend to." I almost glanced toward the gym to assuage my heart that was already missing them, but I didn't.

They would be okay while I was gone. And I would be okay until I came back. I was more cautious now, and nothing would keep me from coming home.

Dae opened the passenger door, waiting for me to slide in. Once I was in the seat, he closed it and climbed in the back.

Ratio fiddled with the radio, settling on a golden oldies station as we pulled away from the house. They didn't seem particularly fond of each other, in fact, there was a tension between them that spoke of old rivalries. That could explain the first fifteen minutes of pure silence. Then Dae broke it.

He cleared his throat. "So, Vienna, Thackery tells me that you're an excellent chameleon."

I was, because Uncle David had taught me everything he knew. Was he purposely bringing him up to see how I'd react? If Daddy told him my skills, then he would have told him where I learned.

Heat hit my cheeks. Why would Daddy share that with them? We held our talents close to the vest because sometimes, the advantage was the target not knowing what to expect.

"Oh, he did? When did he tell you that?" Ice should have shot up the windows from the frost in my tone.

"Easy," he cooed. "He mentioned it just now before you joined us. I'm sure you can imagine why I would be envious of such a skill." I glanced back to see him motion to his features with a straight but soft hand.

He was exotic in an unforgettable way. Uptilted eyes, smooth golden skin, and hair that was so silver, it looked unreal. Yes, Dae would never be able to be a chameleon. He had too many brilliant features to ever truly fit in. He could cover up one, or even a few, but he couldn't hide his entire self.

"In the Network, knowledge is power. I'm sure *you* can imagine why I would be uneasy with you having any kind of advantage over me."

He laughed, and the low, rich sound slid over my skin like honey. "My apologies, Vienna. I did not mean to offend, but I get what you mean. I think, however, as we're going on a job together, that this secret is safe with me. And one that is most appropriate for me to know."

I studied him, and when the seconds turned to almost a minute, his lips twitched.

"Dae, give her a break. She just found out her only parent that she'd been mourning for over a year is back from the dead." Ratio chastised Dae.

This was the opening I needed. "Speaking of that, Daddy seemed very adamant that I should leave this hunt to him. Why the sudden turnabout?"

Ratio hesitated before shrugging. "I'm not sure what his motivations are. Thackery is a very private man."

"I don't believe that. Just in the few times I've seen you both in his presence, I can see he's confided in you. Maybe you don't know everything, but you know enough." I gripped the handle on the door, but slowly loosened my hold as Ratio's gaze dropped.

Never give away your emotions. I knew better.

"Perhaps."

"Then tell me, Uncle David was behind Daddy's disappearance, wasn't he?" I started to say more, but I stopped. I didn't need to justify my suspicions to these men. I needed answers.

"Yes, David was the reason Thackery was captured. You were the reason he stayed." Ratio's voice was grave.

The floor dropped out from under me as chills erupted over my skin. That couldn't be.

"I need you to explain that to me," I said, my words shaking.

"Do I? I feel like it's self-explanatory. David held your safety over Thackery's head, so he stayed put, allowed David to torture and starve him. David was waiting for Thackery to crack. He wanted Thackery to be the perfect assassin, carrying out any job David handed him."

I heard Ratio, I comprehended the words, but they were

fuzzy, distant as I turned and watched the trees pass on the side of the road. Ratio seemed certain, but I wasn't convinced that was what David wanted.

Otherwise, he wouldn't have told me that Daddy was dead. He never intended for Daddy to escape. Was Uncle David a sadist who got off on having power over one of his oldest friends?

"If Daddy allowed himself to be kept, why is he so distant now?" I asked myself rather than to Ratio. Dae remained silent in the backseat, as if he was more than happy to let Ratio run this conversation.

"You're asking the wrong question. What you should be asking is what did David tell Thackery while he was locked away?"

I snapped my head toward Ratio. "What was he telling Daddy?"

Ratio blew out a breath. It pained him to deliver this message to me, but whether he took pity on me, because Daddy hadn't told me, and maybe never would, he continued. "David taunted Thackery that you were going to be the assassin he needed. That he was already grooming you. When you took out the journalist, Thackery heard all about it."

"I had to take her out. She would never have let me go without killing me, and she never would have stopped searching for Daddy," I argued.

That was the hardest decision I'd ever had to make in my life. I still woke up in a cold sweat reliving Sandra Jane's death. Yes, she was a civilian. But she wasn't innocent. Not when she abducted me first.

I gave her an opportunity to live.

But she wouldn't take it.

"You know I can't let this go."

"That's the most unfortunate part of it all." I squeezed the *trigger and the sound exploded through the basement.*

Everyone made their choices.

This was mine.

I jerked when Ratio spoke. "That's not what he told Thackery. In fact, he gleefully told him how you took out a civilian under his orders."

Fury started in my toes, then swept up my legs, through the pit of my stomach. As the raging heat threatened to overtake my entire body, I cursed David in my head.

That mother fucker was playing both ends to the middle.

"You helped us with the cleanup. Why haven't you told Daddy the truth?" The sudden anger vibrated through my words and I fisted my hands on my thighs.

Uncle David was going to pay. By my hand. I would make certain of it.

Another hesitation. A quick apologetic glance. "How do I know what the truth is?"

HOW DID he know what the truth was? Seriously? I frowned at Ratio, but it was Dae who actually responded, "Tell me about the scene."

I twisted to sit as sideways in the seat as the seat belt would allow in order to meet his gaze. My questions about Ratio aside, I at least felt like Ratio and I had some common ground.

Dae was an unknown element, an X factor. The fact he was drop dead gorgeous with features that were both delicate and strong, and a gaze that utterly captivated, only aroused my curiosity more. Aesthetically, I couldn't admire him more. But people were more than their looks.

Far more.

"I'd like Horatio to tell me," Dae said, his soft tone firm as he glanced from me to where Ratio drove. Instead of sitting behind Ratio, Dae had chosen to sit behind me. I didn't particularly care for having him at my back.

"I bet you would," Ratio responded with a shake of his head. "But I don't discuss past events. Once they are done, they are done. The less mention of them the better."

"Tell me about the body." Dae shifted gears. His head canted as though he waited to hear something in particular.

Or maybe he just wanted to needle Ratio. "If the lovely Vienna was going to tell me, you aren't violating confidentiality."

With a look that bordered on incensed, Ratio said, "With all the sincerity I can muster… go fuck yourself."

Dae laughed, genuine humor rumbling out of him as he leaned back. "Unfortunately, Vienna, truth is often subjective. What are the facts?"

"Leave her be," Ratio ordered. Dae merely lifted a hand like we had all the time in the world. Maybe we did. The drive ahead of us was fairly long. So rather than fill the silence, we drove for another three hundred miles without saying anything unless we were asking for a bathroom break.

It was dark when we crossed the stateline and refilled the tank. I sent a message to the boys, letting them know how I was doing. Their responses made me miss them all over again. They were working and Cash asked for an ETA. I didn't have one, but I did share my location. Rick's heart emoji filled me with fresh warmth.

Lowering the phone, I caught Dae staring at me broodingly. I met his gaze and considered him for a long moment.

"You wanted the facts?"

"Yes," he said, straightening, fresh interest on his face. When he held open the door to the car for me, there was no mistaking a flash of eagerness in his eyes. Ratio gave me a quiet look of reproval, but this was my story. He didn't have to like it.

"Fact, David gave me Sandra Jane's info because she had access to files on the Judge. Old notes from a former FBI profiler."

"Your former federal agent lover's father," Dae said as though he'd already been briefed on that part. "What did David want you to do?"

"Eliminate the problem." My mouth twisted. That suggestion hadn't sat well with me at all. Still… "Before you say then what he told Daddy was true, understand that just because I told him I'd take care of it doesn't mean anything."

After a brief pause, Dae said, "Accepted. We must choose the work that suits us and perform the task to the best of our abilities with the merit it deserves."

For some reason the even tone he used rankled, but I put aside my personal feelings. "Fact, Sandra Jane was a civilian. I set up an approach to make my own decisions about her. Just because she claimed to have something on the Judge, didn't mean she did. Also, it didn't mean I needed to act."

"Because in acting to silence her," Ratio said. "You would be proving her story to the masses."

"That's part of it," I agreed, then rubbed my lip.

For some reason, I didn't struggle to discuss some of the finer aspects of deciding if someone lived or died with these two. Their opinions of me mattered only insomuch as I needed to break this impasse with Daddy, and if it meant bleeding David out to get to the real issues, I'd do it.

"The rest," I said, focusing on the landscape as we accelerated on the highway. "The rest depended on her. I'd checked out her place, checked out her, she seemed one hundred percent normal so I left her alone. Headed home."

Still not looking at either of them, I grimaced.

"I made a mistake. She followed me, she used a Taser on me and when I woke up, I was shackled in the basement of her secret sanctum cabin." Distaste twisted through every word. "The civilian tried to torture answers out of me."

Now I looked at Ratio, his hands had flexed on the steering wheel, knuckles white as his lips compressed into a thin line.

"She tortured me for over a week..." I glanced back at the landscape but I couldn't miss the reflection of Dae's stony countenance visible briefly in the side mirror. "She had no intention of letting me go. She had no intention of letting anyone she brought there go. In the end, she left me no choice."

I needed to make my peace with it.

"While you may not know what the truth is, I do. David has done nothing but lie to me. Why the hell would he do anything differently with Daddy?"

"You believe David has done nothing but lie to you?" Dae asked in a thoughtful voice meant for reflection.

"I do," I said, breathing through my nose. Looking back, I saw a million places where I should have done things differently. But there was no going back. I could only make things right going forward. And the start was figuring out exactly how Uncle David had ruined my relationship with the single most important man in my life until these past few months.

"You questioned his motive when he asked you to take care of the reporter?" Dae pushed, and Ratio growled under his breath.

I stopped. I hadn't questioned him *exactly*. More like, I knew he operated on a different moral code than Daddy and I always had. I knew, whether Uncle David realized or not was irrelevant, that I wouldn't actually have taken out Sandra Jane unless I absolutely had to.

But she'd taken that choice from me, damn her.

"Vienna, you questioned his motive when he asked you to take care of her?" Dae's soothing, cultured voice shocked me out of my thoughts.

"The thing about Uncle David, is that he never operated on the same code as Daddy and I did. He didn't have any problem about taking an innocent life. But I placated him to buy time to figure her out on my own." I rolled my lips together. "I would have found a way to get her off of his radar if she was harmless."

"But she wasn't," Dae finished the thought for me.

"No, unfortunately, she wasn't." I faced forward again, fighting against the rush of unwelcome feelings coursing through my body. Daddy had taught me how to disguise my feelings, to don the perfect poker face. But these two, who seemed at odds even while they seemed a pair, would see right through it.

The best thing I could do, was minimize the opportunity for them to see into the core of who I was.

"So, now that Vienna has so graciously told me about the journalist, why don't you tell me about the scene. I'm sure you've shared what you saw with Thackery?" The light note in Dae's voice seemed to irk Ratio.

He ground his teeth, and gripped the steering wheel.

Interesting.

I wasn't the only one showing my hand unwillingly.

"Of course I didn't. As much as you'd like to paint me as Thackery's puppet, I assure you, I am not." Ratio glanced at me. "I appreciate your father, Vienna. He taught me everything I needed to know to survive in this particular life—"

"Ditto," Dae said.

A quick glare at the backseat, then Ratio caught my gaze again. "I would not betray your trust or the confidentiality of a job. That is my promise."

Dae grunted, but I simply nodded. Ratio was a lot of things, most of which were probably still hidden from me, but I did believe him. He might not go against Daddy for me, but he wouldn't tattle on me to get his favor either. For an unknown reason, he was fond of me.

Maybe because I was the one person Daddy had willing ties to, but regardless, the affection was there and plain to see in his blue eyes.

"Fine, we'll move onto another topic. How did David convince you that Thackery was dead?" Dae was too happy to break up the moment with Ratio.

"What do you mean?" I bristled, knowing exactly where this was going. Cash had gone down the same path. But where I welcomed Cash's opinion, I did not welcome Dae's. He hadn't earned the right, and frankly, he never would.

"If you were suspicious of David's motives, why didn't you question him when he told you Thackery was dead. He couldn't have shown you the body."

"How is that any of your business, Dae?" Ratio snapped, showing an unusual amount of ire.

"Because Vienna would have received the same, if not better, training we did. Thackery would have taught her not to take David at face value. *Especially* David," he stressed.

Embarrassment heated the tips of my ears as I continued to stare forward. How had Daddy taught them not to trust Uncle David, and not me?

"You see, Dae. There was one person, and one person only, who Daddy let into his circle. For all intents and purposes, David was the only person to be trusted. Even Mart did not get the time to train me like Daddy allowed Uncle David to have. Fucking forgive me, if I received the most devastating news and didn't immediately think to question it.

"Yes, Daddy trained me to know better. Yes, I should have asked for proof, dug deeper into Uncle David to confirm the information. But I am fucking human too." I seethed, and at some point, my hand curled around the seatbelt, gripping it in my fist.

The silence in the car grew far too loud as the night stretched out before us. While I didn't plan to sleep, I let myself take light doze breaks—enough to rest but not enough to actually let myself go unaware. The minute the car shifted in acceleration, I sat up in the seat. It only took a few more turns, then Ratio pulled up to a gate.

He cleared his throat, then said, "We're here."

"What's the plan?" I only asked because they failed to discuss what we were going to do when we got here. Daddy sent me to assist but I didn't get the feeling that either of them *needed* my assistance.

"How good are you at improvisation?" Ratio asked, a secret smile tugging at his lips.

"What did you have in mind?"

"You'll see." A moment later, he reached out to press the button on the intercom. Dae seemed to sink into absolute stillness. The absence of movement was in and of itself, a tell. One that had me on high alert.

"Yes?" A gruff voice asked over the intercom.

"Good evening," Ratio said in a smooth, *butter wouldn't melt in his mouth* tone. "I am here at the request of Mr. Lennox to deliver a special gift to Mr. Daryawesh."

"Yeah?" The voice sounded skeptical. "He don't like dudes, even if they are pretty like your passenger."

Ratio shot me a look. The urge to roll my eyes was profound, but I slipped into the role like a comfortable old shoe.

"He's not here for him," I said in a baby doll voice that took my own up a little higher. "He's here for me. Where I go, he follows and Mr. Lennox wanted to show Mr. Daryawesh just how much we appreciate everything he's done."

I added a little titter of laughter to the last as I leaned into Ratio and stroked his suit jacket.

Nothing happened for the longest moment. Then Ratio said, "If you intend to keep us waiting, I will return the gift to Mr. Lennox and you can explain the rejection of his goodwill."

This was all a gamble. Uncle David could look like anyone, become anyone. He was a chameleon, just because Daryawesh was his benefactor, didn't mean he knew him as David Lennox.

"Bring her up to the pool house." The gruff voice wasn't the first guy at all. The gates also swung open.

Without a word, Ratio continued up the driveway. No one impeded us, despite the level of security, and there was a conspicuous number of cameras on us... there had to be.

Bypassing the main house, Ratio pulled up to a portico in the back. The pool house was visible just behind the fence.

Not saying a word, Dae exited the back and shot the two men approaching us. Both went down like rocks. The lack of blood puzzled me.

Before I could ask though, Ratio just sighed, "Really? I had us all neatly set up and now you want to do this?"

Dae gave him a bland look. "I'm going to scrub our presence and remove all potential witnesses. You deal with Daryawesh."

He ghosted away like he hadn't been standing there. "If I'd known we were just going to shoot people…"

"He's loading them up," Ratio said as he stepped over one of the bodies. "It's a toxin, takes them down for ten to twelve hours. They'll recover…eventually…it's not pretty."

Oh.

"They are also paralyzed while their nerves scream." Ratio shook his head. "Brutal, but effective."

At the door, Ratio motioned to me when the door opened to a butler. Or some other manservant. Ugh. I didn't want to hurt anyone who didn't deserve it. So I took the man down with two swift blows.

Ratio stared down at his collapsed form and then at me. "Some truths have to be seen."

"Cryptic."

"Sometimes." But he led the way through the pool house like he knew the layout. Maybe he did. We found Daryawesh, high as a kite and palming his very flaccid shaft when we walked into the bedroom.

I grimaced. "Some truths we really don't need to see."

"Agreed." Then he motioned to our target. "Ladies first."

FLETCHER

"HMMM." I pulled the window of basic details over to my far left monitor to maximize the next juicy bit of information. This time, instead of his birthdate, previous addresses, and schools attended, I enlarged the articles about his torrid affairs and lawsuits that were squashed before they ever saw the inside of a courtroom. This Edgar Daryawesh was quite the hacker's dream. And what kind of name was that, anyway?

"That better be a good hmm after we let Vienna go with two unknown men endorsed by Thad." Cash bit into a crisp apple as he popped a lean against the door.

"You better hope Drew never hears you say that you *let her* do anything." I returned with a fake grin. I didn't have to try for Cash like I did for Rick, but the fake it til you make it motto was really to help me keep my sanity.

The anxiety of watching her leave had leveled out some, but even though it was hours since she left, my hands still shook, and it wasn't from the caffeine.

A dark grin tipped up the corners of Cash's mouth as he tucked his head down. "Oh, I hope she does."

"You crazy fucking bastard," I muttered as I turned back to the screen. He seriously got off on their dominance fights. Drew did too, although I wasn't sure she realized it.

"You still didn't tell me what the hmm was for." Another crunch of apple assaulted my ears.

"Edgar Daryawesh is chock full of dirty secrets."

He moved into the office. "If you tell me he's into some dark shit, we're packing up to go get her. I don't give a fuck that Thad wanted her to go with them."

I pulled up another screen on my fourth monitor. "For what it's worth, I did some looking into Dae Hyun. He's a vigilante on crack. Or maybe a Robin Hood?" No, that wasn't a good analogy.

Cash's brows pulled low over his eyes.

"Look, he's efficient and skilled. And he doesn't kill indiscriminately. If we had to let her go with someone else, he's not a bad option." Fake it, fake it, fake it.

Cash's vibe was really starting to mess with the world I'd built for myself to make this okay. I needed to keep him away from Rick, or he'd get stabbed with the grilling fork.

His face lost all of its expression, even his ears drooped, as he just watched me with an unblinking stare. "There are no good options outside of me and Rick."

"Hey! That's the second time you've intimated that I'm not an asset. Do I need to remind you that I knocked your ass out?"

"When I wasn't facing you. That doesn't count."

"Oh, it counts. Not all opponents are going to be facing me." I pulled up my shoulders and lifted my chin. Let him get a look at the Reed arrogance.

"All right, whatever. What did you find on Daryawesh?"

I blew out a breath, expelling some of the bluster and turned back to the screen. "He's your average corrupt run of the mill businessman. He accepts bribes, sabotages projects, and has a really disturbing hobby."

Tilting one of the screens toward him, I pulled up the folder of pictures I'd hacked into. "There's nothing illegal here, but it definitely flirts with the line."

Each picture I clicked through was of a young girl. Nothing indecent, but of legs, barely there curves of the waist, bare feet. Isolated enough that I had an off the charts ick meter going off.

A crash jarred the walls as Rick's muffled curse floated through the house.

"I'll be right back." Cash darted out of the office.

For the next few minutes, I clicked through the rest of the photos that had downloaded, checking the info stamped onto each one.

"Oh shit."

Minimizing that folder, I pulled up another that had almost been forgotten on my server. I said forgotten, more like I wanted to burn the images from my brain because they were so creepy.

I checked the info.

Both sets of photos were shot with the same make and model of Canon camera—the EOS 5QD.

The door snicked behind me, and when I twisted around, Daddy watched me as he pressed his back against the door, and turned the lock on the knob.

"Daddy!" I screamed like a little kid. He might as well kill me now. If not him, I'd die of embarrassment.

Every hair on my body stood on edge. I had weapons in here. Drew had told me to keep something on hand. A knife or a gun tucked somewhere I could access. I wasn't terribly comfortable with the first and I really didn't want to deal with the second. So she'd put a taser in and secured it right below the keyboard.

The progression of panicked thoughts stumbled through me like they were doing a conga line of terror. Daddy studied me from eyes that seemed chipped from ice. Flat. Cold. Implacable. I thought once that my father's disappointed gaze was the worst thing on the planet.

One look from *Daddy* dispelled that notion. "Drew isn't

here," I said when he didn't move or stop staring at me. "You shouldn't be here either."

Right, maybe telling the psycho-killer-daddy where he should and shouldn't be, wasn't the best idea.

"What are you doing with *that?*" The question came out on a hushed exhale of breath that did absolutely *nothing* for my nerves. He would make a great voice for a horror game. Oh, that could work in the right app.

Since he looked past me, I took my life in my hands and tossed a glance over my shoulder. The image of a young Drew was on the screen. Jaw tightening, I wrenched my attention back to Daddy.

Drew wanted all info run past and through her or Cash. That made sense. We were on nebulous footing with Daddy. Still… in this case, the truth just might suffice.

Forcing my shoulders to relax, I straightened. I settled a hand on the back of the chair. More so I could yank it forward and slam it into Daddy if I needed to buy time.

"Research," I told him without a single quiver or qualm. Well, there were some internal shudders and I was pretty sure my hands were trembling, but none of it reflected in my voice.

"What are you researching that involves a picture of my daughter?"

"Anything that touches her," I told him flatly. "You sent her after a target that we knew nothing about. You didn't think we wouldn't make sure we learned everything about him? Drew doesn't need to go into a situation blind, no matter how intent you are on hobbling her and keeping her from looking too closely at you."

I really didn't mean to say all of that, but the words spilled out of me like I blew actual fire.

"So, are you researching the boys or the target?" Daddy transferred his gaze back to me. Ice shivered over my skin at the laser-focus in his eyes.

I lifted my chin. "I meant what I said about researching anything and *anyone* who touches her. Or could touch her. No more ambushes. No more surprises. Drew doesn't deserve that. I won't let anything happen to her if I can prevent it."

"Tell me what *that* photo has to do with your research." The hard notes lining the razor-edge of his voice blunted as he took a step toward me. No, not toward me, but the screen. Right, he wasn't touching the keyboard or my mouse.

"We came across this on Dion's servers," I told him, measuring the words. Nothing to betray Drew, but maybe Daddy needed the reminder that his little girl still loved him. "It's bugged me since I found it, but I wasn't sure where it came from…"

"And you found something regarding this while researching Dae," he asked, ticking off the names slowly. "Horatio? Or Daryawesh?"

Something in my expression must have given me away on that last one because Daddy frowned and moved from being a couple of feet away to right in my space. When he would have reached for the keyboard, I slapped his hand.

"Don't touch my stuff," I snapped.

Daddy jerked his hand back and the ice in his glare threatened to impale me like it was some physical blade. "Then show me what you found. Now."

The order and the implied "or die" on his sentence had me torn. "Give me one good reason I should help you," I said in a show of bravado I really didn't feel. "You don't like us. You don't want us here. You've been borderline cruel to the woman I adore. So, convince me."

The silence following my challenge was so loud, the manic beat of my heart seemed really loud in my ears.

Hand lowering to his side, Daddy straightened to his full height. "Are you feeling brave, boy?"

"Nope," I admitted without an ounce of shame. "You flat

out fucking terrify me, but I'll do anything Drew needs me to do. Even take you on, Daddy."

I was so dying tonight, but Drew would know I went out in her defense.

"Interesting." A thoughtful expression settled on his face. "I will kill anyone who threatens her. Any. One. Over-indulged rich boys with families who pay off their crimes to bury them rather than let them take the heat included."

The declaration didn't shock me. He knew. Knew what had happened. Probably knew what I'd done. Didn't matter. "She knows everything about me."

"Good. Now, show me what you found about that image."

"Daryawesh took it or had it taken." Despite having him at my back, I turned to hit a couple of buttons on the screen. This was either an inspired idea, a terrible mistake, or a calcu-lated risk. "I found these…"

We spent at least ten minutes reviewing the pictures that were on Dion's server and the photos I'd hacked on Daryawesh's cloud. There was no mistaking he was somehow connected.

With each picture, Daddy got colder and colder. So cold in fact, the room seemed to drop in temperature. His fury was ice and his patience was a temperamental surface on a newly frozen lake. One small bit of pressure and it would shatter his loose composure.

"Show me that screen." He nodded to the monitor that had all of Daryawesh's basic details sorted.

"Why do you want to see this? Didn't you say that you had someone looking into Daryawesh?" I snarked as I glanced up at him.

He leveled me with an intense and slightly unhinged stare. "Show me."

"Okay. I just want you to know that I'm doing this because you are Drew's father and I want to believe you're on her side." I really, *really* hoped Daddy was on her side. "But if you betray her again, I'll send Rick and Cash to slit your throat in the middle of the night. Cash would dance in the puddle of your steaming blood while Rick made fancy crumbled coffee bread for a midnight snack. And me? I'd erase you so you aren't even a memory."

I got chatty when I was afraid. It was a character flaw.

It must be working though, because Daddy wasn't saying anything. If he were offended, he would have snapped, maybe even broken my neck. But when I peeked up at him, he studied me with one eye squinted. Then he slowly nodded.

Yeah, I was getting through to him. I was the threat here.

I scrolled through the contents on the screen. Outlining the different points of interest to his favorite hang out spots, most used credit cards, and high frequency of certain meals. But when I got to the layout of the ranch, he stopped me.

I explained the map to him, and then he asked questions.

Were the blueprints outdated? Nope.

Had any additions been made? Not unless they did them under the table.

How likely was a house this size to be on one breaker system? Not likely. I'd guestimate two or three breaker boxes.

Daddy asked me to run from the top again, and I did. Because I had already sufficiently warned him what the repercussions were. It would have been quicker if I printed this stuff out for him, but when I asked, he waved my question away and continued to stare at the screen.

I think the crazy bastard was memorizing the data.

"I need to call Drew," I sighed.

"You *will not* share this with Vienna," he said in a voice that shocked that fear right back into my system. Okay, this creepy under the bed voice wasn't working for me. I was right back to feeling like I was going to piss myself.

"I don't keep secrets from Vienna." I used a slow measured voice to let him know, while trying to control the trembling in my words, that under no uncertain circumstances was I going to keep her in the dark on anything. That was not how I operated.

He was studying me again. Now I knew what it felt like to be an ant under a microscope. Zero out of ten, I did not recommend.

"You can call her. But this information on Daryawesh, you'll keep this to yourself until she gets back and you can tell her in person."

I returned the squint, feeling something like Popeye. "Why would I do that?"

"Because she's with two unknowns and you want this information to reach her ears only. You don't want to slip and give up information to other people. That would compromise her safety, and if she's compromised, you die."

What the hell? Was he being serious, or was he trying to scare me into doing what he wanted?

And why did I care? I could get this information to her a million different ways without shouting it down a burner line. But fuck, if he didn't want her two temporary partners in crime to hear this information, why did he send her out with them? Alone and without backup?

"Go through the information again." He turned toward the screen, leaning one hand on the desk, and waited for me to start at the top.

The pictures started to blur together as I worked on autopilot. I assume the words coming out of my mouth made sense, but my brain was buzzing trying to determine what his game was.

"You know, *Daddy,* I think you're trying to manipulate me, and a Reed can't be manipulated. We've eaten men smarter than you for breakfast." My heart started racing little circles around the inside of my rib cage. I might as well go for a thousand and really let Daddy know where I stood. I'd just do it while not making eye contact. "And I'm not fucking going over this information again. I can print it out for you like a normal fucking person."

"Okay…" Cash drawled.

I jumped and spun around. That wasn't the voice I was expecting.

Cash stood with his arms loose at his sides as he looked between me and my sweet setup. A scowl formed on his face. "Who are you talking to? And what are you printing out?"

"Fuck." I scrubbed a hand over my face. He was about to lose his shit. "Daddy was just here reviewing the information about Daryawesh. But before you go ballistic, we have to call Drew."

"You fucking gave him information?" Cash yelled.

Holding my hands up, I scrunched down in my seat. "Hey! I said before you go ballistic! And I laid the law down! He's not going to be fucking with us anymore! I mean, at least me. He's not afraid of you."

"Stop fucking babbling and get Vienna on the phone." He motioned to the burner on the desk. I nodded, ignoring the throbbing vein in his temple.

"Dialing. I'm dialing."

"STOP," I said when Fletcher stalked back and forth between the window and his office. "You're giving me a headache."

"That's easy for you to say," Fletcher declared as he pivoted. "You didn't just tell her that her father wanted info on their target and he didn't want me to tell her while she was with her new friends."

I leaned back in the chair and kept a hand over my face as I turned the most recent facts over in my head. The target Vienna had gone to see was also the same man who had either taken photos of her or had photos taken of her when she was barely a teenager.

No way her father knew beforehand. I couldn't see Thad approving that, even for a job. The fact he'd squeezed Fletcher for all the details indicated he was definitely not on board. Since he'd disappeared on Fletcher, I'd headed over to check out the house Thad had been using.

He was gone.

Where? My bet said he was after this pedophilic jackass. Vienna hadn't said much on the phone, only that they were on their way back. Or would be soon. Fletcher had a tracker up on a screen I could see. It showed her coming closer and closer to us.

I really wanted more details and I wanted them now. But I

would wait until we had her back here and our audience was gone. Fletcher spun on his heel to stalk back to the computer. Before he got there, Rick intercepted him and Fletcher let out a squawk of sound.

"What is that?"

"Coffee," Rick said and Fletcher plucked it from his hand. He knocked back about half of it in one swallow. To be honest, I said nothing and just waited. So did Rick.

"Holy shit," Fletcher let out a breath then shook his head. "That's loaded coffee."

"A generous measure of Kahlúa. Vienna will be here soon and she doesn't need to worry about you vibrating at the speed of light."

Fletcher glared at him but Rick was so placid in his declarations.

"She also doesn't need to worry that her father scared you this bad."

"I'm man enough to admit to my terrors." The indignant sniff actually made me laugh.

"Yes, you are," I assured the hacker. He wasn't afraid to admit any emotion. He wore all of them like a neon-colored hair shirt that we could see for miles. "You're also safe. We're not leaving you alone, even here."

Rick nodded his agreement. It had been Rick who talked Fletcher down from his super sonic speed earlier, panicking about what he'd told Thad.

After the first cup of coffee, Rick brought Fletcher a second one, as well as offered to get me a first. I passed on it. If he started dosing Fletcher with melatonin on top of the alcohol, I better stay coherent.

As it was, Fletcher did calm down from his semi-violent outbursts. At least he did until an alarm sounded. "Yes," he said abruptly as he stood. "She's back."

In a snap, both Rick and Fletcher took off toward the

garage. I followed behind, ready to break anyone's neck if they so much as breathed on them.

I also wanted to let them have their moment. It might give me a chance to have a nice friendly chat with Ratio.

The cool night air raised the hair on my arms as I stepped outside. Vienna opted not to park in the garage attached to the house, but took the car to a garage down the street.

She appeared just as Rick and Fletcher fell on her. Fletcher was talking non-stop, although at a much slower speed than an hour ago.

"We've got a problem." She looked me dead in the eyes as Fletcher wrapped her up in a big hug.

"Yes, Drew, we absolutely have to tell you—"

"No, inside." She pulled away and strode toward our house.

Where were Dae and Ratio? Why was she coming back alone? If she took care of them, I couldn't say I was overtly upset. Ratio had already proven I couldn't trust him, even if Vienna and the others did.

Fletcher was right on her ass, and Rick on his as they went back to the house. I scanned the yard, took one last look at Thad's house, then headed inside. After locking us in, I found them in Fletcher's office.

"All right, Dark Saint. What happened?" I crossed my arms and leaned against the wall.

"Wait. Before you get start—"

"Hold on, Fletcher. This is important." Vienna brushed her fingers against the nape of Fletcher's neck in apology. Then she moved those bright tawny eyes to me. Every single time I made eye contact with her it was a punch to the gut. "Tell me what you know about Lescheva."

Without question, I jumped right into the facts. "He's a consultant for the FBI. He specializes in patterns and tracking, and he has an uncanny ability to predict both. He was friends with my father for the last... decade. I've worked a few jobs with him myself." I paused. If she wanted more details, I'd happily give them to her, but those were the basics.

She ran her tongue over her top teeth beneath her lip as she nodded. Vienna didn't immediately start talking.

Something had spooked her. If it was Ratio, he was about to die. Although, rationally, I knew I was just looking for an excuse to get rid of the fucker. He enjoyed breathing her air too much.

"Where are Ratio and Dae?" Rick asked, looking out into the hallway as if they were about to walk through the door.

"They asked to be dropped off. After what we discovered on the job, they said they had some things to look into. They didn't appear to be running to Daddy, so I guess there are small mercies."

"Speaking of Daddy—" Fletcher tried to cut in again, but Vienna shook her head.

"Give me a minute, my little pincushion." She stroked a soft hand down his hair, and he preened under her touch. "There's something that you all really should know. I just needed a few minutes to process it now that I'm home."

"You are home. Let me grab you a glass of wine while you decompress." Rick spun toward the door, but she called after him.

"Rick, no wine please. As much as I would love to indulge, I think for this conversation I need to be absolutely sober."

"Okay, Dark Saint. No more stalling. What do you need to tell us?" Something about Lescheva based on her initial question.

"During the job, we interrogated Edgar Daryawesh. Unfortunately, he has no idea *where* Uncle David is. He doesn't stay that close to him, although he did have some ideas on where he could have gone. The more interesting piece of information, that I don't believe Ratio or Dae caught, and if they did, they kept their shock under steel poker faces…" She looked at me, holding my gaze captive. "Uncle David has a few aliases. The most important of which is Gregory Lescheva."

Even as I processed exactly what she was saying, I couldn't quite wrap my mind around the facts she presented. "Did he admit it aloud or was it just on documentation somewhere?"

"Both," she told me before turning her phone over so I could see the paperwork she'd photographed.

"May I?" I asked closing my hand around hers where it cupped the phone and then pulling both her and it closer to me. She slid her arms around me without me having to ask more as I enlarged the photo on the screen.

It definitely said Gregory Lescheva on the papers, along with a handful of other names I didn't recognize.

"More photos on here?"

She nodded then swiped through them for me. The images included a number of downed individuals, all good facial shots, as well as multiple locations in a large house from an office to a kitchen to a wine cellar.

It was the room hidden in the wine cellar I focused on. As I rubbed a hand up and down along Vienna's back, I enjoyed the tactile reminder that she was back with me.

"Shh," Vienna murmured and I spared a glance for where she tangled her fingers with Fletcher's and gave his hand a squeeze. "I know I asked you to wait, pincushion, but let Cash process this information."

"I'm good, go ahead and tell her," I urged Fletcher before kissing her lips lightly. "Did you record your interrogation of this guy?"

"I did." Vienna's tawny eyes seemed to shimmer with all her secrets. "Check under the voice memos. I thought you'd want to hear. The time codes are also marked."

"I love you," I muttered before dragging her back for

another kiss. One she returned with laughter and a smile before slipping away to let Fletcher tell her about her father.

I half-listened to his hurried explanation before I studied each of the shots again. Vienna offered Fletcher comfort and reassurance. A presence at my side had me glancing at Rick.

"Problem?" With the situation? For Vienna? For us? With this new detail?

"Yes," I said, answering all of his questions, even those he hadn't voiced. I gave Vienna a long moment to finish comforting Fletcher. The guy really had been beside himself at the thought of "betraying" her on some level. Even after speaking to her, albeit briefly, his nerves had begun to fray. He'd done good in telling her and telling us.

I had my bets on where old Thad had disappeared. If he didn't know that sack of shit had taken pictures of her as a child or that he wanted them? Yeah, I know what I'd be doing. It would also explain why he didn't want her to know until she came back.

He wanted to deal with the man.

Vienna shifted from where she leaned into Fletcher and looked at me. "What do you think?"

"I think I need to listen to the interrogation and I will, but do you have a photo of Uncle David?"

"No," she said slowly, then frowned. "Maybe. I know there was one in that file…" She was looking around the room.

"Or I can just pull up Gregory Lescheva," Fletcher offered. "Oh wait, I can't because the man literally has no pictures of himself *anywhere*."

That was weird. "None?" I frowned. "At all?"

"Nope." Fletcher gave Vienna a squeeze and then moved back to his computers. For her part, Vienna slid over to Rick and he wrapped her up, his whole expression growing far more content. I appreciated that feeling. Especially now that she was back with us.

I could function in her absence. I didn't shut down like Rick or grow frantic like Fletcher. Brooding, however, I did rather well.

And I brooded when I had to wait for her. I'd much rather be out there with her. Especially if she was going on jobs with people I barely knew, even if I had called one of them friend for a while.

"No social media footprint or images of him. He's got this picture of a horse as his profile pic."

"That's Sadie," I told him. "Lescheva had the horse most of the horse's life. Even after it got lame from an accident, he kept the horse in relative comfort and visited her whenever he went home to Kentucky."

"So home is Kentucky?" Fletcher asked.

"One of them. I didn't really pay that much attention. But he talked about that damn horse all the time. Thought she hung the moon. She was the best companion in life, because she'd do anything for him and she wouldn't stop until her heart gave out."

On the one hand, it sounded romantic—on the other? Eh. I didn't really care for it.

"What about the FBI website?" Rick asked. "He's a consultant, right?"

"We don't even list all the agents up there," I told Rick. "Consultants definitely wouldn't be. Check…check NYPD, he was a consultant with them for a couple of years. Can you get into their servers?"

"Can I get into their servers?" Fletcher gave me an incensed look.

"He wasn't insulting you," Vienna soothed him and I just grinned. Fletcher liked a challenge. Not that getting in proved to be much of one for him.

Sure enough though, there was no photograph for him. It said no known image. Not there. Not in Illinois or Indiana where I knew the man held a private investigators license. He had one in California too, but there was no photo of him or recent address. In fact, his license in California had expired.

After I had Fletcher go through a few agents' private socials that I knew for a fact Lescheva had worked with and no photos showed up, I scowled.

"I'll find David's," Vienna assured me. "Just give me a few."

Rubbing my jaw, I said nothing while she and Rick went hunting through files. Instead, I stared at Fletcher's screens as he continued his hunt.

"I'm really not liking this lack of digital footprint for your friend."

No, neither did I.

"I'm starting to think he's not my friend…"

"Lot of that going around," Fletcher told me with an air of sympathy.

I bumped his shoulder with my fist then moved to take a seat and listen to the interrogation. At the sound of the first scream, I paused it.

"I have headphones," Fletcher assured me before he tucked them on. "Noise canceling." Then he lifted his thumb and I hid a smile as he went back to work and I went back to listening. The guy seemed to know more than he realized, but the information was pretty disjointed.

Pain did that.

VIENNA

"ARE YOU CALLING HER AGAIN?" Rick stopped next to me and placed his hand just above the swell of my ass. For any other man it would have been sexual, but for Rick, he wanted the contact. It didn't matter where that contact was, he needed the closeness.

"I'm trying. She hasn't answered any of my calls since the day she had it out with Daddy. I've tried all of her burner phones. Now I'm cycling through." I blew out a breath.

We didn't have the typical relationship a mother and daughter would have. If it wasn't for me stumbling onto that argument of theirs, I doubt I would have ever known. And that was okay. I didn't need her in my life as a mother figure, but I did care about her as a person. She'd always been there for me in her own way.

At least once I was reintroduced to her as a teenager.

But she was hurting from Daddy's decision to remain in captivity for a year, and I wanted to make sure she was okay. With everything going down in the Network, it wouldn't be bad for her to disappear for a few days either.

I punched the numbers of her primary burner that she ran her less than ivory white business through. It rang once, twice, then three times.

A click flipped down the line, and her tired voice met my ears.

"Vienna," she sighed.

Rick raised his brows, kissed my temple, then walked away, leaving me to handle this conversation on my own now that Mart was on the line.

"Mart, I wanted to check in on you. When I last saw you… a lot of information was being thrown around…" I turned and leaned on the edge of the dresser in my bedroom.

"Dollbaby, I'm sorry. I'm not in the headspace for this conversation right now."

I'd talked to Mart during various times throughout the years, and she had never sounded so worn down as she did right now.

"That's okay. I'm not calling to rehash anything from the past," I paused when she drew in a sharp breath. "But I did want to check on you, make sure you're safe."

"Oh honey. I'm sorry. I wish things had been different. I have a thousand regrets over the way things played out."

"Hey," I said softly. "I don't need any apologies. I had a great life with Daddy," current situation notwithstanding. "And my friendship with you as I got older was a bonus."

I could practically see her slowly nodding her head, absorbing what I was telling her.

"Regardless, I still wish things were different. I also wish Thackery wasn't such an asshole," she said, her words tinged in fire.

Chuckling, I crossed one arm under my chest and looked down at the floor. "That's between you and him. But the one thing I do know is there's more upset about to hit the Network. Can you lay low for a bit?"

"I don't have any current or pending jobs. Maybe I'll just take a short trip down to the Gulf for a few weeks. We can catch up when I get back, and hopefully I'll be in a better mood." Even as worn out as she sounded, her voice was full of sugary sweetness.

"I would enjoy that." We disconnected, and Rick popped his head back in. When he saw that I was off the phone he stepped in with water and snacks.

"You take such good care of me." I lifted a salted cracker covered in brie and raspberry jam.

He didn't respond. He didn't need to validate that comment. But he did ask about Mart. "Everything went okay?"

"Yes, she's safe for now. Might take a trip south for a while."

"That was a short call…She didn't ask why you wanted to make sure she was safe?"

"Mart knows better than to ask. I won't give her details, and she doesn't expect me to. The warning call is enough."

Rick nodded and wrapped his arm around my shoulders, fitting me to his chest. "I'm supposed to tell you Fletcher has something to show you."

I smiled against the soft cotton over his chest. "But you're not ready to let me go?"

"Never," he vowed, stroking a hand down my back. "And that will never change."

The declaration wrapped around me like a warm embrace. Rick never failed to make me feel the comfort of his presence. Settling back against him, I soaked in his nearness. Eyes closed, I let the constant hum of agitation singing in my veins calm.

"When we finish figuring all of this out," I murmured. "We really do have to look for a new place to live."

I'd been wrestling with that idea since discovering not only that Daddy was alive but that he'd been keeping so many secrets. Secrets like Dae and Ratio. Secrets like sending Ratio to be Cash's informant. Secrets like purchasing our property through those boys.

Secrets like the cameras and listening devices stashed all

over my home. Our home. Fletcher had cleaned them all out and started tracking where the devices had sent their information. It… irked me that there was that kind of threat to them. A threat that occurred under my watch.

"Whatever you need," Rick murmured. "Just need to make sure we have the right equipment for you to be comfortable."

Laughter threaded through me and I tilted my head back to smile up at him. "The three of you absolutely have all the equipment I need."

A genuine smile tilted the corners of his mouth. "Then we shall be fine."

Yes. Yes we would. "I like this plan."

He brushed the hair away from my nape, then pressed a kiss behind my ear. "Are you ready?"

I curled my fingers against his cheek, holding the contact for a few long moments before I nodded. "Yes, you said Fletcher found something?"

"He did," Rick said, shifting his weight to drop a hand to my lower back. I carried my water while he brought the snack tray.

In the office, Fletcher and Cash were both focused on Fletcher's monitors. Well, Cash had part of his attention on the monitors and the rest of it focused on the photos on my phone. He hadn't returned it while he went through the interrogations and the search photos.

I didn't mind, Cash had his process just like the rest of us. But Fletcher's attention seemed far more lasered on his screen than on his surroundings. Then again, he glanced right at us when we came in.

"Oh, a cheese board treat!" Fletcher grinned. "Thanks, Big Guy."

"You're welcome," Rick said easily. "Cash, you need to eat too."

"Yep," Cash said without glancing up. "Let Fletcher go first."

"I already planned on it," Fletcher told him with a grin, he looked so thoroughly pleased with himself that I had to wonder what he'd found.

Cash glanced up when I settled on the edge of Fletcher's desk. The former FBI agent gave me a once over, concern filtering through his gaze. I touched his knee with my toes and a hint of a smile kicked the corner of his mouth up higher.

"If I may have all of your attention," Fletcher said as he popped a cracker with brie and raspberry into his mouth before he cracked his knuckles and motioned to the screen. "Our loveliest of ladies and my fine fierce gentlemen…may I present the Red Death network."

The screen flickered as names, locations, and dotted lines began to spread out across the U.S.

"How did you crack the Network?" Rick asked, leaning around me to get a better look at the screen.

The smug grin gave Fletcher a cute and boyish air. He was pleased with himself, as he should be. "I would have cracked it sooner or later, and I was already on the right path. Then I listened to the interview you had with Edgar Damp ass and he mentioned some very interesting names. To open the Network, I just needed the right passcode.

"Not only does Red Death have their own network, they have their own *network*. It's just as sophisticated as the system you're using, Drew. It makes me wonder who set it up. Think this was Dion's work?" He glanced at me, and a memory flashed through my head.

A black and blue Fletcher with one eye swollen shut, as he looked at me like his savior.

"Dion had no code of conduct, and operated under selfish motives. It would not surprise me." The screen was still lighting up with new locations and names. Red Death rivaled the size of the Network. That was alarming. "Dion did have photos from Daryawesh... He was at least connected to the right people."

"Wrong people," Rick quietly corrected.

"The wrong people," I repeated.

"The question is, how are we going to shut down Red Death?" Fletcher took his seat again and started tapping furiously on the keyboard.

"From your shit eating grin, I imagine you have ideas." Cash smirked, his attention going between the screen and the photos on the phone.

"Oh, do I..." Fletcher spun in his chair and Rick smiled down at him. Rick was proud of our little pincushion. I couldn't hold in my grin either.

Even with everything going on, all the stress pulling my mind in different directions, and uncertainty if my relationship with Daddy would ever be the same, these men made everything okay.

They brightened my dark moments and gave warmth to the cold. Each one brought something unique and different to our family dynamic and I couldn't see this bond we built ever breaking. My men were each irreplaceable.

"Well, what is it, Pincushion?" I propped my hip on the desk and braced a foot on one of the legs of his chair.

"I'm currently downloading the information for each data point, whether it's a person, business, or location. Within Red Death, they're ranked by skill and level of competency in a very simple color coded grid. The very easiest step is inserting a virus into their network. We can choose to do one of two things.

"The first, we could have the virus crash the system so they are disconnected from their internal network and pick them off one by one, or as needed, with our soon to be printed Red Death Directory. Or..." he punched a few more keys like he was playing a symphony solo. Rick and Cash both laughed. "We could have the virus lock onto their devices and track their movements. It would be a slow process but we could put tags on certain words and codes, really build up our data on who Red Death is and what they do. Although knowing that it's a secret sub network, I imagine the jobs they organize aren't kosher. If we do this, then we'll still be able to pick them off as desired, but we'll have more ammo in our back pocket, and maybe blackmail information as we need it."

"Second option. Then, we cut off the head of the snake," Cash said as he pointed at the screen with the hand holding my phone. "What's that bar at the top?"

"Oh, this baby? This is essentially a search bar. You drop in your price range and desired skillset and it matches you up with specific people who meet your criteria. Kind of like Bad Guy Bumble. Hey!" Fletcher spun around and slouched down in the chair. "What about the Bad Guy Brigade? That has a fun ring to it...although it doesn't incite fear," Fletcher muttered and dropped his gaze to his lap.

I ruffled his hair. "With all the affection I feel for you... no," I said with a smile.

He grinned, rolled his eyes, and turned back to the screen.

"I'm with Cash. We need to take out David, because we can at least be sure he's the head." Rick pushed away from the desk. "I'll go work on dinner while you three decide the best course of action." Then he was gone.

"The issue is finding him," I murmured, studying the screens. The Network was impressive, but not unmanageable now that Fletcher hacked the system. "And we still need to vet the information about Uncle David's aliases, specifically Gregory Lescheva."

"Talk to me about that. What does he look like?" Cash asked.

"I can give you a base description, but Uncle David's best

talent is morphing his appearance. Every time I see him, he looks like a different person."

Cash shook his head. "There are certain things that a person can't change. Not really. How tall is he? His eye color? Any disabilities that affect the way he works?"

I thought of Uncle David. "He's about six foot. Maybe six foot one. His natural eye color is light blue but he wears contacts often. No disabilities that are noticeable or known. He's somewhere in his fifties, but I've seen him appear anywhere from early thirties to late seventies." Then because I adored him but some things he needed to remember. "You can change height with lifts in your shoes, a slight stoop to your shoulders, even the way you hold your head. Think Christopher Reeve in that Superman movie. The difference between his identities was how he held himself."

"And the fact he wore pajamas," Fletcher offered up. "But I see your point."

"Fuck, that doesn't help at all." Cash turned back to the monitors, lost in thought. I let him have time to process because it was written all over his face that he had an idea.

With Cash, there were only two modes. Recklessly jumping into a dangerous situation because he could, and processing an idea until he'd figured out all the different angles. And never both as far as I'd observed.

"Do you trust me?"

I glanced at Cash. "You know I do," I said softly.

"That's a very sweet moment," Fletcher heckled, but we both ignored the comment.

"I've disengaged from my contacts so I wouldn't be tracked back to you. But I do have friends I can trust. I want to put feelers out. See if I can find Lescheva's location." He leveled his gaze on me, waiting to see how I would respond.

Daddy's words rang in my ears, that Cash was a liability and the FBI would be looking for him. But I pushed it aside.

Cash was far more capable than anyone I'd met in the Network. And more than that, I did trust him.

"Do it. We need to find Uncle David, and we need to do it before Daddy finds him."

A slow grin spread across Cash's face. "That's what I was hoping you'd say."

RICK

AFTER CHECKING MY WATCH, I glanced to where Vienna sat in her favorite chair staring sightlessly at the television. The show she'd turned on was a documentary, but I doubted it even registered with her. Since she and Cash returned with Mr. Drew, Vienna had been… *different*. A difference, I suspected I noticed far more keenly than the others.

Vienna was *off*. The moment I strode into that alley intent on saving this ethereal being, I discovered an all too earthy woman waging a personal war against the monsters lurking in the darkness. Fletcher and Cash both described her as complicated and powerful. They worshipped her as she should be worshipped.

They loved her like I did. Like me, they'd seen the changes. It wasn't like she hid them from us. The long silences pregnant with heavy emotion. The troubled eyes shimmering beneath a sheen of tears. The ferocious possessiveness when Mr. Drew suggested she couldn't trust us.

My beautiful love was hurting. Suffering from wounds inflicted in a way I couldn't stop or defeat. I hated it. Anger flared in me all over again. Her *father* hurt her with his actions, abrading her already torn soul. From those first few days, the mourning had been there. The shadows in her eyes, shadows I hadn't quite understood but I desperately wanted to defeat.

For a short time, after we found her and before we found her father, those shadows had begun to dissipate. Cash burned them out with his brash attitude and bluntness. Fletcher charmed her with his playfulness and vulnerability.

And me?

I just did my best to look after all of them. The problem with Thackery being the one to hurt her...I couldn't just kill him. Not when she clearly loved him. Not when I fought to understand the *why* behind his choices.

Planting my hands against the marble countertop, I forced my breathing to slow. Between her father's rejection, the arrival of Horatio and Dae as allies her father cultivated, and now the suspicion that Cash's friend Lescheva and her uncle might be the same person, she was truly off center.

Cash had left on a research excursion, possibly to meet with contacts he said he could trust. Still, he'd taken Fletcher with him as backup. When Fletcher had given him a shocked look, it had been Cash who said with a shrug, "you don't need to fight, you just need to make sure they don't record me or track me."

That pleased our hacker to no end. Vienna trusted Cash to play this hand and I trusted him to bring Fletcher back to us. No more losses.

Not for her.

Not for us.

"Vienna," I said when the silence in the room grew almost claustrophobic. I waited until she turned those luminous eyes on me before continuing, "Would you like to train?"

She lifted her brows and tilted her head as though she needed a moment to process the question. Patience was not a struggle for me, except when it came to her hurting. I possessed no patience for that.

"It's late in the day for training," she said slowly, sampling each word with the same kind of care she showed when she tested the flavors of a new meal I'd prepared. "Are you alright?"

"That's a question I should be asking you," I said, fighting the need to just go drag her from the chair and drown her in passion until she sobbed out everything she needed.

Maybe I should have started there, but I would never wrest control from her. Vienna decided when she needed me to take over. Until she asked, I would respect those boundaries. Still…

"I think you are asking me." A long, nearly forlorn sigh escaped her. "I'm sorry, Rick. I haven't been much company for you."

Leaving the kitchen, I circled the column to go into the living room. Once there, I took a seat on the coffee table so I could face her without looming over her. For all the power she possessed and all the capabilities she demonstrated, she was still so much physically smaller than me.

"I do not need you to entertain me," I assured her. "All I've ever needed is to keep you safe." Exhaling a long breath, I examined my own frustrations. Bottling them was useful when I had a direction. At the moment, I rather expected she needed more than just my control. "I need to help you."

Leaning forward, she reached for my hand and I scooped her up. The movement was all the invitation I required to cradle her to me before I took her seat and settled her in my lap.

To my delight, she curled into me and rested one hand against my shoulder before tucking her head against the other. Palm sliding down her back, I marveled again at the strength housed in this delicate frame.

"I love you," she whispered and I basked in the warmth of those words. "I genuinely don't know how I would get through all of this without you. Without all of you."

As much pleasure as I took in those words, I shook my

head. "Vienna, you are the capable one and so very strong. You would persevere and discover all the answers with or without us." I didn't care for the idea of her being alone again. "And we *will* find them now."

The muscles of her back were so tight and tense. I continued to massage slow circles from along her shoulders then down her spine and back up again. Getting to know her body had been a sweet privilege. It allowed me to help ease her discomfort as well as give her pleasure.

If I had my way, she'd never know discomfort again. Since life was never that kind, I would take every opportunity to look after her whether it was cleaning the house, preparing meal, fucking her against a wall, or dismembering a body.

Where she went, I would follow. What she needed, I would deliver. What she wanted... we'd damn well make sure she got that too.

Cash, Fletcher, and I were united on this front. Fletcher had been stalking Thackery online and off. Cash would pull all the strings he had. Then there were the interlopers—I agreed with Vienna that Horatio seemed trustworthy and that his loyalty to her existed.

As for Dae? I shrugged him off mentally.

If he became a problem, Cash would probably kill him for us. He'd shown restraint with Ratio so far because Vienna seemed fond of him and he'd come through for us repeatedly. Well, he'd come through for *her*.

That was the important part.

Another sigh escaped her, the sound so forlorn and lost it shredded me. "Tell me what I can do to help?"

"You're doing it," she assured me, patting my chest as she rubbed her cheek to my shoulder. "It's... I don't even know how to describe what I'm feeling. Daddy and I—we never talked feelings. We talked the work. We talked about loyalty. We talked about trust and the hunt. We talked about the things that needed to be done."

"But not your feelings." I tried to understand that. My parents hadn't been perfect, but they had been good people. Kind people. My father had been demonstrative with his love. Acts of service, my mother had called it. Mom had been the one with the sweet words and the hugs. She also taught me to cook.

They showed their love in so many ways. Vienna's love language was complicated. How could it not be?

"No," she said after a long moment, tilting her head back to look up at me. I drank in the sight of her. The hint of sassiness in the tilt of her smile, the softness adding to the shimmer of her tawny eyes.

"I know Daddy loves me." She paused again, a thoughtful look in her eyes. "I know he loves me because of how he raised me, the choices he made, the fact he's always put me first. I know Daddy has always protected me. I think that's what makes this hard…he *chose* to stay away. He chose to let Uncle David control him…because of me."

"Do you truly believe he was being controlled?" Because something about that whole idea did not sit well with me. If I were her father and placed in a cell, would I obey someone to keep her safe? Yes, but not before I tried to kill the person threatening her. Could Thackery be much different?

Really?

The weight of the sigh she released filled the room.

"I want to believe it," she said slowly. "More than I thought I could possibly. But… if someone did that to me? Choosing to threaten Daddy to keep me in line? I'd kill them myself."

Raising my hand to cup her head, I said, "Then why else would your father stay? What could your uncle have used to control him?"

It must have been the right question, because her eyes narrowed and her lips compressed. Shadows danced through her expression, then she locked her gaze on me. "I told you I love you, right?"

The warmth that ballooned at that declaration was the most heady intoxicant I'd ever encountered beyond her smile itself. "Yes, but I treasure each time you say it. The word has never had the value it possesses when it crosses your lips."

A soft laugh escaped her as her lips curled upwards into a smile. "I need you in my life, Rick. I didn't know how much until you came into it. Now—I never want to imagine my life without you."

Some distant part of myself relaxed. Vienna had become home, safety, and the one to nurture and protect. But with that statement, she brushed away the remnants of anxiety that I wasn't enough. That I couldn't be enough. I didn't have to be her everything, I just had to be here for her. Understanding kindled in my soul. I was enough for her.

"You will never lose me," I swore. "I'd never let anyone keep me from you and if they threatened you—I know what you would do."

"Kill them all," she swore. And on this, we were agreed. "I would kill anyone who threatened to hurt any of you."

"Yes. We will have to look after Fletcher though. I know he would do anything for you, but he really doesn't like blood."

A throaty laugh bubbled up from deep within her and it eased more of my concern. My beautiful Vienna was a survivor. She'd survived the year without her father. The week with Sandra Jane, and now she would survive her father's return.

Gradually, her humor dried up. "For so long, all I wanted was to avenge his death. Now…he's not dead and I should be over the moon. I was so damn relieved to see him and it's just…"

"It hurts more because you don't understand it all."

"Yes," she admitted and then burrowed against me. At the unspoken request, I wrapped her up tight. "I'm trying to understand, but he's shutting me out. Judging my choices when it seems like his choice was to stay away. Would he have come back if we hadn't found him? Would he have stayed away forever?" The lost note in her voice damn near undid me. "I won't apologize to him for finding you. Or for Fletcher. Or even Cash. Even when I want to throttle Cash."

It was my turn to chuckle. "You only want to throttle him because he challenges you."

"True," she admitted as she raised her head. "He pushes me in all the ways I didn't know I needed to be pushed. Just like you take care of me in all the ways I didn't know I needed. Fletcher…"

"He makes you smile, frees up your laughter, and lets you live." I saw what Fletcher did for her. As much as he'd annoyed me in the beginning, I appreciated him on so many levels for what he did for her. What he did for all of us, really. He even softened up Cash.

With smooth control, she shifted in my lap and I adjusted my grip. When she straddled me, I rested my hands on her hips.

"What do you need?" The darkness clouding around her had been pushed back and there was a glimmer in her eyes that had been missing before.

"All of you," she whispered.

"You have us." If they were here, they'd say it themselves. For now, I would say it for all of us. "What else do you need?"

The soft curve of her lips deepened as she traced her fingers over my face then to my hair. I wanted to lean into the contact and close my eyes as she stroked her nails over my scalp. It relaxed and invigorated me in the same instance.

"Rick…"

I waited as she studied me.

"Why don't you want me to punish the driver who took your family?"

The question didn't startle me so much as just deepen my love for this remarkable woman. She didn't need to worry about the drunk driver, yet she'd clearly been thinking about it. She'd clearly been concerned.

That she was asking now, said it still troubled her.

"Because they have been punished. A drunk driver took them. He made a terrible mistake with a painful cost to me and to himself." I shrugged. "I could hate him, but that's a lot of energy and investment in a person who acted carelessly. Getting revenge on him wouldn't bring my family back. While jail may not seem like equitable justice…he didn't mean to do it. His crime was without malice."

Sucking on her lower lip, she chewed it thoughtfully.

"I love you for wanting to extract that justice for me. But I have made my peace with it. I will always miss them…but you're my family now. Fletcher is. Even Cash. Maybe…" I considered this a moment before finishing the sentence. "Maybe some day that family will include Thackery and Mart. Whether it does or not, I have all I need with the four we are now."

"I hate that you were hurt."

"I hate that you have been hurt too. Just being hurt doesn't mean we must extract a pound of flesh."

For the first time in our relationship, Vienna pouted. It was adorable. "True. Very well, then if you see no need for further justice, I will accept that. But careless or not, if anyone hurts you again…"

I gave into the impulse and dragged her to me. The ferociousness of her protection warmed me all the way through. Pouring every ounce of my loyalty and admiration into the kiss, I squeezed her tight. She ground down against my rigid erection that had swelled at the first contact of her ass.

"We will protect each other," I said against her lips. "We will see that we're all given the justice due." Another biting kiss. "And we won't allow anyone to hurt or use us again…"

Then words weren't needed. Not when she rolled her hips or when she tugged at my shirt.

Fisting her hair, I held her captive to let me fully explore her mouth. The wonder of kissing her would never get old. A groan vibrated from her. The sound traveled through me until I echoed it as she dueled my tongue with her own. It wasn't a battle for dominance.

No, she didn't make me fight for it. Surrender tasted sweet on her as she arched her whole body. I pulled away only long enough to shed the shirt before I rose and carried her up the stairs.

"The sofa…" she complained.

"…will be there," I assured her. "What I want to do to you needs the bed."

A delicious shudder traveled through her. "I need you…"

"And you're going to have me." Upstairs, I went straight to our room. Though I still had a room of sorts, I never slept in it anymore. My place was with Vienna, always.

I lowered her onto the bed before I went to work peeling her out of her clothes. She'd been dressed casually, comfortably and there was no bra. I paused to admire the tips of her rigid nipples where they peaked.

Wrapping my mouth around one, I teased the pebbled skin. It was a sweetness to taste these breasts. To massage them with my fingers and with my tongue. She raked her nails over my scalp, the movement equal parts provocative and inciting.

I cut my gaze up to find her watching me with wet, parted lips and eyelashes lowered. Her breath came in sharp pants. When I scraped my teeth over nipple, she let out another sound. This one went straight to my cock as if she'd wrapped her sweet hand around it and squeezed.

Wanting, no needing, to drown out the voices in her head, I alternated between nipping, sucking, and laving my tongue over her nipple until she shook. Then I moved on to the other.

It took only a bit of maneuvering to strip away the leggings and then her long, bare legs were trying to curl around me.

Having learned just how clever and strong my Vienna was, I planted a palm against the inside of her thigh, pinning her to the bed. If she wanted up, she would tell me. I used my thumb to tease along her slit.

Oh, the dampness there was inviting. I could smell the sweet musk of her arousal and I nearly abandoned the nipple torture to feast on her pussy.

I could dine there all night, until she was hoarse from the screaming, and it would still not be enough. She thrashed, writhing as I moved back to the first nipple. They were both puffy, and deepening to a rosy pink from my ministrations.

One thing I'd noticed from her liaisons with Cash, she preferred the bite of pain with her pleasure. She'd liked it when I spanked her. She'd liked it when he marked her up. She liked it when I filled her ass until she sobbed from it.

I let my thumb graze her clit and she reacted like I'd pressed a taser to her skin. Bucking, she let out a scream that made me pursue her pleasure even more ruthlessly. Back and forth, I moved between her nipples until they deepened to a dark rose shade, and glistened from the strokes of my tongue.

Her breathing came in sharp pants. All along, I would let my thumb barely brush along her clit, never quite making contact, until I lifted my head and blew cool air against her nipples, even as I pressed against that bundle of nerves with far firmer strokes.

Vienna came apart beautifully, her lusty cries sending a thrum through my blood to pulse into my cock.

"Nipple play...I've never come from that before," she admitted after several minutes while I savored the reactions she didn't mask from me. I'd taken the time to strip off my clothes and suck the flavor of her from my thumb.

Real pleasure shone in her eyes and I stroked myself as

she began to focus more on me. When her gaze went to my cock, I smiled.

"We're far from done, my sweet beauty. Unless you need rest…"

"Never stop." It was a plea and a command.

One I was more than willing to fulfill. Catching her thighs, I pulled her to me, setting her ankles to my shoulders and bending her as I settled my cock against her pussy.

Angling my cock, I lifted her and thrust at the same time. She was more than wet enough to take all of me, but the soundless scream she emitted and the way she squeezed my engorged dick encouraged me. I gave her a few seconds to get used to my intrusion, then I pulled out slowly, dragging it out for both of us.

She was so fucking beautiful and so damn sweet, but even more, I could feel her wrapping around my soul with the same warmth and ferociousness with which her body held onto my cock. It was like she didn't want to let me go. When I slammed back inside, we both let out a ragged breath.

I locked eyes with her and her smile was wild and sweet. "More, Rick…give me everything…take everything…"

"Yes," I promised as I began to rock my hips, there was no finesse to my movements now. Only the desire to be as deep inside her as I could be. I wanted to pound my scent into her skin, pour my essence into her until we could never be separated.

The thrusts rocked her, trying to force her up the bed, but I held her to me. She wanted more. So did I. Locking one arm over her legs to keep her with me, I dropped my free hand to play with her clit.

Her writhing screams climbed in intensity until she spasmed around me. I didn't wait out her orgasm this time, just kept going, fighting against the intense pull of her cunt fisting me inside of her and thrusting in until she arched her whole body and clawed at the sheets.

When the world finally narrowed only to her and my balls dragged up tight, I let myself come, but only when she was screaming, so I could orgasm with her. When I collapsed down over her, I braced one arm on the bed to keep my weight off of her.

"More?" I whispered, aware of the wet heat I still nestled in and the way she spasmed, squeezing my cock over and over. My orgasm had only softened me some and if her inner muscles kept it up, I'd be hard again in no time.

"Yes," she groaned, but I'd let down my guard and even boneless and shaking, she flipped me over onto my ass. "More, Rick, my sweet love. More for me. And you're going to let me have it…"

Yes, I absolutely was and when she rose up above me, my cock went to stone. Tawny brown eyes, so golden they beckoned for me to plunder their depths, teased me. She could do whatever she wanted to me.

I clasped her hips and when she began to roll and move, I thrust up. The motion made us both gasp.

More.

Definitely more.

"ARE you sure you want to do this?" Fletcher asked me as we filed into his office. When I would have settled on the desk next to his computer, he slid his arms around me and tugged me toward his lap.

The past seventy-two hours had involved a lot of clandestine electronic and telephone meetings for Cash with Fletcher covering his back—until the day he went to meet one of his former colleagues. Then we'd all gone.

By request, I'd taken a high position with a rifle. It had surprised, I suspected, then tickled Cash when he realized I intended to literally watch his back and I would eliminate any threat to him. Fletcher went to work in his new van set up— one he'd declared made him Benji to Cash's Ethan.

At my blank look, Fletcher had looked downright offended. "Movie marathon. You bring your sexy ass while Rick makes all the treats and we'll even let Cash massage your feet."

"Thanks," Cash deadpanned, but it still made me laugh as I agreed. I liked making plans for the future. His former colleague as it turned out, was a woman, and five minutes into that conversation and it was clear they'd been more—at one time.

Their conversation had been brief, her forensic observations sharp, and her tone absolutely abrasive. Cash admired her and I could see why. She'd asked him only one question—was he sure he wanted to do this? When he gave her a firm nod, she'd turned over two huge files and then taken her leave.

Maybe when we were in the clear, he could introduce me. She reminded me of Mart in a much saltier way. His expression when we met back up had utterly charmed me. The intensity in his eyes and the determination in his jaw.

"I like that you're not jealous," he murmured as he kissed me.

"Good," I told him, before pressing a hand to his chest. "She's your past."

"And you're my present and future," he confirmed with a wry smile. "Cheesy as that sounds, it's also perfect."

"Aww," Fletcher added in undertone. "You guys are gonna give me cavities."

It was Rick who smacked him in the back of the head, but it clearly didn't hurt and we were all smiling.

After Cash went through Lescheva's files, we'd compared descriptions using a program Fletcher had pulled up. I could do some sketches but it wasn't anywhere near that artistic. Still, Uncle David could look like anyone, it was hard sometimes to remember what he looked like without prosthetics.

Disturbing thought.

"Yes," I finally answered Fletcher's question from when he tugged me into his lap. "We've done research, we've begun to pull apart the tendrils that comprise this hidden network, but at the end of the day, the only one who can answer these questions is Uncle David."

Fletcher studied me for a long moment. To my surprise both Rick and Cash said nothing. They, like me, understood that until we caged and interrogated—quite probably eliminated—Uncle David, this would never be over.

"Okay," my sweet pincushion said before pressing a new

burner into my hand. It was hooked up to his computer by a cable.

"This is the burner you use with a few modifications. It's going to send a message to his phone, let me track it through the cellular network. We'll start with the packets going to his messages, it's like casting a lot of different fishing lines. We're going to see where we get nibbles."

Gripping the phone lightly, I kissed the tip of Fletcher's nose and his eyes sparkled with humor.

"That's almost a cookie, but if I do this real well, I would like to say I prefer the original reward."

"You want me to suck your cock?" I asked lightly, before tightening my ass against his fledgling erection. It took almost no encouragement for him to stiffen right up and I swore my core went soft. "That can definitely be arranged," I promised him. "Work first."

"I adore you," Fletcher declared with a smirk. "I find your system of rewards to be somewhat perfect." This time, he kissed me. Hard and fierce. The stroke of his tongue on mine sent electricity skittering through me. The feel of his piercing always did the most interesting things to me.

Maybe I should get pierced.

When I groaned at the thought, Cash cleared his throat. "I did the first good boy job, so I'll take my blowjob later."

Fletcher grunted, then bit my lower lip. For all his loving playfulness, my pincushion knew how to keep amping up the anticipation. "Gonna be a full meal for you," he whispered.

"Especially if I have Rick for dessert." A delicious shudder went through me. I loved their dicks. Not a thought I ever imagined having. Before a cock had been something to ride and get myself off. Now, I got to delight in theirs. I loved the way they felt on my tongue, against my lips, pressed up inside of me, in my cunt or my ass.

I wanted—all of them. Every inch of them filling me. Another shudder rippled up my spine until my nipples went taut. A hand fisted in my hair. With a gentle tug, Cash tilted my head back and I grinned up at him. His kiss was all sharp and biting.

Stop playing. The message came through loud and clear.

I bit down on his lower lip, sucking it hard against my teeth until he rumbled and Rick said, "Vienna," in that deep, sexy-throated way.

Yes. I needed to work.

Jerking my thoughts away from their beautiful bodies and even lovelier souls, I focused on the cell phone. My libido checked itself as I typed in the number.

Sex was the last thing I had on my mind by the time I entered the last digit. Knock, knock, Uncle David.

"How are you going to convince him to call you back?" Rick asked before I hit the call button.

I glanced at his completely earnest face. Concern radiated from him.

"I'm going to tell him I think I found something on Daddy's killer. Drop Daryawesh's name."

"You don't think he's going to know that Thackery escaped and is back with you?" Rick spread his attention between the three of us.

"David absolutely knows Thad escaped," Cash said as he swiped his index finger over his brow. "But he won't know that he came back here, or that we were the ones who busted him out."

"I wouldn't be so certain of that, MacGyver." Fletcher removed one hand from my waist as he typed a code onto the keyboard. A new screen popped up filled with lines and lines of text. He hit another key and footage overtook the rest of his monitors. "I put up surveillance and the place has been a ghost town and he had no equipment of his own to track Daddy's extended stay. Rookie mistake." He typed out a few more codes and the screen flipped through different tabs almost too fast for me to track. "Now, it could be that he had equipment up and removed it once he realized Daddy had sprung the joint, but I don't think so. There was no evidence of any type of advanced technology set up. So...unless *Daddy* has been parading down the strip with a "pick me, bitch" sign, or leaving his calling card on asshole bodies as a big fuck you... I'm not convinced Uncle David knows anything."

Fletcher sat back and loosely locked his arms back around me. I smiled at him, proud to have him on our side. Hackers were a dime a dozen. What they could do was one thing, but more important than what they could do was be the person who could be trusted and really knew their shit. Fletcher had the critical thinking skills to back up his work and that was what made him dangerous.

"Okay, so say David doesn't know Thad escaped. That works in our favor. Just like it works in our favor that even if he does know he escaped, Thad wouldn't necessarily come back here. As far as David is concerned, Daddy believes Vienna killed Sandra Jane on his command. He would believe Thad would lie low, hunt him, kill him, and do his own research into Sandra Jane's death, before seeking Vienna out. The voicemail to draw him out is still our best plan." Cash laid it all out. He'd been thinking this over for a while.

"All right. Next time *Criminal Minds* needs a script writer, I'm going to anonymously put your name in the hat." Fletcher's face lit up. "Hey! We could be the Profiling Party of Four!"

"No," we all chorused together.

"Fuck, you guys are no fun. You don't deserve a fun and catchy name," he grumbled as he rested his head on the back of his chair and started twisting us side to side.

I hit the dial button, and after three rings it went to voicemail. Perfect. The standard time before a call went to voicemail was twenty-five seconds. That meant Uncle David had this burner on him.

The computer-generated voice asked for a message and at

the beep, I dove in. "Uncle David! I just broke a nail and it's terrible! Darby talked non-stop during the appointment and said some crazy things about Dad! Call me back when you get this." I added just enough affronted entitlement to my voice, sighing hard between sentences.

To anyone else, I was a spoiled kid complaining about a poor nail job.

"That was...not what I expected." Fletcher seemed impressed with the way he regarded me.

I opened my mouth but Cash beat me to it. "You never want to leave a legitimate detailed message. Too much rope to hang yourself with in case the phone is ever confiscated by authorities. She complained about a job gone wrong. Getting a disturbing message about her father from a man with the first initial of D. Did I get that right?"

I raised an eyebrow. "Why ask me, you're doing so well on your own."

Rick and Fletcher chuckled as Cash outright grinned. If I'd been standing, I'd have gone a bit weak in the knees.

Fletcher bent forward, jostling me against his now dying erection. He tapped a few keys. "It would have been better if he'd answered, but we can work with this."

Cash and Rick crowded around the back of the chair to see the digital map on the screen. It started as the world, then zeroed in on the US. After a few seconds it refocused on our state, and finally a town that was about forty-five minutes away.

"What are the odds?" Fletcher said as he opened his phone.

"You said Uncle David has never been here, correct?" Cash closed his fingers around my palm and helped me from Fletcher's lap. He smoothed his hand down my side before stepping back.

"Right," I said, but pursed my lips to the side. It was too coincidental that he was so close after Daddy was out.

"Let's go. I have a lock on his location. There is a small chance he's using some kind of VPN to settle on a random tower that's closest to our physical location, but we won't know until we check it out. And let's not forget, I have my own sweet van set up for situations like this." He winked as we strode out of the office.

We put on our shoes and headed for what Fletcher had so nicely dubbed his kidnapper van and the Wi-Fi on it was set up as: FBI Surveillance Van as a big middle finger to the world. It was adorable.

About fifteen minutes outside of the town where Uncle David was supposedly hiding, I noticed something in the rearview. Or should I say someone.

With more calmness than I felt, I pulled over into the back parking lot of a dying shopping complex.

"What are we doing?" Fletcher poked his head between the two front seats as I parked next to the dumpsters. No matter where we were, it was always a great spot to get privacy. People in general hated the smell of garbage.

"We have a visitor." I unbuckled my seatbelt and threw my door open just as Daddy parked behind us.

"Shit," Fletcher mumbled and ducked back into the back of the van. Cash and Rick appeared from the other side as Daddy turned his car off and climbed out of the driver's seat.

"Vienna," he greeted, this time only a slight disappointment tinged his voice.

"What are you doing here?" He must have been watching the house. Did he know where we were going or was this just luck?

"You need to go home." He braced an arm over the top of his door, keeping his body completely relaxed.

"Sorry, Daddy. You don't make those calls for me. You haven't in a very long time, and you definitely don't have that power anymore." I started to turn around to walk back in the van. If he wanted to follow us, fine. But we weren't going to waste precious time.

"You're not going to chase after David. I told you before, I'll take care of it." His voice was stern, allowing no room for disagreement.

Still, that wasn't going to work for me. "And I told you that I had a job to do, and I'm going to do it." I tossed up my hands. A rookie mistake. I was letting Daddy get to me. Just the slight disapproval radiating from him had my heart rate climbing.

He shook his head. "You have no idea what you're doing. I didn't raise you to get yourself killed because your emotions are too much for you to handle."

Steam poured out of my ears as the edges of my vision dimmed. Cash and Rick started to step forward, but I held up my hand. It wasn't worth it for them to cause a scene in a parking lot. Whether anyone was within hearing distance or not, this was still an open area.

"I'm not the naive girl you think I am. I'm not going to let Uncle David manipulate me. I don't follow anyone *blindly*. You taught me *that*."

Irritation rolled through his eyes. "You believed him when he told you I was dead."

I stumbled back. The icy pain lancing through my chest was an actual physical ache.

I had believed Uncle David. Cash had told me that was a mistake, and yes, it was. I knew it now. But then? I was over-wrought with emotion and Daddy had never given me any reason not to trust him. That was *his* mistake.

"Uncle David has to be taken care of. If you won't do it, I will." This time I did pivot, but Daddy didn't let me get far.

"He knows I'm with you. If you go, you'll be walking into a trap. Is that how you want to lose your men? Because you can't take a beating to your pride?" He shook his head and my cheeks burned.

"I always do the research. Always. I never walk into any situation unprepared."

"Then consider this. I sent him a message on Daryawesh's body. He knows I'm free. He knows I'm back home, and he knows I'm coming for him. Don't get yourself killed because you don't know all the facts." He dropped back into the seat, started the car, and politely backed up before turning toward town.

I watched the road until the car disappeared, and then some.

How could Daddy have built me up all my life, just to tear me down now? All the pain I thought I'd compartmentalized broke free of its confines and rushed through my body, to settle in my fingers and toes. It *hurt*.

Fletcher stepped up next to me, gazing in the same direction. "Are we following him?"

"No," I rasped. "We're going back home."

He nodded, and my men were silent as we climbed back in the van. It was a brutally silent drive back to the house.

VIENNA WAS NOT HERSELF. From the moment her plan had gone awry or, better phrased, her father had ambushed us and derailed it, she'd alternated between unspoken depression and silent rage. While not a single syllable passed her lips, there was no mistaking the rigid line of her shoulders, the tight compression of her lips, and the distance in her eyes.

It was the return of her father all over again. She didn't talk, she didn't "react," she just—went through the motions. Cash went for a run with her, I followed her into the gym, and Fletcher settled in with his laptop to work next to her when she'd delved into research.

Previously, we'd given her time. Pushing her wasn't acceptable when she was this wound up. Or it hadn't been based on what I'd known then.

Now...

"You have a plan," Cash said as he joined me in the kitchen. I'd made a fresh pot of coffee and poured his when I heard him on the stairs. After their rather *lengthy* run, he'd paused to talk with me before showering. She'd showered alone, then come down with her laptop.

"I do," I admitted after a long beat of silence. Until he'd said anything though, I hadn't even realized the thoughts I'd begun running. "We can't do this like we did when he came home."

"Agreed," Cash said. His knuckles paled to white as he closed his grip on the coffee cup. A muscle ticked in his jaw and for a split second, the sound of his grinding teeth carried before he shut it all down. If I hadn't seen Vienna do exactly the same thing when she needed to focus on the tasks at hand, I'd have been concerned.

It was a method. A tool. One he shared in common with her. One that we could use to our advantage now. That said, I wasn't sure he was going to go for it.

"What do you want me to do?" Cash asked after he'd packed away all of his anger and agitation.

"Something, I suspect, neither of you will enjoy." And by neither, I meant him and Fletcher. Then again, it wasn't about enjoyment, it was about taking care of the woman we loved. If we could make room for each other, we could make room for a little discomfort.

Stretching his head from side to side, he popped his neck then looked at me with his cool, unreadable gaze. "What do you want me to do?"

"Follow my lead," I said, as I finished the tray of coffee with mugs, and some cookies I'd baked the day before. A little something sweet to help with the bitter. Inclining his head, Cash motioned for me to go ahead and I nodded.

As I passed behind the sofa where Vienna and Fletcher were at work, I caught what was on their screens. Vienna read through the files Fletcher and Cash had compiled on Lescheva, David, and any other aliases she was aware of.

Fletcher had his surveillance screens up and stared broodingly at the house where Thackery had set up… and was currently sitting on his porch, making no pretense of watching our house.

I paused to consider that for a moment. Despite all his attempts to contain his emotion and be enigmatic, worry seemed present in his expression. Maybe I projected that, but why else be out on his porch, in plain view, where she would see him watching her.

"Computers up," I said as I continued around to set the coffee and cookies on the coffee table. Cash took a seat in Vienna's preferred chair while I poured the coffees.

Fletcher blinked at me and then over at Vienna who stared at me with the same expression her father currently possessed.

"What?" Confusion, not anger, filled the single syllable and I gave the top of her laptop a gentle push to lower it.

"Computers up. We need a break, all four of us, and I need you to focus on something that isn't those files." Rarely did I give her orders. Then, I only did it when she asked me to take over.

There had been no request this time, not verbally or nonverbally for that matter. But Vienna was fighting to keep her head above water. She didn't need to wage that battle alone.

"Thirty minutes," I told her. "No time at all, but enough to breathe, drink the coffee, and enjoy the peanut butter fudge cookies I made."

A hint of light flickered in her eyes. She happened to love those cookies. While it wasn't enough to brush aside all of the hurt she was drowning in, it did elicit at least a hint of a smile.

With a long sigh, she closed the lid of her laptop before she handed it to me.

"Thank you," I murmured, trying to infuse each word with all the affection and gratitude I felt for her. Fletcher still eyed me skeptically, but when Vienna put her hand on his arm, he closed the screen and put it on the table next to him.

Once we all had mugs of coffee, I took my seat. Vienna played with dipping one of the chunky cookies into the liquid. The various emotions that danced over her face seemed in a fight to take purchase, but none lasted very long.

Exhaling a breath, I said, "I wasn't sure about bringing Fletcher here or Cash. Not in the beginning. Not even after the first few days. I understood the need for both, but it made me question my own worth. You shouldn't have to reassure me, yet you took the time to do so when most others would have just gotten impatient with me. The need to take care of you, to be enough for you, to make sure nothing touches you that you don't wish is so overpowering at times..."

I debated how to phrase this next piece.

"I need to be needed by you even if you don't need me. I love being in your life and a part of it, but if you had no place for me...I think I might kill to make that space available again." No, I would definitely kill to make sure I was in her life.

"Rick..." Concern lifted the syllable of my name and I held up a hand as I shook my head.

"You don't need to offer me comfort, I know my own flaws and weaknesses. I know myself. I know...*you*. What I have with you, I've had nowhere else. Even Fletcher and Cash have made a space for me, a space where who I am is accepted and liked. Most of the time."

"Don't cut yourself short, Big Guy," Fletcher told me with a faint smirk. "I couldn't survive without you. Cash *definitely* couldn't have survived without you."

The rumble of sound that came from Cash's direction didn't sound like disagreement or assent.

"Thank you," I told him. "However, I'm not saying this because I need you to make me feel better." Once more I tracked my focus back to Vienna. "I'm telling you that since I met you...my life has changed in ways I haven't fully comprehended. I could smother with my need for validation before. I don't need it now. Or maybe...I know I always have it with you."

Yes, that sounded far more accurate.

"When I met you, I'd just left the latest program. I don't know if it was successful this time. My need for you has not wavered. Not an ounce, but my confidence? My security? They are incomparable. You've given me that. I'm not the man I was before you. I'm not even the man you took with you that night to the gala…"

Every word was the truth and until I put my mind to it, I hadn't even realized *how* true it was.

"I'm not Merrick Wright. I'm not even the Rick Drew that Fletcher created… but I am the man that loves you and will protect this family we've built. I like that man. If no one but the three of you see me, that's all I need." Especially her.

A gleam entered the soft golden sheen of her eyes, sparking a real smile for the first time since her father's ambush.

"I'm not the same Vienna you saved that night," she admitted softly. "I don't think I've been her for a very long time."

Cash gave little start at her words. But it was Fletcher who grunted and let out a breath. "Well, I'm definitely not the same idiot dilettante who managed to piss off the bad guys so much Dion was going to shoot me in the head after he beat the shit out of me."

A ferocious look crossed her face as she turned to Fletcher. "I would never have let him hurt you."

"And you didn't," he said, tapping two fingers to the arch of his brow. "You didn't know me, but you saved me. I'm not the guy who gets saved…I'm the guy who gets bailed out, then shuffled off out of sight before I embarrass the family any more."

"You don't embarrass us," I assured him. "Even at your most irritating." That would be useful to me to know, so I wanted to make sure he did.

"Good to know I can still irritate you," Fletcher said with a hint of a grin, but then he sobered. "Honestly, I don't think either of you…" He motioned to me and to Vienna. "Neither of you have any idea of the kind of man I was… the kind of family I came from."

"But I do," Cash volunteered. "You're not your family, Fletcher. You're arrogant, but you have heart. You're brilliant, but you have humility. You're dangerous, but you have compassion."

Gripping his chest, Fletcher stared at Cash. "You really care about me."

"Don't make me take it back."

"Nope, no take backs. We're bonded. We're like boyfriends in law or something."

Cash just rolled his eyes, but Vienna let out a soft laugh. "Be nicer to him," she admonished Fletcher. "But I agree. You are not your family."

"Neither are you," Cash said, snaring her full attention even as her smile erased. "You aren't the Vienna that Thad left behind when he went on that mission. You haven't been since the day your uncle told you he was dead."

She pursed her lips.

"Truth is, none of us are the people our parents expect us to be or who they left behind, whether they died, disappeared, or just moved on. We're not supposed to be." The former FBI agent rubbed his palm against the stubble decorating his cheeks. "We shouldn't be. Who we are changes through our experiences, our trials, our triumphs…and even our losses."

"He was my best friend," Vienna said softly.

"So was my pops, even when he was a bastard. He figured out pretty early on that nothing scared me. He'd push me to do more, to take on harder challenges and where fear would put caution in some men…it didn't in me. Didn't happen the first time I was shot, or broke a bone, or even had a woman walk away because I was more interested in my job than her."

With his gaze lasered onto her, Cash lifted his chin.

"You didn't have relationships when your father was here, did you?"

"No," she said slowly. "Dirty hookups..." At his arched look, Vienna shrugged. "I like sex. Daddy didn't like it when men looked at me. Sometimes... I would test the waters without him and I can take care of myself. No one is going to make me do something I don't want to do."

"Damn right they won't," Cash growled. "And there won't be any more dirty hookups."

"Is that so?" Despite the fact this had been about confiding in each other, and building our bonds, Vienna's dare was almost playful. "Going to enforce that, are you?"

"I will share you with him," Cash said, pointing to me and then to Fletcher. "And him. They're it. You and me? We're facts. So are they. You want to flirt with another man and lure him to his doom, I will happily end his life before he puts his hands on you."

The shiver she gave suggested she liked that and I couldn't really disagree with it. I didn't like the idea of anyone touching her. Not without her permission. I accepted Fletcher and Cash, like me, they were guardians of her heart...

"Your father expects you to be who you were when he left." I needed to bring us back to where we'd started.

Cash sighed and leaned back in his chair as he studied her.

"I want him to be the daddy I remember," she admitted and it wrenched my heart. With a glance down at her hands, she twisted her fingers together. She wasn't focusing on us. She didn't see Cash's knuckles go white or Fletcher's eyes narrow. "I want...*him* back but I'm not his little girl. Not the way he wants me to be."

She sucked her upper lip between her teeth.

"I hate that it took losing him for me to find any of you..."

Then she lifted her eyes. "But I won't give you up. Not even for him."

"Can you stop beating yourself up for changing?" I had to ask, because her pain hurt me and I wanted so badly to end that pain for her.

"I can try," she said and when Fletcher claimed one of her hands, then interlaced their fingers, she summoned up a smile.

"Your father terrifies me," Fletcher told her. "But nothing is scaring me away from you. Not even him."

"Good," Cash said, and then he grimaced. "In the interests of this group therapy session… I've never felt fear until the day we discovered Thad in that cell."

Vienna wasn't the only one to stare at Cash. Fletcher blinked and I frowned.

"You're not afraid of Daddy," Fletcher protested and Cash gave him a sliver of a smile.

"No," he said. "I'm not. The fear I felt was at the idea that with him back, Vienna wouldn't need us anymore. She could retreat to that safety of what she'd known…and I'd have to fight to stay in her life."

While he spoke to Fletcher, his gaze never left Vienna.

"You're worth every battle. Whether it's your father's handpicked suitors." Cash grimaced and I shook my head. I didn't like that description for Dae or Ratio, no matter how accurate. "I make no apologies for what I will do if they try to take you."

"They can try," Vienna said, looking every inch the dangerous woman she was. "No one is taking you away from me or me away from you. You're mine."

"And you're ours," I returned softly. Those words were the right ones.

The only ones we needed. Fletcher squeezed her hand and she held out her free hand to us. I don't know who moved first, but Cash and I abandoned the chairs to join her.

"Thank you," she whispered as she wrapped her hand around my nape and pulled me down for a kiss. "Thank you for loving me and showing me that I can love all of you…" She sighed against my lips. "For accepting that I love all of you."

"He loves us too," Fletcher said almost sotto voce. "We just love you with more dick."

Laughter erupted.

Those were the right words too.

"At least I know I'm not the only crazy bastard in this relationship."

I slapped Cash on the back and he shook his head, but he was also smiling.

They were all the right words because these were the right people.

Our people.

Our family.

I STOOD on the small back porch off of our home, bracing my hands on the railing. With drones and satellites being what they were today, I rarely spent any kind of time outside. The tall shade trees should prevent any unwanted spying, but with our life's work, one could never be too careful.

In fact, it was better to be on the defensive. Three steps ahead at all times.

Daddy had taught me that.

Yet, in the late evening, with the low storm clouds hiding the setting sun and the scent of rain in the air, I couldn't help the desire to soak in as much fresh air as I could.

For the first time in days, weeks maybe, I felt like I could breathe. Not just with relief that life was as simple as it could ever be right now, but that I had what I had always wanted. Even if I'd never admitted them to myself.

Experiencing the fullness unfurling inside my chest felt... like nothing I'd ever felt before.

The Red Death network was still active, for the moment. My relationship with Daddy might never be the same. Uncle David taught me a lesson on how those closest to you were sometimes the most deceitful.

If we were splitting hairs, that was a lesson I learned from Daddy too.

Still, what I had with Rick, Fletcher, and Cash? It eclipsed all that.

"Dark Saint, what are you doing out here?" Cash rumbled against my hair as he wound himself around my body, molding his chest to my back.

I hummed and lifted my head to tuck my face in his neck. "Just being…happy."

He chuckled. "It feels weird, doesn't it? I can relate." Cash left his answer at that and propped his chin on top of my head.

I breathed in this moment, wanting the calm serenity coursing through me to last forever.

"While you're out here, Rick and Fletcher are both inside worrying their asses off. You should go comfort them. After that intense session, they're worried about how you're processing."

Turning in his arms, I looped them around his neck. "It *was* intense, but I loved it."

One corner of his mouth hooked up, and his white teeth flashed in a smile. "Rick does love his therapy, doesn't he?"

I swatted his chest. "Leave Rick alone. It was good for us."

"Oh, I'm not saying it wasn't. It was a…very Rick thing to do." He dropped his head and sucked my bottom lip into his mouth, biting the soft flesh just hard enough to sting. "Let's go inside, Dark Saint," he whispered, his turquoise gaze burning.

Nodding, I dropped my arms but he caught my hands and walked us backward. He led me to the house, keeping the entirety of his sharp focus on my face. It was heady, being the center for this man. For any of them.

When we reached the door, he let go of one of my hands to twist the handle. Cash tugged me over the threshold, and yanked me against his chest as he took care of locking the door. Then he wasted no time to slide his hands under the cheeks of my ass and picked me up.

Immediately, I locked my legs around his waist and cupped his neck. The whole process was so smooth and coordinated. A masterful show of skill that didn't surprise me one bit coming from Cash.

He started a sweltering path of open mouth kisses down my neck as he walked us through the house. I pushed my fingers through his hair and held him close as he moved us up the stairs.

Our trip to the bedroom was a dream, and when he set me on my feet and gently spun me around, I noticed what I'd missed while under his spell.

Soft light flickered over the room with fresh scented candles scattered across the dresser and nightstands. Fragrant rose petals dotted the floor and bed, appearing black under the dim light.

And my loves? They stood in opposite corners, stripped down to their boxers, gazing at me with lust-filled eyes. When I turned to Cash, he was slowly, and deliberately, slipping out of his clothes.

His strong hands unbuttoned his shirt, sliding it off his broad shoulders. Then his hands went to the belt, the sound of the metal prongs being released so obscene in the quiet space. My pussy throbbed.

"Uh-uh. This is an equal opportunity space, Drew. If we're foregoing our clothes, you have to as well." Fletcher tutted as he and Rick appeared on either side of me. They'd been working on their stealth. I hadn't heard a rustle of movement as they closed the space between us.

"Fletcher is right, and we're happy to help you." Rick grabbed the hem of my shirt and pulled it over my head as Fletcher tucked his fingers in the band of my pants, sliding them over my hips. As they fell, he shifted his hands around to my ass, squeezing the globes with firm pressure.

I laughed. It was such a Fletcher thing to do.

"I love you." I happened to be looking at Fletcher, but I

moved my gaze to Cash. Then Rick. Standing there in my bra and panties, I repeated myself. "I love all of you so much, I can't breathe without you." My hand somehow found its way to my chest. "No matter what, no matter what happens as we take down Red Death, find Uncle David, or whatever else this life brings us, I need you. Each of you."

My breath caught. All the warm and wild emotion that had been building throughout the day, that hit so hard on the porch, peaked. Tears pricked my eyes.

Fletcher turned me into his chest as he banded one arm across the top of my shoulders and smoothed the hair at the back of my head with the other. "Shhh. It's all right, Drew." His voice was warm and low. I allowed myself to sink into his embrace for a few moments, then I pushed back enough to see his face.

His hair was loose with a few unruly strands framing his angular face. The proud lines of his face softened with a hint of vulnerability he only showed with us.

"You know I love you?" A sudden desperate need to ensure they realized just how essential they were to me crashed against my chest. I cupped his face, the soft stubble pressing against my palms as I pulled his face toward mine.

"Yes, just like I love you, Drew. More than anything." His lips met mine, and we spent minutes exploring each other's mouths. Gentle kisses, licks, and nips did more to ease my soul than anything else could have.

No, that wasn't true. Hearing he loved me did that too.

Rick peeled me away from Fletcher's hold and walked me back toward the bed. "You don't need to say it, Vienna. You already know I love you more than any person has a right to love anything. And I know you love me the same."

As soon as my back hit the bed, Fletcher pulled my hands over my head, and Rick hooked his thumb in my panties to tug them down my legs.

"Vienna," Cash said as he prowled toward the bed. It wasn't even a prowl. It was a seductive show of flexing muscle and sleek skin. A dangerous package that no one could ever mistake for anything else. And it was all mine.

"Yes, Cash?" My voice came out husky, from the emotion. From the lust.

"I don't love you." My heart stopped, but he continued. "That's too soft a word for what I feel in my soul. It's pure, unadulterated obsession. People in love would let their partner go if that was what their partner wanted. They would tear themselves up if it meant their partners would be happier without them." A sinister smile curled his lips and the flickering light deepened the darkness exuding from him. I loved it, I loved him.

"I will never let you go. I will never let you walk away. No matter what you do or have done. Nothing could change my mind. Your place is with me, always. That is my promise to you." He dropped to his knees, grabbed the back of my thighs and spread me wide, then buried his face in my pussy.

The tortured scream that worked up the back of my throat ripped from my mouth as I tossed my head back. He had no mercy, wringing every bit of pleasure he could with his masterful fingers and tongue.

"Damn, Cash. I'm obsessed too. We could have practiced our speeches so we could all look good," Fletcher mumbled above me. The words barely registered. I was too lost to the terrible rapture licking over me.

Rick swung a leg over my stomach and settled his thighs against my sides. At some point, he'd lost his briefs, and his angry, turgid erection stood stiff against his stomach. I licked my lips as he reached over to the side of the bed. When he straightened, he had oil in his hands.

His shoulders bunched as he stroked himself, his head tipping back.

"You're drooling, Drew." Fletcher's grinning face appeared over mine. Cash must not have liked the talking because he bit the inside of my thigh before pushing two thick fingers inside me. He fucked me so good with just his fingers, my eyes rolled back in my head.

"Here Big Guy, I'll give you a hand," Fletcher said as he shuffled his knees on either side of my head. Then he pushed my breasts together as Rick used his thumb to force his cock down low enough to fit in the crevice. "You see, Drew. We thought about making this all about you, but we know you. For tonight to be perfect, you'd want us to feel wanted too."

Rick started moving his hips, his cock gliding through the oil. The sight so erotic, I forgot to respond to Fletcher. Hell, I couldn't even remember what he said.

After a couple thrusts, Cash timed his movements with Rick's and fiery heat blanketed my body. Sweat broke out over my skin as I writhed beneath them.

"Prime her for me, will ya?" Fletcher called down to Cash, tossing the bottle of oil to the foot.

I didn't have time to fully appreciate what was happening before cool, slick fingers probed my ass. Without thought, I relaxed, and he pushed one finger inside, twisting and pulling out, all to the same rhythm as Rick.

Then another finger was added.

All I could see was Rick's beautiful, strained face. He gripped the tops of my shoulders to deepen his thrusts and I grabbed onto Fletcher's thighs to keep from scooting up the bed.

The fingers disappeared, and Cash's hot, hard cock pushed into me. His hands smoothed up my legs and he shackled my waist in his grip. "Feel how hard you make me, Vienna? You'll never leave me. You'll never leave us. We won't let you."

Cash started bucking into me, using my waist just like

Rick was using my shoulders. I thought Fletcher would have made a smart comment, something to break up the intensity of the moment, but when I glanced up at him, his brows were pulled low and mouth was set in a firm, taut line.

He massaged my breasts, then pinched my nipples almost to the point of pain. "Cash is right, Drew. We're all in this together."

Rick grunted, his movements erratic. One pump, then two, and three. His face reddened and a vein popped in his neck as streams of hot cum shot over my chest and under my chin. He kept moving, jerking with each backward pull until he shivered.

"You're beautiful like this," he said and swiped his hand through his cum. He didn't wipe it away, but rubbed it into my skin.

I didn't say anything as we locked gazes. Everything was in his eyes as he climbed off. He bent down to press a kiss on my waiting lips.

"My turn." Fletcher's voice was strained as he slid his hands under my arms and dragged me up his chest and away from Cash. He settled us against the pillows as he used his legs to push mine wider. "Hand me the lube."

The open bottle was placed in his hand and he dribbled some over himself and me.

"Sorry, I don't have enough control to save you the mess."

"She's already a mess," Cash supplied as he settled between my legs. "Those are the best fucks, aren't they Vienna?" He adjusted his cock and pushed in, pausing while Fletcher started to work himself inside.

I moaned. The pressure of feeling so full dispelling all thoughts from my head.

Fletcher passed the tight ring, and sighed as he flexed his hips and bottomed out. "This is the best place I've ever been."

"Agreed," Rick grunted as he laid back next to Fletcher.

He placed one arm behind his head and relaxed, ready to watch the show.

"Look at me, Dark Saint," Cash demanded, setting a slow, steady rhythm, so unlike the frenzy from a few minutes earlier. "What do you want?"

"You," I whispered. "All of you."

"You have us," he said, groaning as he pushed back in. "What do you need?"

"All of you. It's the same," I gasped as he thrust back in, hitting my g-spot with his angle.

"And what will you do to keep us?" His voice deepened and his breath quickened as he and Fletcher worked in tandem.

I loved Fletcher's hot pants against my ear as his arms tightened against me. I loved the darkness that only I seemed to pull from Cash during sex. The devotion Rick gave that seemed to make him just as happy as I was to receive it.

Cash was right. This was more than love. I would never let them go.

"Everything. Nothing will take any of you from me. I'll destroy the world first."

"Damn fucking straight," Cash growled, and that was all it took for wave after wave of ecstasy to completely wash over me. I clutched at Fletcher's arm and Cash's hip as I pulsed and twitched in their arms.

Fletcher groaned and Cash snarled something unintelligible under his breath as they both followed after me.

Once I came back from the high, Cash pulled out and fell on the other side of Fletcher. We were all gasping for breath and goosebumps erupted along my skin as cool air hit my sweat slicked skin.

"Here, let me take care of you," Rick said. There he was, a warm washcloth in hand as he cleaned me up from my chin, all the way to the crevice of my ass. He left no place untouched as he did exactly what he said he would.

He handed Cash and Fletcher each their own warm cloth, and once everyone was cleaned up, we snuggled under the sheet. Even Cash, who usually didn't cuddle me when we were all in the same bed.

But tonight, nothing could have forced us away from each other.

CASH

MY PHONE DINGED with a text message from Ratio, as Fletcher and Vienna came down the stairs. I couldn't have planned it better myself. Not that I was trying to keep Vienna out of the conversation, but if I had to watch her father break her fucking heart one more time…

I twisted my head to the left, satisfied with the series of pops, then twisted my head the other way.

Yeah, that wasn't going to happen again.

And I wasn't about to set up a meeting for Dae and Ratio to be in her presence unless I absolutely had to. Rick had a secret little laugh at my expense, but I didn't fucking care.

Vienna loved us, and she had no attraction for those two. But that didn't change the fact that they each watched her with an unusual amount of interest.

"I packed you snacks and some water in case it doesn't go well and you get hungry." Rick picked up the bento style lunch boxes and handed Fletcher and Vienna each their own, then dropped a kiss on Vienna's smiling lips.

It had been dangerous to let Rick go wild on the credit card. As soon as Vienna gave the green light, he picked up boxes upon boxes from Amazon at the local grocery store. He'd ordered cute themed toothpicks, different color cupcake liners, and various forms of meal prep containers. Then there were the boxes of different cooking utensils I hadn't even heard of.

"You're sure you want to go?" I asked, because as much as I wanted to do this without her, meeting some of Fletcher's family sounded painful. People like us? We didn't do the meet the parents thing.

Thad was the exception. We could all agree he wasn't a typical parent. From the way Fletcher nearly pissed his pants in his presence every time he came around, he was worse.

It was probably best they both were gone.

Vienna faced me, her hair bouncing in large loose curls around her face. She'd applied more make-up than I'd ever seen her wear, giving her a haunted but beautiful look. When she stepped closer, a waft of sensual musk met my nose and my cock thickened.

That wasn't out of the norm in her presence.

"These are the family members he likes. Mostly," she added when Fletcher choked.

"Listen, I wouldn't take her near most of the Reed family if we were drowning and they had the only door. Those bastards would push us off even if there was room. Give me a little credit when *I* invited her along." He tugged on the suit jacket that he wore like a second skin.

Fletcher had a little bit of chameleon in him too. An incredibly useful skill.

Ignoring him, I spread my fingers wide across her waist and yanked her into my chest. I loved the softness covering the honed muscle on her body. But not as much as I loved the way her mind worked. Only a fool could look in her eyes and not see a deadly predator.

"Call me if you need backup. Rick and I will drop everything to come get you."

"You're forgetting I knocked you out." Fletcher sniffed and I rolled my eyes.

"You came up behind me."

Vienna smiled only with her eyes, and when I tasted her lips, she pressed her breasts against my chest. I absolutely loved being coated in her any way I could.

Yeah, she was the perfect mate for me.

"Okay, okay, it's time to hit the road." Fletcher caught her hand and pulled her away from me. There was a lot of that going around lately. She never had space to herself between the three of us, but from the happiness shining from those gorgeous fucking eyes, she didn't mind.

"We'll check in, and if we don't, you have our location on your phones. We'll be fine." She gave Rick his kiss, then they were out the door, lunchboxes in hand. The image was hilarious, but I didn't laugh.

I opened my screen.

Ratio: We'll be there in thirty minutes.

We were cutting it a little close, but that was fine. This wasn't going to be a secret anyway.

"What is that look on your face for?" Rick asked.

I raised my brows. "What look?"

"The one that says you're about to slice someone up and enjoy it."

I grinned, putting my phone back in my pocket. "That look has benefited me more than I can count when working with informants. We're about to have guests, this is your thirty minute warning."

He grunted under his breath, and started zipping around, wiping non-existent dust from the house. Fletcher would be sad to miss this.

By the time twenty minutes had passed, I headed outside. And what do you know? Ratio and Dae were just pulling up. How convenient he had given me a later arrival time.

Their nondescript car pulled up in front of Thad's place. If I needed any evidence that he had his own surveillance on the property, this was all I needed. He was on the porch before he could have heard the car if he were, say, in the study.

"Ratio, Dae." Thad frowned, not at all pleased they were here unannounced. Good. I wanted him off kilter, if even just the slightest for what I had planned.

"I invited them," I cut in before Thad or the others could say anything. I leveled Thad with a hard stare. "I'm sure you know, Vienna just left with Fletcher. They'll be gone the entire evening. Why don't we go over to our place and have a chat."

Ratio squinted behind his thick-rimmed glasses, and after a few minutes he shrugged. Turning to Dae, he said, "He's a bit of a hard ass, but he's a solid contact."

While Dae was trying to figure out if he liked Ratio enough to believe him, I turned to Thad. Mainly because Dae and Ratio had issues they wore on their chest like badges. I had no idea what happened to get them to that point, and I didn't care. It was just curious, because they'd been spending quite a bit of time together.

And I was a man who liked puzzles, so that part of their dynamic intrigued me.

Thad crossed his arms, planting his feet shoulder width apart. "We can go inside if you'd like to chat."

"That's not going to happen," I shook my head. "This is my meet, and we'll meet in my location of choice. If you don't feel comfortable, you can sit out."

We locked stares, his jaw grinding a mirror image of mine.

Yeah, I haven't forgotten what a fucking asshole you are.

Finally, he nodded. Dae begrudgingly followed, most likely because he looked at Thad with stars in his eyes. He'd follow Vienna's father anywhere. Ratio would too, although they had both convinced Vienna that they were their own men.

Inside the door, we took our shoes off and arranged them neatly on the plastic covered rack. So they'd been working with Thad long enough not to question these practices.

Rick poked his head around the door to the kitchen, then disappeared.

"Was that Rick?" Ratio asked, a hint of humor bleeding through his words, even though his face was blank.

"It was. This way." I showed them to the living room. If I was going to extract the information I hoped to, being comfortable was key. Once in the living room, I sat in the armchair. It was closest to the door, while blocking anyone from sneaking up on my back.

Dae and Ratio took the couch, and Thad hesitated before leaning against the wall so he could see out the window. A smirk nearly broke free. He was off balance, but hiding it.

"I'm surprised you didn't ask what I wanted to talk about outside." I pinched my jeans and lifted my ass to adjust the crotch.

"It wouldn't have mattered." Thad waved a hand. "You clearly stated this was going to be your way. As Vienna's father, I didn't fear that you would try to attack me."

"That's where you're wrong," I said, dipping my chin just enough to increase the intensity of my expression. "If you hurt Vienna one more time, I'll happily slit your throat and dance on your grave. But Vienna does love you. And whether you admit it or not, you love her too. So it won't come to that, will it, Thad?"

His top lip curled. "I don't take kindly to threats, boy. Don't forget who I am. You won't succeed."

"So you're admitting you will hurt Vienna again? Because for a father, I can't imagine how you've allowed yourself to hurt her as much as you have since you came back."

Dae and Ratio's heads bounced back and forth, following the action. Annoying, if unavoidable. We had to get this out of the way first.

"Of course not. But some things can't be helped. If her feelings are hurt, that's a better option than David getting his hands on her."

I pointed at him. "That's exactly why I called you here. I'm going to take your answer as a promise not to do anything to risk Vienna either emotionally or physically. However, I think we can all agree, David Lennox is a thorn in everyone's side and he needs to die."

"That's very colorful language coming from an ex-FBI agent," Dae broke in. His soft, melodious voice sliding over my skin like broken glass. Yeah, I still didn't like him.

I shrugged. "The key word there is *ex*. But ask Thad or Ratio. They'll both tell you I've always followed my own path, politics and policies be damned."

Dae glanced between Thad and Ratio. Ratio stayed quiet, not willing to impart any information, but Thad gave one firm nod.

"Back to why you're here. I believe everyone in this room would never want to see harm come to Vienna." I glared at Thad. "With the recent information that's surfaced, we know he's a threat. Maybe not directly, but because she now knows what a piece of shit he is, I doubt he would hesitate to take her out." I paused, then added, "If only because she's the one way to hurt you. Right, Thad?"

He ground his jaw and his shoulders tensed. Vienna had so many of his physical features, most noticeably the tawny eyes, but they even showed their anger the same way.

"Consider this an open forum. You show me yours, I'll show you mine. We'll be able to end the threat much quicker if we're unified." I leaned back and waited for their response. They didn't seem like the kind of men who went for open session therapy, but with one common denominator, it was my best course of action.

The smell of bacon and sweet cheese alerted me to Rick's presence before he appeared in the doorway. All at once, the entire attention of the room focused on the empty space.

When Rick appeared, he grunted, completely straight-faced.

I had to love him. When he was with Vienna, he was an eager puppy lapping up her attention and melting at her feet. Without her, he gave off incredible psycho vibes. And yet, here he was, fierce and over muscled, carrying a medium-sized tray of dainty snacks and a pitcher of fresh homemade lemonade.

Thad was unimpressed as Rick arranged the food and drink on the coffee table. Dae and Ratio, however, couldn't hide their surprise.

"Is that... bacon-wrapped dates?" Ratio scooted to the edge of his cushion.

"And melted brie with some type of fruit preserve?" Dae sat forward and took a discreet sniff.

"Yes. I find that hard conversations are sometimes easier with good food and a full stomach." He shot me a ghost of a smile that would terrify most people. "I'll grab the glasses."

He opened the buffet set against the wall and pulled out several glasses and doilies.

I scrubbed a hand over my face. This was an intense conversation and he was breaking out doilies.

When Thad caught sight of those frilly white circles, he almost cracked a smile.

Well, well, well. Maybe he didn't hate us as much as we thought he did. Then he gave me his signature death glare.

As long as he was nice to Fletcher and Rick, I didn't give a rat's ass if he liked me. In fact, I'd rather have him fear me.

Rick squeezed my shoulder as he left the room. He didn't say the words, but he was excited I'd taken a page from his book. I'd have to tell Vienna later. Get a proper reward.

"I have to say," Ratio said through a stuffed mouth. "We'll have all of our meetings here from now on if this is the standard."

We laughed, and just like that, the tension in the room evaporated.

"Listen, I'm not trying to step on anyone's toes. But my

first priority will always be Vienna. To keep her safe, we need David to be a non-issue. We can even discuss who handles the job. But we have to know all the details or else, we're spinning our wheels and chasing our asses. Let's work together."

"David is mine."

I raised one brow. I'd love nothing more than to shove those words down Thad's throat with my fist, but I didn't act on it. "Fine, we can negotiate jobs. To get started, we need to go over all of David's aliases. We have our suspicions, but he's covered his tracks extremely well."

Ratio and Dae cleared half the tray in a few bites, happy to let Thad run this part of the conversation.

"And what aliases have you uncovered?" Curiosity curled around his words.

"For starters, we believe he's the consultant to my old unit. He worked under Gregory Lescheva. Can you confirm?" I cupped my knees and sat straighter. Thad would know this answer. It was written all over the storage wall. I just needed him to say what we already knew.

"Yes." Neither Ratio or Dae was surprised with his answer. "He has a list of constant aliases and an even longer list of one time use names. I have them all. Before he abducted me, I had spent five years compiling evidence against him."

That caused Dae to pause. "If you suspected him for that long, why not act on it sooner?" The corner of his wide mouth turned down.

"Because, son, he was my closest friend for years. I needed to be absolutely certain he deserved the punishment." Thad walked over and sat on the loveseat, reaching out to take one of the bacon-wrapped dates.

"And the crime?" Ratio canted his head. As much as he had shared with them, this wasn't information they'd heard.

Thad glanced between us, and a moment of guilt pressed on my shoulders. Vienna would have wanted to be here. The best I could do now was fill her in when she came home. And given the way both of their tempers frayed in each other's presence, there was no telling we would have had this outcome with her here.

"The short answer is David is a psychopath, and doesn't discriminate on crimes to get his way. His ambitions were to be king of his own dirty network. As far as he's concerned, he's achieved it."

He had. David had built out a vast network that flew under the radar for most of the cleaner members of the Network. Unfortunately for him, his reign was about to end.

"Now, tell me what you've learned, and the boys and I will fill you in. But remember, you made a promise. I will take care of David. Not Vienna."

I nodded. Thad was right. I made the promise, but Vienna hadn't. She had just as much of a right to get her pound of flesh after the way David manipulated her, and I had no intentions of taking that opportunity from her.

"I have the file," Rick sailed in with a familiar manila folder. He handed it to me, and left, taking the now empty tray with him.

"All right," I said, flipping open the folder. I was taking a gamble, sharing what we'd learned, but sometimes, the bigger risk was not taking one at all.

"Here's what we have…"

FLETCHER

THE CODE SCROLLING over the screen was more an abstract exercise than real work. I had a dozen different search protocols running, even more trace programs. Somehow, Cash's contacts had come through, as had the sit-down with *Daddy*.

We had brand new lists of identities, aliases, and accounts. The programs I had going were going to dig down through the complicated layers of a network overlaying another network, letting us dissect it for every single juicy morsel.

With Ratio's tracking as a jumping off point, I'd already located, rerouted, and then closed with a middle finger emoji a dozen different sources for pooled funds. A system of charities designed to launder the money before filtering it back through a dozen business shells—including two for laundromats and another for a dry cleaners that didn't exist anywhere beyond paper.

If I wanted to finesse the money, I could have set up a dozen different funnels to shave the funds off in a slow, damn near untraceable format. It would keep my head down and net us a good profit.

After meeting with my cousin, I had set up something similar to deal with another part of the Network. While I hadn't said anything directly to Adam, he'd handed us access to another piece of the puzzle. Drew asked me if I trusted that he had nothing to do with the rest of it and I did.

Reeds could be absolutely brutal in our ruthlessness. But Adam's only targets were other Reeds and those who went after his sisters and their friends. Those people weren't even worth the cost of a pine box if they got in his sights.

Still… I swung my attention away from the searches to where I was currently draining the near two hundred and seventy-nine million, eight hundred, forty-one thousand, six hundred and sixty-nine dollars from the Red Death slush fund in the Caymans and poured it into different abused women's shelters and teen crisis centers up and down the east coast.

We didn't need this money, not with the over five hundred million I'd already siphoned off for a rainy day, and the various caches of tens of millions I'd invested for Drew. She would be quite wealthy, and the Red Death network really fucking broke, before I was done.

It was also happening rapidly. If someone stared at their accounts, they'd notice the drain. Then they would try to stop me. I spun in my seat once with a little laugh. I really wanted them to try and stop me.

With all the electronic traps I'd set, I was ready for Uncle David and his crew of bad boys to come after the money. This minefield was my playground. I'd invade their equipment with worms and tracers until I could shut them down with a touch of a button.

Kind of like a special bonus in my…

Sitting up abruptly, I jerked my attention from where I was decoding and tracing details and tabbed through a series of screens to bring up the latest update to the game I'd been working on.

Now that I was intimately aware of Drew's type—where her targets were concerned—and a list of contacts for her shifty-shit of an uncle, I could actually push an update out to my game that would work like a sniffer on their personal data.

There were lines in the terms and conditions that granted me—the programmer—with easy access to all the private data on the phone. I would, of course, never sell this data. It was primarily to improve the game's functionality and maybe... just maybe, to get the dirt on allies and enemies alike.

It never hurt to invest in insurance and a bail-out package. Okay, no maybe about it. It was how I'd gotten into Dion's systems and earned his attention in the first place. But I could sniff for more than just porn or bank account numbers or trace emails back to human traffickers.

Between the collective knowledge on the Network and the Red Death network including the Venn garden where they crossed, I could actually track down David in a way he'd never see coming.

Excitement threaded through me. Pushing back from the desk, I started to go find Drew but she wasn't here. She and Rick had gone to check on Mart. The live-wire had been... quiet enough that Drew had grown concerned. With *Daddy* now seeming to work with us instead of against us, she'd absented herself from the interactions to avoid starting a fight with Daddy.

Neither Cash nor I looked on this favorably. Mostly because Drew didn't run away from anything, so she was making a calculated decision to keep her father engaged by disengaging. And I didn't like that it left its own wounds on her.

I'd explain it to Cash and get his thoughts. I paused though when another alarm on my desk setup went off. Tabbing over, I watched Daddy pull into the garage at his house. But rather than close the door and disappear inside, he left the car and started toward *our* house.

Shit.

Run to get Cash or get Daddy on board first. Frankly, he'd be the hardest sell. Right, get his thoughts first. Then I could pop the air out of any of his objections. Energy drink in hand, I headed straight for the front door.

The rain the last few days had left a definite bite in the air, but it felt good after the stuffiness of my office. As soon as I was outside, I paused when I found Dae, Ratio, Cash *and* Daddy basically standing in a loose circle facing each other in the driveway.

"Oh," I said, frowning as they all swung their gazes to me. "This looks flat out uncomfortable, but put a pin in whatever dick measuring contest we're playing. Side note, Rick would win, but that's not what 's important right now."

My stomach lurched as cold sweat dotted my back and forehead. Yeah, if I were honest, the sweat wasn't that cold and it was more drenching me than anything else. But I locked my gaze on the eyes that were so like Drew's and so absolutely foreign at the same time.

"I have an idea," I said, spitting out the syllables before anyone—Daddy—could interrupt. It was bad enough he was staring at me. "I'm running the numbers and the accounts. I've already begun draining their largest accounts. Not doing it stealthily either. Within a day, if they have any kind of monitoring, they are gonna know their money is gone."

Pride flash-fired through me. I got all of that out without stuttering. Swallowing, I fought to get moisture back in my mouth.

"That's the stick," I said. "They are going to be pissed when they figure it out and unless they have someone better than me—and Drew killed the only guy I know who might have been *slightly* better than me when he wasn't stoned out of his mind—then they aren't going to be able to claw it back."

Which was part of the beauty of my plan.

"While they are chasing their tails trying to get their

money back, psychopaths are probably more likely to turn on each other. I mean, clearly they are going to blame each other, who else knows where their money is?"

Ratio actually looked thoughtful as he took his glasses off. He cleaned them slowly as he considered me then glanced at Dae. The Asian man was far too damn good looking, it was annoying. Right. Not focusing on him, because that would be distracting.

Daddy raised his brows.

"Right," I said. "The plan then is to strike while their attention is elsewhere but via a method they would never consider. Granted, I don't know how likely it is that all of them have downloaded my game, but statistics are on my side. If only one of his super secret death Nazi network has the game, that's *all* I need to get into their equipment."

Now I had all of their attention.

"The game?" Cash prompted me and I spared him a look. Good, I could take a deeper breath and get more oxygen. Fundamental for thinking. Knocking back the last of the energy drink, I pulled it together.

"The game," I said with a nod before explaining to them the game I'd created and what I could do with it thanks to the terms and conditions.

"Really?" Dae said, opening his phone and pulling up the app store. After he typed in the name of the game, he went through the steps and then began to review the terms and conditions.

"I'll be damned," Ratio muttered as he leaned over to read his screen. The two managed to make "not touching" a thing even though they were that close. It was like putting two magnets together—they were repelling even as they leaned in. "How is that legal?"

"You can't be forced to agree to them, but ninety-nine point nine percent of all consumers never read the fine print."

"So he installs it and you have access to his phone?"

Daddy questioned, his fierce expression easing. Not that the chills running up my spine were happy with him talking to me.

"Yes." Then because they hadn't truly been introduced to the wonder that was me, I added, "Shall I show you?"

Cash's expression didn't change, but Dae and Ratio glanced at each other. The silent conversation they shared was deeply hostile but it ended the moment Daddy said, "Do it. Download it, Dae."

"Yes, sir."

I didn't get any closer. I just pulled out my phone and opened up a couple of browser windows and then FTP'd over to my server. I could track installs, and did, I just zeroed in on our location once Dae had it downloaded.

"There's no way to proceed without agreeing to all of this." Consternation filtered through Dae's tone.

"No one reads the fine print," Ratio murmured.

"I do," Dae stated firmly but he was tapping away. The air shifted next to me and suddenly Daddy was at my side. Not what I expected and my pulse leapt to a mad rate.

All the spit in my mouth dried up. The minute Dae finished the install, his phone appeared on my FTP screen, along with the basic data from GPS location at the time of install.

With a couple of taps, I sent out the update. He gave a little curse.

"It crashed," Dae said. "But I have it open again."

Of course, it did. The crash forced the update and then I had access to his contacts—there were only three—, his social media accounts, of which there was only one on that phone, and his email.

Punisher5by5.

Punisher.

"Shit, you're the Punisher?" I'd seen that reference in

Dion's files. The shock that rippled over their faces was almost worth the fresh jolt of real fear.

"That's a terrifying amount of access," Dae said in a frosty tone. "You would be well reminded to stay out of my files."

"Go deeper," Daddy instructed me. "How much can you mine just from that particular burner."

"Everything," I said without an ounce of conceit. "And because he has the same email on another phone..." I tracked it and pinned it on the screen. "Not as easy to crack into it, but one email with a tiny worm and I'll be in."

"This will help us track and trap David," Daddy said slowly. "Even if *he* doesn't download it."

"That's the idea," I said, pivoting so I could face him. "I have his aliases, we have the shadow network they were building mapped out. All I have to do is start working my way through the web. Statistics say at least one of them already has it and even if they don't, I can send out some random junk mail, targeting them and use a few key phrases to get them to install."

I blew out another breath as I lifted my gaze to meet Drew's father's.

"Here's the thing, Daddy, this is a way to cast a huge net in the ocean of data. They won't be protecting against it, because really, who would hunt anyone via a game app?" I was rather proud of this. "It gives you David and you can end that piece of shit before he gets anywhere near Drew again and we can dismantle the rest of the Red Death network. Win. Win."

Exhaling, I tried to concentrate on slowing down my insane heart rate. Contrary to what it thought, I had not just run a damn marathon.

The silence expanded for so long as Daddy met my gaze and seemed to peer right into my soul. Gradually, it also registered that I'd called him Daddy.

Today was as good as any other day to die, I suppose. But maybe he'd wait until after my plan worked.

"I like it," Daddy said after that pause, then gripped my shoulder and I didn't have to worry about my racing heart. It just stopped altogether. "Do it. Dae—stay with him. Keep him safe. If they do manage to track it back here, I want them feeling the bite and not us."

Wait.

What?

Daddy glanced at Cash. "We should talk."

"We should."

Then Daddy was walking away and I debated whether I was going to throw up or not.

"You did good kid," Cash told me, gripping my shoulder where Daddy had.

"Yeah?" I questioned then summoned up a smile. "I think I need to throw up."

"At least you waited until after," he told me with a grin then he glanced at Dae and Ratio "Not a hair on his head."

"I'll take care of him," Dae promised. That oath added to the significant dread coiling in me. But instead of looking annoyed or put out, the Asian gave me a long, assessing glance before he nodded. "You're a valuable asset, Mr. Reed. I see why Vienna treasures you so."

She did treasure me.

Oh, fuck if this worked—that blowjob would be epic.

"What do you think of the Digital Defenders?"

"Is that some anime show?" Dae asked and I sighed.

No, it wasn't. "Right, work first. Names later."

Despite the trembling in my hands and the sweat soaking my shirt, I was feeling pretty damn badass. After all, I'd called the Judge *Daddy* and survived.

RICK

IT WAS TIME.

"Hell yeah, mother fuckers!" Fletcher hooted from the office. He'd spent the last hour racing around his office like Quicksilver.

The edges of my mouth twitched. He would be proud if he knew I was making a movie reference about him.

"Who's dying?" Ratio slid up next to me as I carried a coffee carafe toward the office.

"No one, yet," I shrugged. It wasn't what he asked, but people would die soon. Fletcher was uncovering too much about the Red Death Network. The air was buzzing with tension. The more that was revealed, the less time it would be before we took some kind of action.

Before, we had discussed taking out the Network now, or waiting and watching, biding our time.

With every new piece of information, I was certain we wouldn't watch. There would be no letting these men and women get away with another crime.

"Don't you think more caffeine is a bad call right now?" Ratio mused as he clasped his hands behind his back and tilted his head toward the carafe.

I looked at him, until he shrugged. He didn't need to know this was decaf.

"Got you this time, you weaselly little toe biter!" Fletcher pounded over his keyboard like Beethoven during an intense encore. "Fuck you in the ass, worm!"

I couldn't believe he was treating his keyboard that way. Although, it was probably a once in a lifetime event to crack this big of a network. He was lost to the endorphins.

"Does he always act like this?" Dae cast a concerned look over Fletcher's erratic behavior. Our new friend was the epitome of unbothered, standing regally in the corner with his hands loose by his sides. If he hadn't said anything, he could have been mistaken for a statue.

"No," I said as I poured the steaming coffee into Fletcher's empty cup.

"Thanks, Big Guy," Fletcher said absently. "I know I can always count on you."

I dipped my head and moved to the chair in the corner. Later, I'd have to dust and disinfect the room. Everyone had been coming and going all day, and there were new smudges of oil left on the doors and desk top. The room was also getting muggy from all the hot air crammed into the small space.

"How long do you think this will take?" I didn't actually take a seat like I'd originally intended. There were crumbs just outside the door. If I left them there, they'd bother me.

"Maybe a day. We should have everything sorted tomorrow." He tucked his hair behind his ear before stepping back to watch the different screens. Dae crossed his arms, the slight rustling of his shirt as loud as an oncoming train.

Fletcher didn't acknowledge him at all.

"When was the last time you ate?" I paused at the door to look over my shoulder.

"You know there's no time for self-care when we're taking over the world!" His head rocked back as he laughed gleefully.

"Maybe you need to give him some bread to soak up the caffeine," Ratio said quietly from the door.

"You!" Fletcher twisted his torso to point at Ratio. "If you talk about me in the third person, I won't be responsible for what Rick does. Not me, I'm not the fighter. But if I'm offended, you need to watch out for Rick." He pressed his lips together. "Maybe Cash too."

I shook my head and ushered Ratio out the door.

He never said what he came this way for. Maybe just to check in on Dae, but he left the house while I headed to the cleaning closet.

That night, I served a light dinner. It wasn't a sit down affair, but a rotating door until the house settled down around nine. Vienna seemed shocked that Thackery had stopped in for a plate and left. But after the other day, I knew he wouldn't skip out on family meals in the future. It would just be baby steps before he actually sat down at the table instead of grabbing a plate and running.

Cash slept in his old room for a couple hours, while Vienna and I took turns sleeping and sitting with Fletcher. Needless to say, by the next day, we had more than enough information on the Red Death than we ever imagined. In Fletcher's words, they were stupid to house so much of their data on one set of servers.

Although, I think sometimes Fletcher didn't realize how talented he was. They could have had ten servers, twenty servers, and Fletcher would have still cracked it.

"Big Guy, we're having a family meeting." Fletcher ran into the kitchen, grabbed a handful of grapes I'd set out on a morning snack board, then ran back out.

I met Vienna in the hallway, and she smiled up at me. "Are you okay?"

"Yes." I dropped a kiss to her temple and massaged her shoulders with one hand as we headed toward the study. It was just before lunch, and everyone we'd managed to kick out of the house yesterday was back.

Inside the office, Fletcher sat at his desk as Cash stood at his back. Ratio and Dae were silent sentinels on the wall. The odd one here was Thackery. He stood behind Fletcher's other shoulder, almost competing with Cash for the space.

When Cash glanced up and saw everyone was here, he straightened.

"Fletcher was able to amass an insurmountable amount of evidence and information on the Red Death network. He's moved their money, rerouted their communications through his system so any jobs they are asking for come through us. They will never know it's not the intended party responding. And more than that, he's pinned down their locations."

Cash was in full leader mode, giving the brief of everything Fletcher had accomplished. I thought Thackery would chime in, or try to take over, but he didn't. He stepped back, and leaned his ass against the desk.

"There are two locations with a high concentration of Red Death members. From what we've gleaned, they're high on the hierarchy. We should hit those places tonight." Cash let his gaze touch on Vienna, waiting for her approval.

She pulled in a soft breath and nodded.

"I suggest two teams—" He started to turn toward Thackery, but Thackery beat him to it by holding up a hand.

"I have a different job to take care of. You six run it without me, but I want to know what happens when you're back."

I held my breath, waiting for an argument to break out. It didn't happen. We were making so much progress, it seemed that no one wanted to jeopardize the fragile trust we'd built.

That was how I ended up in the driver's seat of team one. Dae was in the passenger seat and Cash in the back. Neither were great conversationalists. It wasn't until we pulled up outside the swanky hotel that Dae spoke up.

"To confirm, basement level three is Red Death only, and the elevator code to get there is 5469. We can agree that no one leaves?" Dae pulled his silver white hair back into a low ponytail and clipped it with a plain barrette.

"Agreed. My thought is we'll—" Cash started but was interrupted by Dae as he checked his weapons inside his suit.

"Sorry, I don't work in a team. I'll go in first, and head to the back. Someone else cover the door. We'll meet after the job is done."

Cash chuckled. "Works for me. Rick, you want the door?"

"Yes, I won't let anyone past me." I turned off the car and unsnapped my seatbelt. I'd parked us down the street instead of in the parking garage. Too many cameras and opportunities to get locked in.

"Great. Let's roll," Cash said through a grin.

We silently climbed out of the car, and Cash pulled out suit jackets that were hanging up in the backseat. Once we were put together, Cash and I each grabbed a leather tote bag, and started the short walk to the hotel.

The street was fairly empty, but there were a few people here and there. I took out my phone and texted Fletcher, letting him know we were about to go in.

He sent back a thumbs up. Perfect. They were ready too.

At the hotel, we went to the service entrance. I led the way, just in case the cameras weren't on loop. Dae was too recognizable and Cash was still considered missing.

Just as Fletcher had prepped us, we found the back hallway with no issues, and jumped on the elevator. The buttons were like any other elevator, numbering the floors up to twenty-five. There wasn't even a button for basement level three. But when Dae entered the code, it beeped three times, then descended with a light jolt.

The doors slid open, revealing a purple lit murky hallway, with intricately carved wooden doors at the end. R was carved in one door, and D in the other. Not very subtle of them.

As we approached, Dae snapped the elastic bands of his

gloves in place as he pulled a carefully packed bag out of his pocket. I stopped to watch what he was doing, and then jolted forward when I was left behind.

"What is that?" I asked, nodding to the brass knuckles he now held.

"Ricin coated knuckles." He held his hand up for just a second, long enough for me to catch a glimpse of the needle thin spikes sticking up. Then he dropped his hand and pushed the door open.

Smoke wafted out, and the low base of some type of exotic music. Tinkling laughter from women and harsh chuckles from men tumbled out as Dae slipped through. I caught it, and stepped inside just in time to see him punch the doorman twice in the face. Blood spewed from his nose. Dae was quick enough, or skilled enough, to avoid the splatter.

Then he was gone.

The doorman collapsed on the ground, and Cash nudged him with his foot. When he didn't move, Cash kicked the bastard in the stomach.

I shut the door and pressed my back against it.

No one out.

We'd all reviewed the files for the members invited to this cell. They were all monsters. I didn't feel one bit of guilt about what we were about to do. We were making the world a safer place. We were bringing justice to those who avoided it. And we were cutting off their easy access to continue their work.

"Should we take care of him?" I touched the gun in the shoulder holster under my jacket, then the short knife tucked in my waist.

"Nope. Ricin is incredibly toxic. This man won't die right away, but soon he'll have a fever so strong, he'll be incapacitated. He'll probably die in a couple days depending on how much poison got in his system."

"That's…brutal." But expected from the Punisher. Fletcher had filled me in after he left that first day. He didn't take jobs, but he doled out punishments. Appropriate punishments that matched the crimes.

"Fitting." Then Cash dropped his bag by the wall and was gone too.

Arranging mine next to his, I made sure they were both far enough to avoid any mess.

I pulled the man's body in front of the doors. If someone did get past me, I'd have extra time as they tried to get the door open.

Wherever Cash and Dae had gone, no one was aware of their presence yet. The music changed to a slower, more enthralling beat. From what we could gather, this location was a poker lounge and dance club. The only people who were allowed to work it were members of Red Death. No opportunities for their secrets to leak.

Another five minutes passed, then the screaming started.

Both men and women were fighting for their lives.

Then they started to come.

I tensed. Did I go for my knife? My gun? Nothing at all?

In the end, I settled on the knife.

A man stumbled through the hall, his face a mask of horror as he watched whatever scene played behind him. He was within feet of me when he turned around.

"Oh shit!" He started to backpedal, but I made a last minute decision to stow the knife, and I reached for his head, giving a stiff jerk to the side. He didn't make a sound as he tumbled to the ground.

A small group of three came running next. Two men and one woman. Unlike the first man, they noticed me immediately. And I recognized them.

We had files on each one. I'd been helping Vienna keep tabs on them for months.

The one on the left was slightly heavy and balding. Troy Rutger, leader of an underground fighting ring, and a high valued customer of trafficking to source his fighters. Mostly young men from third world countries.

In the middle was Darren Jones. Short, stocky, with a permanent eye injury that left his eye constantly watering and unable to close. He was the son of a man Thackery took care of over a decade ago. We'd suspected he had taken up his father's work but he was too good at covering his tracks.

Until Fletcher brought their network down, revealing all their files.

And the slender pinched faced woman, Denise Stodger. Trophy wife in public, cannibal in private. She started up a cult for wealthy influencers who ate the bodies of the less fortunate to show their superiority. Another strong client of the trafficking industry.

"Move," Denise demanded as she stomped her foot.

Darren and Troy stopped on either side of her back, placing her in the middle, and conveniently for them, in the front.

Instead of answering, I smiled. They weren't leaving through here, and they wouldn't get out the back past Dae and Cash. I waited to see what they would do.

They must have realized their options were more than limited, because Denise screamed, and raced toward me on teetering heels. I caught her upraised hand, spun her around so her back was to my chest and her body was trapped by her own arm. Then I pulled the knife out, and slit her throat.

Warm blood spilled over my hand as she gurgled, gripping at her throat. I gently lowered her to the floor, keeping my gaze on the two men. One of them—Troy—dashed back down the hallway.

But Darren gritted his teeth, sneered, and charged. His moves were sloppy as he punched at me. Only one of the blows landed and glazed off my shoulder. He yowled and gripped his hand. No one had taught him how to punch properly and how to tuck his thumb.

Shaking it out, Darren charged again, and this time I punched him in the throat. Satisfaction filled through me as he gasped. I didn't give him time to recover and stabbed the short knife right through his rib cage the way Vienna had taught me.

He crumpled too.

When I glanced up, a few more people came running through the door, then a few more, and a few more. Every time I dispatched someone, I moved farther into the hall and away from the growing pile of bodies. Eventually I pulled out my gun, aiming for head or heart.

The set up here was like a maze, making it too easy for three men to take out the entire cell. But I wasn't complaining.

I glanced down at the mess as soon as the last person was down. Blood pooled under the targets, staining the glossy floor. Sweat dripped down my temples. I hated stains. Good thing we'd brought my tote bag with fresh changes of clothing as well as my favorite cleaning supplies.

"I didn't realize so many had gotten by me," Cash panted as he walked through the door at the end of the hall-way. He took off his jacket and used his sleeve to wipe his face.

"That's going to stain." I furrowed my brow at the blood and grime now streaking his sleeve.

"It's fine. We'll burn these clothes and get new ones. You're not looking so hot yourself."

I glanced down and huffed. I had more than a little blood decorating my suit. "We'll burn them," I agreed.

Dae strolled back into the room without a mark on him or a hair out place. I wasn't sure what to make of him. He was too even, not enough personality or expressions for me to get a read on him. And now, I was a little jealous.

"Quite the mess you made there," he observed in his quiet voice.

I didn't like that he rubbed it in. "We need to start on the body removal." I stripped my suit jacket and dropped it on the floor next to our tote.

"Most of my kills aren't actually dead yet. They deserved to suffer...I'll stack them in the back, and Ratio can take care of them." He dipped his chin and then disappeared again.

"I'll check in with Fletcher while you start here." Cash backed away like he was being sneaky to avoid the cleanup. That was fine.

I didn't enjoy the killing...most of the time. But it never bothered me to get rid of those the law couldn't, or wouldn't take care of. That was what we did here. The cleanup was just a natural part of the process. I unbuttoned my cuffs, rolled my sleeves up, and started rearranging the room. The handheld vacuum would come out next.

FLETCHER

THE TIMER on my watch alerted me via a mild vibration. Not a sound. Since we'd gotten into the car, I'd parked it in the back, laptop open and working as fast as I could on the various technical aspects of our evening.

We were team two. Drew drove, with Ratio riding shotgun. My position put me behind Drew so I could protect her back and if necessary, I could whale the accountant with my computer if necessary.

Not that I thought I needed to protect Drew from *physical* harm. The only physical intentions from the blue-eyed fox had seemed more—well, friendlier than I'd like them to be. But he didn't put any moves on her *and* he wasn't an icy dick like Dae.

The man was downright chilly and I hadn't expected him to follow right to the fucking bathroom door when Daddy put him in charge of looking after me. It had taken Drew to get him out of the house and the next morning—he'd been right outside.

"We're on schedule," Ratio said over his shoulder as he glanced at me.

"I know." Then I blinked. "Did I look worried or something?" It was kind of dark in the car, we were hitting just after three in the morning when our targets would be partied out.

Rick had actually made me a Red Bull Recharger before he left with the others and I was practically vibrating. It had tasted obnoxiously good. It worked though and that was all that mattered.

"You look like you were calculating how hard you'd have to hit me to render me unconscious." The light comment seemed almost teasing except… "If you really want to be in a better position, you should be directly behind me," he continued. "From this angle, I can catch most of your movements in my periphery which would give me a chance to respond with a—"

A faint click of sound registered and Ratio turned a rather wide, and very warm, smile on Drew. My sexy death angel would always protect me, and it took a lot not to smirk.

"Hypothetical situations only," Ratio promised. "I wouldn't truthfully harm him…"

"Really?"

"Well, I might incapacitate if he truly tried to knock me out, but since he belongs to you, I would endeavor to *not* hurt him."

"Suck up," I commented and Ratio laughed.

"Well, our lovely Vienna has a knife pressed against my dick. Honesty and sincerity seem prudent."

I grinned again. Ratio was alright. "I'm good, Drew," I promised. "Just going over the last minute security items. All the cameras in all locations will begin their loops in about sixty seconds. It's gonna be another thirty minutes before we're in, so we'll know if anyone's noticed before them."

"And team one?" she asked as she shifted her arm as though putting away her knife and Ratio smoothed down his shirt.

"They're moving right on time. They'll be hitting their location in fifteen minutes." Rick and Cash were on team one

—with my icy guardian. Maybe they'd leave him behind. Daddy wasn't with any of us.

He had his own job tonight. Speaking of which, I changed screens and pulled up his location. He'd agreed to the tracking software so we could leave a little breadcrumb trail for Uncle David. Okay, he'd agreed *after* I asked him to let me track him. The fact I had access to his phone meant I could run a program using the Bluetooth to look for connections around him and... The phone was currently downloading the contact data from all the phones in range of him.

Daddy said there were places he preferred Drew didn't go, and he would take care of visiting them to track down the stragglers of the Red Death network.

Tonight, we were hitting the two largest cells for the RD Network. There were more around the world but Dae and Ratio both said they could clean up the underlings, it was better to cut off the heads.

David kept most of the power, but there was a hierarchy. Where there was power, there were greedy, questionable people. While the bad uncle might want to be the sole ruler over his domain and to control everything, not everyone was as controlled as him.

Even psychopaths had blind spots.

Apparently.

"We're nearly there," Drew commented. "Finish up and then shut that down. I don't wanna light up our approach."

"Yes, ma'am." I murmured. "Have I mentioned how hot you are when you give orders?"

Her soft chuckle was all the answer I needed. Ratio said nothing at all, but no judgment seemed to roll off him. Good. Cause I was allowed to flirt with Drew whenever I wanted.

She'd said so.

With her words in mind, I finished the last electronic sweep, then shut it down so the screen was dark and put the laptop away. Like Drew and Ratio, I was dressed in all black.

When Ratio pulled a dark mask over his face, hiding everything but his eyes, I did the same.

A moment later, Drew dragged on her own while Ratio drove one-handed from the passenger seat. It was a remarkable show of trust, but then, Ratio had been earning points with Drew for a while now.

All the lights in the car went off, as well as the headlights. The car slowed to a crawl and made no sound at all. Now I understood why we'd taken these. Hybrids. Under twenty miles an hour there was no need for the gas-fueled engine, so the car went silent.

Nice.

Adrenaline spiked as we pulled off the smooth road onto a gravel-lined one. Why did the bad guys have to live in such a rural area? Couldn't they have done this somewhere closer to civilization? The bouncy road, even as slow as we were going, was damned uncomfortable.

First world problems, I scoffed at myself. The fact I managed to filter myself should earn me a cookie. I went to open my mouth and say so when I remembered we were running silent.

Miming zipping my lips, I pretended to toss away the key. No idea why, I had no real audience and even if they did see me, it was so damn dark in here, I could barely make out my hand.

No moon tonight. Dae and Drew had both been pleased by that fact. Then Cash laughed. I mean it made sense, and I appreciated the logic, but those three were way happier about it.

That did make me question whether it was just pride in their work or pleasure when their work was made easier that delighted them more. The minute that thought took root, I had to shake my head. I could almost picture the patient look Rick would give me before he slapped tape over my mouth.

But I wasn't talking. At least not out loud. The only person who could hear this merry-go-round in my head was me. So, this was me being good.

Could you really irritate yourself?

The answer to that was yes, apparently.

We stopped the car just off the road behind a couple of large cypress trees. I slid out of the car almost as quietly as they did, but Drew caught my hand and we didn't "close" the doors fully. They wouldn't be latched.

It made for a speedier escape if we had to escape. The plan didn't call for it. The plan called for scorched earth. The two establishments we were hitting tonight were centers of information and finance for the Red Death network. The beast wouldn't be dead, but it would be blinded. Then we would begin the cleanup of all the tendrils that would try to go to ground.

And by try, I meant Cash was already looking forward to that hunt with more glee than he looked at anything. Well, except Drew.

Drew put me between her and Ratio. I had a hand on his shoulder, she had a hand on mine. It sounded way cozier than it was. The walk to the building at the end of the drive didn't take as long as it felt. It was a lot larger in person than it had been in the satellite pictures I'd found.

"It's huge," I murmured.

"It would have to be," Ratio stated in a low voice as he continued to move like he could see in the dark. Maybe he could. A Clark Kent based on his look, but I really hated to think of him as Superman.

Right. So more… Batman than Superman.

That did not help my case. Drew would probably enjoy a dark detective with brutal tendencies.

I almost tripped at the thought. Nope. Ratio couldn't be the big bat dude. We already had one of those.

Guess that made him the sidekick.

There might be something there…

"Pincushion," Drew's breath whispered against my earlobe as gently as her voice. Goosebumps prickled my flesh and blood pounded right toward my cock.

Death didn't usually make me horny, but my sexy death angel just needed to glance at me and I was harder than these thick bodied trees around us.

"I need you to not throw up in there," she continued in a voice that couldn't have been more than the barest of whispers. "I need you to trust me and close your eyes if you have to and stick to me like we're bound together."

Oh, that was a firm squeeze on my cock.

"I'll do my best," I managed, swallowing the drool. "I've been practicing and Daddy told me to use the menthol rub."

Her teeth scraped my ear and my thoughts spasmed briefly. "Good boy, Pincushion. Hold it together and I promise you, there will be a reward."

The urge to whoop and smirk was real, but I handled it like a mature man. I gripped my cock to shift it a little and did a little mental fist pump. Daddy said the menthol rub would help with the smell. Cash told me not to look directly at anything, that would also help.

I'd been mentally practicing.

I could do this.

With a kiss to the spot behind my ear, she slid around me. We were right to the edge of the trees. The building loomed before us and there were lights on it, motion-sensor lights that kicked on to track the security team strolling along, having a smoke and chatting.

"Pathetic," Ratio murmured.

"Good help is hard to find," Drew said with a hint of laughter.

I barely caught the movement of Ratio's arm but he fired twice. The suppressor reduced the sound, but it still made me jump. One bullet for each of the patrol. They went down without a word. I dug the little jar of vapor rub out and put a swath right under my nose before capping it and shoving it in my pocket.

Holy crap, that stuff was strong, but I could breathe, and I couldn't smell *anything*. Not even Drew's sweet, earthiness. My dick wanted to protest, and truth be told, so did I, but I could smell Drew anytime. She needed me to not puke now.

I fell in just one step behind her as they both moved. What impressed me over the next fifteen minutes wasn't just how hot Drew was as she moved like a slash of darkness with a subtle sway to her rounded hips. No, it was how lethal my sexy death angel was as she delivered sentences to every single person we found inside. Damn, was she ever.

No, what impressed me was that Daddy had been right. Without the smell, this was so much easier. Although I did not want to look at anyone who had their face blown off. My stomach barely trembled.

But following the plan, I stayed with Drew and I had my own gun. Granted it was a stun gun, she didn't want me to have to use it but I refused to be useless at her side. What was a few thousand volts when it meant keeping her safe?

Ratio headed upstairs while Drew angled down. She wanted the down because that was where the computers were. As it turned out, it was also where the cells were.

The vapor rub almost didn't help when I had to pull the guard off the keyboard he'd fallen on, but Drew just yanked that keyboard and brought me another.

Yes, that helped.

Mouth breathing hard enough to practically taste the rub, I plugged my thumb drive crackers into each of the servers. There were seven.

Nice system.

After popping my knuckles, I pulled up a chair.

"The door locks," Drew whispered against my ear. We didn't have to be quiet.

"Fuck," I exhaled. "I appreciate the offer, but I still need to finish my part."

The corner of her mouth quirked upward.

"You didn't mean my reward right now."

She gave the very gentlest of headshakes before pressing a kiss to the top of my head.

"Right, I'll lock the door and use the cameras to guide you two. Be careful, Drew." The last came out an order and that smile of hers deepened. Then she was gone, waiting right outside the door until I locked it.

When she turned those tawny eyes up toward the camera, I swore I could see their sparkle, despite the low-res and grainy quality of the black and white video. Then she winked and was off. I slid back into the chair and went back to taking down their main servers.

This definitely needed to be an inside job, but I took the time to encrypt and pack up a full set of disc images for all of the drives. Spreading the packets out to a dozen different cloud accounts, where I had a program that could retrieve and put them back together.

In between each keyboard stroke, I flicked my gaze to the cameras. Drew cleared the basement. Most of the occupants were not members of the Red Death network, but prisoners.

In some cases, they were prisoners from powerful families. I recognized more than a few. Upstairs, Ratio methodically went through each room, eliminating targets until he got to the underboss.

"I have him," Ratio said simply over our communication line. "Ladies first?"

"I'll be right up," Drew answered in a purely professional tone. "Pincushion? Anyone else in the building?"

"Haven't found anyone yet and I'm searching for secret or hidden rooms. Have Ratio bring your guest downstairs so you're closer to where we can seal off if necessary." Their dungeon actually had a steel trap we could close.

Nice bonus feature.

"Of course," Ratio said. "It will only take a moment and he will be bruised on arrival."

I didn't have to see Drew to know she just shrugged, but I grinned. "Kick him at least once for me."

A couple of clicks and I found Ratio and his prisoner. The very sharp, and swift kick, he delivered to the downed man's ribs made me grin.

This man deserved a *lot* of pain, but Drew also deserved answers. Speaking of which…

VIENNA

THREE DAYS of cleaning house and we'd disassembled more than half of Red Death's network. I studied the last man I'd interrogated. We had the last of anything useful and his biometrics unlocked what Fletcher needed done, so Ratio wrapped plastic over the guy's face and smothered him.

Despite the man's exhaustion, he fought and bucked as soon as the plastic began to cling to his face. Death by suffocation was not pleasant. Not that this man, the most recent on our list, deserved anything better. If only it weren't so quick.

Ratio's knuckles whitened as he maintained control. I didn't interfere. It would be an insult to insinuate he couldn't handle the target. Particularly when the man's broken fingers weren't going to catch on anything.

"I've been thinking about that dinner invitation," Ratio said, tugging my attention to him. "Rick's a marvelous cook."

"He really is," I said. "Once we've gotten everything settled, we can discuss dinner. But you and Cash need to make nice."

With an exaggerated grimace, Ratio sighed. "If you insist, though I maintain he won't forgive me until I apologize, and I have no intentions of apologizing."

Shrugging one shoulder, I said, "That is between the two of you. But I won't have any of them discomforted. I will say, Rick's cooking is even more exceptional than you realize."

"You drive a truly hard bargain." He paused a beat to flex

and tighten his grip as the man finally began to succumb. "Stubborn one."

"Survival instincts surprise us all sometimes." A phone vibrated in my pocket.

"It's Daddy," Fletcher told me. "He asked for a direct line to you." The "I hope it was okay" lingered in his voice.

"It's fine, we're done here. Wrap up in there and we'll come get you." We'd left him in another control room. This was a distribution center and a trucking company, apparently. It also answered some questions about targeted hits on other transportation companies in the Network.

Once we liquidated this place, I'd have Ratio send restitution to those companies. They'd only kept a small crew here, but we'd gotten some very useful information and access.

Also, backup servers that were transported by truck with a roving signal. Fletcher had a little orgasm when we'd opened that up. His excitement had me claiming that set-up for ourselves. Maybe we could create a traveling household for when we needed it.

Food for thought.

Phone to my ear, I braced myself for Daddy's voice. The past few days had been an organized dream come true, but it hadn't been organized with me. Daddy had worked with Cash. As much as that stung, I also appreciated his taking real interest in the guys and showing them real respect.

Fletcher had definitely impressed him.

"Sweet girl," Daddy said in a low voice. "Your men came up with an excellent plan."

Daddy did not give faint praise, so I just smiled. "Yes, they did. They are very good at what they do."

He made a noncommittal sound. "We have David's location."

Everything in me stilled.

"Dae found a singer. He gave us three addresses. I knew of two, the third was unknown..."

"Did you give it to Fletcher?"

"He did," Fletcher said softly, and he was speaking just to me, not to Daddy or to Ratio. "It's a solid lead."

"Yes. He confirmed." There was a bite of silence, like Daddy forced himself to take a beat. "I won't take Dae or Ratio and you cannot bring them…"

But…? I waited.

"But I want you to come with me. We will take David together. You do not get to interfere, I want him… but you've been right from the beginning. This has been your fight and you deserve to be there."

My heart fisted in my chest as I took a moment to savor the words. "When?"

"As soon as you're done. I can pick you up." This was an olive branch.

What did it mean? After everything he'd said and done since we'd found him, I was hesitant to hope for a better outcome than constant indifference from him. It had gotten so hard for me, that I had started to hate when he referred to me as Sweet Girl.

It had lost its warmth and affection.

But just now, there might have been a small amount of warmth accompanying the name.

"Okay," I agreed. My palms were starting to sweat but I ignored the desire to wipe them on my pants. Daddy's teachings were too ingrained.

"I can finish up here and take Fletcher back to the house." The man in Ratio's arms had stopped struggling, the plastic no longer sticking so far inside his mouth.

Glancing at Fletcher, I hesitated. Cash could handle himself. Rick too. But Fletcher? He was the most vulnerable with the Network.

"It's fine, Drew." He still kept his voice low, maybe to drive his point home or hide from Daddy. "I've gotten to know Ratio a little by now. He's not going to hurt me. He knows you and the rest of our family would rain hell down on him so hard, he'd never recover." At that, he cast a sidelong glance at Ratio in warning.

The corner of Ratio's mouth tipped up. "I am properly intimidated. You're safe with me, hacker."

"Man, I need a code name. You have the Accountant when you're not the Vanisher. Dae has Punisher. Even Daddy has the Judge. I think I deserve something more than hacker..."

Their conversation faded to the background as Daddy spoke in my ear.

"Can you be ready in five minutes? I'm almost there."

I held my breath. It wouldn't surprise me if Daddy had waited until he was almost here to call, to minimize the opportunity for me to change my mind. Not with how our relationship had devolved over the last month.

"Yes, I'll meet you out front." I hung up, and stepped up next to Fletcher. He stopped his rant mid-sentence to give me every piece of his focus. "I love you. And I expect you to be at our house safe and sound when I'm done with Daddy."

His cerulean gaze softened as did his mouth. "I love you too. I'm not a fighter, but I'd give Ratio a run for his money if he tried to prevent me from coming back to you."

"I resent all this doubt about my character," Ratio grumbled as he removed the plastic from the man's head.

Fletcher and I each smiled, but kept our gazes locked.

"I still owe you a reward," I whispered, my voice husky.

"Drew," Fletcher groaned. "You're giving me a chubby and leaving me here with the Vanisher. I don't see good things."

I chuckled and raised up on my toes to kiss the corner of his mouth. As I pulled away, he wrapped an arm tight around my back and crushed me against his chest. His tongue flicked against my lips, the warm metal ball teasing me. He ended with a chaste peck, and slowly lowered me to my feet.

"This is a good sign. Daddy isn't so bad. And I know he

loves you," he whispered, pressing one more kiss to my forehead. "I'll see you when you get home."

Ratio had made himself scarce during our kiss, and I didn't see him on my way out. I didn't have any time to think about where he'd gone, because as soon as I stepped outside, Daddy was idling at the curb.

I slipped the gloves off my hands and into my pockets on my way down the walk to where he waited. The ubiquitous dark sedan with the tinted windows wouldn't stand out *anywhere*. Well, maybe on a farm, but we weren't on a farm.

After sliding into the passenger seat, I buckled the seat belt immediately because Daddy was already pulling away. "David's a couple of states away," he said without any preamble. "Yes, I waited until now to tell you. This is for us, Vienna. No one else."

"They can track me," I reminded him even as I pulled out the phone to send a message.

"I can still hear you too," Fletcher said via my earpiece. "I've got a lock on your phone, and you. Be safe, my sexy death angel."

"You too," I murmured in response before I turned off the earpiece. Sliding a glance at Daddy, I wondered if this was time for a conversation. He nudged up the radio and I sighed.

We didn't stop except for gas and bathroom breaks. When Daddy told me to sleep so I could take over driving, I obeyed. It was how we'd operated once I learned to drive. Each stop, I checked my messages and sent Rick an emoji. He would appreciate it.

Cash's messages were packed with a lot more violence and ire. He was *not* happy to be missing this excursion, but Rick was not persuaded that they needed to force themselves along, so he would give me this time.

I adored his irascible nature and cranky temper. On the road, I rested or Daddy did. He also grabbed food at some of the stops, eating more than I'd seen him consume since he came back.

How long had David starved him?

An hour out from the GPS-marked destination, Daddy touched my arm. "Wake up, Sweet Girl. We're going to get coffee and then we're going to plan."

The ease in his voice, the natural cadence was back. Anger still simmered beneath the surface of every word, but this was so Daddy it wasn't funny. We stopped at a little place on a side street with picnic tables outside for eating.

Over pancakes and coffee, Daddy outlined the plan. Uncle David had built himself a home, one he kept off the books and in a name he was convinced no one knew.

"He used to get drunk when we were younger. We both did. At least until I realized how loose it made your tongue," Daddy explained. That in and of itself was bizarre. Daddy barely drank. My love of wine had developed thanks to Mart. "He told me his real name once, but I don't think he ever remembered doing it."

But Daddy hadn't forgotten. "Did you search on it before?"

"Yes," he said. "Never thought about looking at a residential house purchase." He shrugged. "Unimportant now. This was a bolt hole, a safety net, a place to go to unplug himself from the Network."

To hide.

"Are we sure he's there?"

Daddy nodded once. "I'm sure, but we'll verify before we go in...we don't have time to build a whole operation. He has good instincts and he has to know I'm coming."

Which meant, we had to go in hard and hit hard.

"Just tell me what you need me to do," I said. As much as I wanted to make David bleed for what he'd done to Daddy and to me... I could live with enjoying it vicariously. Daddy deserved dibs on him.

We just had to make it *hurt*.

————

The house was secluded, but closer to town than we'd ever wanted for our homes. In a way, it was beautifully done. The town also gave off the vibe that no one cared what you did, as long as you returned the favor.

Surprisingly, Daddy turned onto his private driveway. When I sent him a questioning look, he said, "He would have surveillance set up around the house and property. He'd have far too much time to prepare against us if we tripped a sensor while coming in on foot."

I nodded, that made sense.

"When I park, go to the front door. I'll go to the back. This house only has two exits and we can cover both."

As soon as he threw the gear in park, I jumped out while the car still jolted from the forced stop.

The house was quiet as I ran up the steps, but Uncle David had to know we were here, just as Daddy said. It wasn't a big house by any means, maybe a thousand to fifteen hundred square feet. I gave Daddy fifteen seconds to get to the back door, then I kicked in the front, taser raised.

That had been our weapon of choice going in. Uncle David would have something much much stronger, but we didn't want to shoot to kill. We wanted to incapacitate to *hurt*.

Uncle David ran toward the door, gun pointed.

I was already dropping as he fired. A bullet went over my head, and I shot the taser as the door rebounded and hit me in the shoulder. I ignored the pain.

The darts stuck in his upper thigh, and he jerked and shot the ceiling again. Short noises escaped his throat as he dropped to his knees and face planted on the floor.

Daddy strolled down the hallway, holding his own taser while I kicked away the gun.

"I'll lock the doors while you get Uncle David secure."

Daddy nodded, and I quickly cleared the house and confirmed the windows were locked, then the doors.

When I came back, Daddy had Uncle David tied to the kitchen table. Uncle David was tall, as tall or taller than Cash, and to see his head and feet hanging off the ends would seem very uncomfortable.

Perfect.

He groaned while Daddy worked his way around the kitchen, checking cabinets and pulling basics out for easy access.

Salt. Vinegar. A meat pulverizer.

When pushed for time, Daddy was an expert at extracting pain with bare essentials. And no one deserved the pain more than Uncle David for what he did to us.

I walked around the table to get a good look at him.

This had to be the real him. He was bald, with only quickly graying brown hair around the sides. His nose was much thinner than I'd ever seen, and his chin pointier. All things that would be easily changed with stage makeup and toupees.

His skin was also much smoother than I'd ever seen. I wouldn't be surprised if he used some type of glue over his face and body to induce wrinkles.

Uncle David really was a master of disguise to make it seem so genuine to the public. That being said, people as a rule didn't pay attention to those who weren't part of their circle. And the unfortunate and homeless? They completely avoided looking at them all together. It had been one of the reasons he loved that particular disguise so much.

"Are you done with your inspection, Sweet Girl?" Daddy's voice held a hint of amusement as he faced me.

A smile broke free as nostalgia hit me square in the chest. This was how it had been when he'd first started training me on the more physical jobs.

"I'm done, but we still have at least five minutes before he's back with us."

Daddy gave me a considering look then back at David. "You're right. Get the plastic from the garage. We have time to do this like I've been considering for the last two years."

Considering was as close to fantasizing as Daddy ever got. In the garage, I found the plastic and a battery charger—with new clamps. When I brought all of it back in, I swore Daddy's grin spread a notch wider.

"Hook him up, Sweet Girl. We don't want him to miss anything."

Uncle David woke up with a pained and pitiful yowl. Granted, I didn't actually touch his junk. In my absence, however, Daddy had stripped Uncle David down to just his briefs, leaving all his pale white skin on display.

He seemed... smaller. Somehow, lesser.

But when I touched the battery clamps to his thigh, singed hair, burnt skin, and the pungent hint of urine filled the air.

Jerking his eyes wide, David glared at me. His eyes were like two empty pits of darkness. Like the predator he was though, he slid a look toward Daddy and then all pretense disappeared from his expression.

"I knew the day she found you that it was over," David said with a harsh coughing laugh.

"Then this won't be a surprise," Daddy said a moment before he snipped off the end of one of his fingers. Pain rippled over his face, but David controlled his reaction—for three more fingers.

Then he screamed.

They always screamed.

When Daddy had finished removing his fingers one joint at a time, he paused for a drink of water while we waited for David to resume consciousness again. When he did, his eyes were wild and spittle flew from his lips.

"What do you want?" Pretense wasn't possible, based on the agony in his tone.

"As usual, this is when bargaining begins," Daddy told me. "In twenty years, bargaining always comes when the denial begins to fray. Soon, desperation will lead to insults, hoping to incite an angry response that will end their pain sooner."

"But that's an amateur's reaction."

It was the correct response and Daddy nodded approvingly. "We're not amateurs."

"No, sir," I said with my own slow smile before we both looked at David "We're not."

"Ladybug… there's so much you don't know."

"Maybe," I said with a half-shrug. "What I do know is that my daddy hunts the monsters. Even the ones who try to look like us."

Especially the ones who tried to look like us. Daddy waited for me to take a step back as he weighed the meat pulverizer. "Rest assured, David," Daddy informed him. "This is going to hurt you far more than it is me."

VIENNA

UNCLE DAVID... David was dead. A part of me might always think of him as my uncle, but the rest of me understood exactly what kind of a predator he'd been. A predator who'd hidden right in front of us, masking everything about himself.

A true psychopath. I remained one of his *only* regrets? I didn't scoff, but my skin did crawl. Daddy had let him rant when the words came, but David made no apologies or excuses. While I'd kept my word and let Daddy handle everything, I was more than grateful to have been present.

I wouldn't have believed his breakdown if I hadn't witnessed it for myself. He suffered from a total lack of remorse, but I was his one regret... I was having real issues with that statement.

"Stop, my sweet girl," Daddy said as he wiped his freshly washed hands. We still had a body to deal with, but he'd changed, disposing of his blood-soaked clothes and washing up once we finished.

I spared Daddy a glance and frowned.

"There's no way you could have known. He fooled me for more years than I care to count." The flat tones carried an unusual element for Daddy—hurt. "I always thought of him as the perfect ally and partner. He was a good teacher for you. The skills he perfected that you took to so easily..."

Daddy shook his head.

"Mistakes were made, sweet girl. But they weren't all made by you."

That almost pulled a smile from me. Almost. Lips quirked, I raised my brows. "I should have questioned him when he told me you were dead."

Rather than react coldly, Daddy shifted his stance and studied me for a long moment. "Let's get ready to clean this up, then will you tell me?"

A request, not an order. Hope surged around my battered and bruised heart. "Yes. Will you tell *me* what happened?"

Disappointment swelled at the lack of immediate response. But we'd been walking carefully around each other, so I bit back the hurt and waited as he considered the corpse waiting for us to deal with it.

David was dead. The only thing we had left to do was dispose of his remains and maybe, just maybe, begin to knit our relationship together again.

"You need to know?" The question held no elements of judgment or anger. If anything, he sounded like he really needed the answer.

"I could make my peace with never knowing." I could. It was possible. A person could do anything. "I want to know though. I want...I want to know how you were taken away because if something like this happens again... I need to know I can be more effective than I was this time."

Bitterness salted that wound. More than a year I'd truly mourned him while I hunted for someone who'd been right in front of me. I'd focused so hard on that loss, on the pain, I failed.

Daddy was right, I knew better. I should have done better.

"Sweet Girl, he fooled us both." Even his choice of words held solidarity. He glanced at the body. "Do you want to do the dismemberment or the disinfection?"

"I'll clean, you cut."

And like that, we both had tasks. "Back here in ten," he

said, before we split up. I had to go back to the car for the scrubs and plastic suits to wear.

Dismemberment was messy business, but if you gave the body some time, it was at least not as likely to spray blood everywhere. You actually needed a pumping heart for that kind of pressure.

Outside, I took a deep breath of cooler air before gathering what we needed. David had chosen this location well. We could *hear* the highway, but it wasn't visible beyond the trees. The foliage here was dense, hiding everything from homes to full shopping centers.

This could be a good area for relocating. The weather was cool, the green beautiful, and there was the promise of real seasons in the air. I'd have to talk to the boys about it.

Speaking of the loves of my life, I sent a message to let them know Daddy and I were fine. The drive through Wyoming had been particularly harrowing in the middle of the night with the raging storm.

Harrowing, but worth it.

Daddy and I hadn't worked a job together in almost three years. Four, if I were being honest. I hadn't realized how used to my independence I'd become or how much distance had opened between us—until it came to the work itself.

There, we slipped into the roles he'd carved out for us over the years. He was my daddy again and we went after the monsters. David had been the biggest and the worst monster ever…because he was the kind of monster we'd trusted, and it had taken us too long to see what he'd become.

Cash wanted to know when I'd be back and I told him I'd let them know when we were on our way back and that I loved him. His response was immediate. Where was I and could they come here?

He sounded like Cash. I just said for him to behave and he could spank me later. For now, though, I needed the time with Daddy. He was still typing when I closed the phone and turned it off. I didn't mind if they tracked me, but I also knew that my message would keep them at a distance so Daddy and I could work this out.

I missed him.

This was a second chance to have him back in my life. We'd changed...both of us. But he wanted my story and he said he'd tell me his.

Back inside, I found he'd already begun taking David apart. I moved to another area to begin cleaning up the blood. "When was the last time we had to do a full site clean?"

"Six years ago," Daddy answered in a crisp tone.

"The runner," I said with a nod as I glanced over at him. "I'd almost forgotten that."

A faint smile touched his lips. "You were perfect that day."

Perfect.

Warmth flooded me at the pride and approval in his tone.

"I didn't want to let you take that job," he said. "I had a bad feeling about it."

"So you insisted we would do it together and you would be my assistant." Daddy had been very particular on that job. "I thought it was just a teachable moment."

"It was," he said, pausing the bone saw to meet my gaze. "It was also to protect my little girl. Jobs...jobs don't always go the way we want them to go. We can plan. We can prepare. We can perform. But what we can't do is always account for the x variable. That job had a bad feel to it and I needed you to come home."

I dropped my chin to my chest, eyes blinking rapidly to hold back the tears that burned. I soaked in those words like the parched land gulps the rain. "Then you didn't come home from a job..."

Melancholy flooded me as that memory swelled up. The bleakness and the silence. Trying to tell Daddy all of that, the feelings I'd barely understood, to the choices I made to continue the work.

For the next hour, I detailed those first few weeks. From what David told me, to what he offered, to what I did.

"Wait," Daddy said as he sealed the last tub with David's torso in it. The head went into a different container. "You finished all of the Bridges business?"

"Yes," I told him. "All five participants of the Bridges' County social worker scam have been located and dealt with. None of the bodies will appear."

There was no need to inform the world of their crime to try and make it right. Everyone knew what they did, but missteps in the investigation had led to a hung jury and they weren't sure they could re-prosecute.

They'd sold children. Sold adoption and foster placement for a percentage of the state's money. Kids had starved, been shoved into closets to live, and in far too many cases, left to die. It had never been about caring for the kids. It had been purely about profit.

Their deaths had been perfect for gluttons. I'd even managed to arrange one so that a cartel took care of it. Not exactly Daddy's style but I wanted them to suffer the appropriate punishment but at the same time, I wanted to get back to finding who killed Daddy.

While I finished detailing those, Daddy studied me for the entirety of it. He didn't interrupt or shift expressions. When I was done, he nodded slowly.

"Creative. Deliberate. Detailed in as much as you varied causes and disposal. The cartel was not something I would have done," he admitted the last but didn't sound upset about it at all. In fact, he seemed bemused. "Interesting choice."

"Effective. Not one I might rush to do again, if only because trusting others to do the work isn't always advisable."

A faint, but real smile touched his lips. "That's my girl."

More praise in such a short window of time? It was intoxicating. Pushing on, I told him about meeting Rick. His reaction to Rick "saving me" was to just nod slowly. Eventually, I told him about Fletcher. The work. The jobs I did in between, and finally, Cash coming into my life.

"I really don't like that you're so tied up on him," Daddy told me. "He had a life that revolved around hunting people like us."

"Did he?" I challenged. "You were apparently working with his father *and* you said you sent Ratio to him."

Daddy frowned.

"You want to know what I think?" I'd had time to think about it over the last few weeks. Not waiting for Daddy to answer, I plunged ahead. "I think his father approved of your work but he couldn't overtly approve of it. So, he protected you and when you realized what he was doing, you reached out..."

Daddy's eyes narrowed.

"Never owe a debt, even if the man doesn't know you owe it."

A long sigh escaped him. "His father wasn't a bad man. He wanted the monsters in jail or in the ground. But for every one he caught, there were dozens out there that got away."

"So a relationship was born, but not one where you ever directly told each other anything. You worked off trust—and misdirection." When Daddy didn't deny it, I lifted my shoulders. "Cash and I want more than that. He has been looking for you his whole life, he thought you were his father's great white whale."

"Moby Dick," Daddy sneered, but there was a faint humor to it. "If you like forceful men, Sweet Girl, Dae and Horatio are more than capable..."

"Daddy," I scolded and he sighed. "I don't want your proteges. You don't want me to have them, otherwise you wouldn't have kept them a secret from me all these years."

"I never wanted you with anyone, Sweet Girl," he said. "I hate the idea of them even thinking about touching you."

"You're going to have to get past that. After all, if I can root for you and Mart..."

He frowned. "What about Mart?"

"Daddy, she's never just been one of the Network. You've always cared for her, even when you didn't want to show it." The one time I could remember Mart being bruised up when we went to see her, Daddy had gone frigid. He asked for a name, told me to stay with her and for us to look after each other, and he'd gone.

No doubt existed in me about what he did.

"She's your mother," he said gruffly. "This isn't a conversation we need to have."

"Well, I'll stay out of your love life and you stay out of mine." Although I didn't want to detract from the fresh warmth and humor between us, I couldn't let it go unsaid. "And it's your turn to tell me what happened."

With a glance to where I was using the peroxide to clear away the blood from the edges of the plastic, he sighed, "Sweet Girl, I trust Dae and Horatio."

"And I trust my guys, Daddy. Don't make me choose."

"No," he said slowly. "I wouldn't...not when you already have." There was a sadness there, one he couldn't quite hide, but I suppose that was more about not being able to make decisions for me anymore than anything else. "Very well... let's finish this up. David... David's fall from grace began for me when you were fourteen and he wanted to use pictures of you to lure out a predator..."

That was new. "Wait, the pictures from when I was ten? Or nine?" I'd been painfully young in those images on Dion's computer and I had no idea where they came from. Not when we first found them. Now? Well, I knew the man Daryawesh took them.

"Yes," Daddy growled. "Photos he found somehow. I

never knew how he did that or who took them... at least until recently. I managed to stop him on that one, but it was just the first in an endless list of jobs that began to edge past our boundaries, when it became about killing people for money and not for justice."

I paused with him on that one. We weren't assassins. We weren't murder for hire. You couldn't just *ask* us to kill someone. Mart, occasionally, pointed us toward someone who did need to be dealt with. There was transport work...

"So, the night of your job?"

"I'd set a trap for David, I didn't trust his information and I wanted to see what he'd do. The problem with the trap was he'd anticipated it. I woke up two days later in an underground cell with no appreciable entrances or exits. David spoke to me over a radio..."

He announced a challenge for Daddy, one where he would convert Daddy to a new system of beliefs. While he worked on him, he would also work on me. I was the more malleable after all, and now vulnerable, with Daddy's absence.

I wanted to kill David all over again. He'd leveraged me against Daddy to keep him compliant. He'd leveraged Daddy's death to make me continue to rely on him...

"Only it didn't work, I never fully trusted his information or what he wanted me to do. I also wouldn't let him help me." It would have made sense, but I'd kept him at arm's length. "Then I didn't need him, because I had my guys."

"Tell me about Sandra Jane."

David told him I'd killed her at his command and for no other reason. "I made a mistake with her..." I began. The mistake of believing she was exactly as she appeared. I hadn't seen the trap before it closed over me.

When I detailed my own incarceration, while editing some of the more painful details, I held Daddy's gaze.

"She left me no choice. I didn't want to kill her, but she had no intention of letting me walk free. She wanted to punish her father's killer, something I understood all too intimately."

Finally done, I carried one of the buckets of hot water over to dump on the space, Daddy followed with one of his own. Between us, we cleaned up all remnants of biological matter, and bagged up the rest.

"If she hadn't pushed you at the end," Daddy said. "If she'd agreed to stop…would you have let her live?"

I hadn't wanted to kill her, but I couldn't leave her out there as a threat to haunt our every step. "If it had just been about me," I admitted. "I like to think I would have."

When he gripped one edge of a tub, I got the other. There were five of them. Each packed tight. We needed to deliver them to Reuben, and he would take it from there. He was back from his "vacation."

"You know," Daddy said. "Dae has…"

I paused to stare at him and he sighed.

"What if I go out with Mart? Would that persuade you to give one of them a try?"

"No."

He nodded.

"No accidents for them?"

"No."

"That's what I thought."

"Daddy, you like Fletcher and Rick."

"That might be too strong a word," he argued.

I laughed. He let Fletcher call him Daddy, and he'd eaten Rick's food on his last visit.

"Come to dinner," I invited him. "Come and get to know them."

We lifted the first tub into the van and he grunted. "I might never like them," he warned me. "But I can accept that they are what you want."

I smiled.

"If they ever hurt you…"

"I'll take care of them and they'll take care of me." Then, on impulse, I wrapped my arms around him. "I promise, Daddy. They love me and I love them."

After the briefest of pauses, he returned the embrace. When he pressed his lips to the top of my head, I almost lost all sense of cool. After one more squeeze, I made myself let him go.

"You'll come to dinner?" I said when we returned to the interior to grab the next tub.

He sighed, then inclined his head with a smile. "Yes, Sweet Girl. I'll come to dinner."

CASH

I ROLLED my cell between my hands as I sat in the gym. It wasn't unusual for me to come grab a quick workout while everyone was otherwise engaged, but today, I had an ulterior motive, and it chapped my ass.

A drip of sweat landed on the floor next to my foot, telling me to hurry the fuck up.

I had run over five miles on the treadmill at a fast pace just to clear my mind, and now that I was sitting here, I was working myself up all over again.

There was no question that this had to be done. The issue however, was who would be the best person to help me. I didn't fucking like it one bit.

But the reward…the reward would be so *sweet*.

I'd initially thought about asking Thad. He had the right resources, the motivation to help me get the job done, if only to protect Vienna, but the asshole that he was, I had a feeling he'd only point me in this direction anyway.

Thad also hadn't made any fucking fans with me. Vienna had seemed to make her peace with his decisions, but I hadn't. How could a father, the center of his little girl's universe, treat her the way he had when she quite literally saved his ass? I didn't get it. If we ever had any girls, shit, if we ever had any kids at all, I'd show Thad how a father was supposed to treat the ones he loved.

Biting the bullet, I dialed the number saved in this burner.

During all the cleaning up, Fletcher had given the seven of us burners with each other's numbers programmed in.

"Cash, I have to say, this is a plot twist I didn't expect." Ratio's humor grated down the back of my neck and I ground my teeth.

"Ratio, I need a favor."

I could practically feel his excitement through the phone. "Funny you should call. I just had an interesting conversation with Vienna. You see, I'd love an invite to dinner, and I'm willing to accept that as payment for a *favor*."

"You don't even know what the favor is."

He chuckled. "True, but I'm sure it's something I can deliver."

I blew out a breath and scrubbed a hand down my face. This was something that needed to be done with a delicate hand. Except, I didn't want this fucker at the table with me.

His breathing filled my ear as I studied myself in the mirror. I didn't think I was a man who was too full of himself to see the bigger picture. And the bigger picture was everything in this case.

"One dinner," I ground out. "One dinner only. I don't like you, so don't think this will become a regular occurrence just because you have Thad's approval."

"I accept. Now, what was the favor?" He was far too upbeat. Over the years, I'd learned many different sides to the Accountant. This was a new one.

"I need to disappear. And leave a body behind to officially die."

"You already have someone in mind?"

I stretched my feet out and leaned back on the bench. "As a matter of fact, I do."

Rick and I had been combing through the files of targets. It was harder than I had hoped it would be, but we finally settled on a man who was of similar height, build, and a waste of fucking space.

"Timing?"

"Today."

No hesitation on his end. "I have something I'm wrapping up now, but we can meet this afternoon. Do you have a plan, or is that what you needed me for?"

"A little of both." I had what I thought was a damn good plan, but this was too important to fuck up.

"Got it. Call me when you leave so we can set a meeting location…Unless you'd like for me to come pick you up?"

That was a hell no. "I'll send you meeting details." I hung up.

I pocketed the phone and closed up the gym, cleaning it to Rick's standards. There wasn't much time before I needed to leave, and part of that would be explaining to Vienna I was going to be unavailable for the next day or so.

Then I saw Thad waiting on his porch as I exited. The fact that he had eyes on this door exactly, and started heading my way, was a clear sign that he was waiting for me.

I met him halfway, and all he said was, "Walk with me."

So, we started taking a stroll around the neighborhood. I didn't say anything as we left the residential street and headed down a runner's path. Fuck that, if he wanted to chat, he could start the conversation. By now, we were far enough away from the subdivision that Vienna couldn't see or hear us. If she knew I had left at all.

Thad had his hands loose at his sides as he watched the branches sway in the wind. He took a deep inhale and let it out. This was something I imagined he did often after we released him.

"I don't like you," he started.

Stopping and facing him, I shrugged, even as he matched me and our gazes locked. "That's no skin off my back. I don't like you either."

"But I did like and respect your father," he continued as if I hadn't said anything.

Was this supposed to be some kind of approval conversation? I didn't need it. Vienna didn't either.

"My father knew who you were." It was a statement.

He shrugged. "If he did, he never said, but some of the things he managed to sweep under the rug made me think he did know."

I shook my head. "I neither care nor need to have this information. What's in the past is in the past. I think we both know where my future is."

He regarded me with a dead neutral face. Except the slight tic next to his eye and along his temple gave him away. Thad didn't like that his daughter was my future. Too fucking bad.

"I see a lot of Casey in you, but then again, I don't. It must be your mother's side."

I bristled. My mother was no kind of mother, and definitely not a wife. Forcing myself to relax, I released a long puff of air. "What you're doing, it's not going to work. You can't get a rise out of me to make me out to be a bad man. You don't need to do that at all." A ghost of a smile flitted over my lips. "Any time you hurt Vienna, I will happily teach you a lesson. Any time you want to spar, I'll be there in two seconds flat."

Thad laughed, the sound dry. "I didn't ask you to walk with me to insult you or pick a fight. This is an olive branch, boy. Vienna has made her choice, and before I sit down to a dinner with your...family," he stumbled over the word like sour eggs, "I wanted to clear the air."

"By telling me you don't like me and I'm like my mother?" I raised an eyebrow.

He smirked and a twinkle entered his tawny eyes. "I never said I was good at this. I deal in truths, and where you're concerned, those are mine."

As long as he didn't fuck up again, he and Vienna were on the clear path to repairing their relationship. I wouldn't stand in the way of that. Neither would Rick or Fletcher. Hell, I think they all even liked each other.

I was okay with being the voice of reason.

"You want to call a truce? Fine, then answer me this. Why did you keep Vienna out of so much before you disappeared? Because she didn't know she had to suspect David, she could have played right into his hands. You caused that. You put her in a vulnerable position."

The humor fled to be replaced by weary acceptance. "I did. Maybe you'll understand one day, and maybe you won't, but everything I did was to protect her. She cared for David because I had let her. I wanted to take care of him and clean it up before she ever found out about it. To lessen the pain she would never have let me see."

I nodded. Understandable. I didn't like it, but I could understand it. "And how you treated her like a pariah after we found you?"

Instead of getting angry, like I had predicted, he sighed. "First, I want to say, this is none of your business. I don't owe an explanation to you or anyone else about my actions. Except for Vienna. But, I will say, I'm human. I didn't want to believe David had gotten a hold of my girl, and the more distance I put between us, the less it would be staring me in the face. On the off chance that he had lied to me, I didn't want to put her in harm's way."

He was trying to extend another olive branch by explaining that. If I would have confronted him weeks ago, he would have tried to go for my throat.

"I can accept that. You fucked up, but I can see why you would do that." I glanced back toward the house and offered my own olive branch. "I love her more than anything. She's my soulmate, and there's nothing anyone can do to change that. I would tear down the world to keep her. And I will kick my own ass before I hurt her. You don't have to worry about her when she's with me."

When I met his gaze, he regarded me with a new light in his eyes. I wouldn't call it appreciation, or even budding respect. It seemed like if he couldn't pick her partner for her, he was happy she had one that would do anything, kill anyone, to keep her safe.

She has three of us. Even if Rick and I would take care of all the killing for Fletcher too.

As a father, what more could he ask for?

———

"Mom, I can't talk right now. I just wanted to give you a call and check in so you wouldn't be worried." Ratio and I watched my doppelgänger climb into a rental car that he'd tampered with. In the mountains, the guard rails were a suggestion instead of a safeguard. He wouldn't be able to stop himself from crashing over the mountain side as he made his way up to his mistress's place.

"Cash! The FBI are looking for you! And the police. What have you done?" She was only concerned about how this would look to her friends that the police were banging down her door for information. Mom didn't give a flying fuck about me.

"Nothing, mom. Listen, I have to go. I'll check in again soon." I hung up and glanced at Ratio, who was on the phone with Fletcher.

"Perfect," his voice crackled over the cheap phone speaker. "That was long enough for them to ping you to this general location. I have the recorded footage of you getting in the car moved up to this timeframe so police will see you getting in the car instead of numbnuts."

"What about his location?" I asked, propping my arm over the steering wheel.

"Already taken care of. He has several purchases happening across the country, you know, where he's actually supposed to be right now. He'll disappear for good on his way home."

"Thanks, Fletcher." Ratio hung up. "Shall we?"

"Yep." We pulled on the road and followed the car as it left town. There was enough brake fluid left that he would make it almost to the top of the mountain.

Just like we planned, he turned on the highway traveling up the mountain. It was good luck that it had rained earlier, making the roads slick.

"You know, the actual killing isn't in my repertoire." Ratio kept his eyes on the brake lights in front of us.

"No, I can do that part. Yours is to make sure he can't be recognized or DNA-tested afterwards."

"He should be losing his brakes right about…now."

The car started to swerve, speeding on this temporary downslope. We slowed, waiting to make sure he was going to go over instead of crash against the rock.

"Three, two…one," Ratio said under his breath as the car slammed into the metal guard rail, breaking through and rolling down the mountain. He pushed a button on his phone, and the boom preceded the wave of heat and smoke by a few seconds.

"You're sure this will take care of it?" I asked, rolling by the scene. Not too slow, just enough to see it for a few seconds. I picked up speed once I could no longer see the fire.

"The bomb was comprised of natural flammable ingredients. The impact of the car crushed the gas tank, adding fuel to the fire, no pun intended." He smirked. "And the seats were recently heavily coated with a sealant that is also incredibly flammable. He's going to burn so hot, his body will disintegrate. There will be nothing left to test. What could be there would be contaminated. But don't worry, I'll come back after you drop me off to make sure."

I laughed. When I had been making plans for this exact moment, I didn't think it would feel any different. Except, it did. I was free in a way I'd never been before. Free from the shackles of society. Free to live my life as I saw fit with Vienna, Rick, and Fletcher. Free to continue work that mattered.

Rolling down the window, I continued to laugh as we drove to the drop off destination.

———

"A picture? Really?"

"What?" It had been three days since we had burned down the remnants of Cash Morgan. My death had been running on all the national news stations, with heavy speculation on why I was missing in the first place or what crimes I had been trying to escape.

To tidy up all the loose ends, I called Krystle. Through my career with the Bureau, she was the only one I trusted. She had never turned me in, even with the many rules I had broken through the years. I owed it to her to give her the truth after she helped us pin down the Red Death network. Vienna even trusts her now...as much as Vienna trusts anyone outside of her family.

But then she threw me off balance as soon as I identified myself.

"The scene was pure ash. Nothing left except melted tires and a few rusty chunks of the car that broke off on the way down the mountain. But there was a picture of you right on top of the ash. It was old. Maybe from a couple years ago, while on that job in Florida."

I didn't want to grin, I really fucking didn't, but Ratio was genius. That was a sure-fire way they'd believe I was dead. Not to mention his big reveal, the crafty bastard. I had no idea he was the Vanisher. Course, after Fletcher figured out he was the source of the electronic surveillance, we'd saved his life by *not* telling Vienna and he'd sworn that once we'd moved in, he stopped listening. I didn't really care if he listened except for the invasion of her privacy.

In our new place? We would have checks in place to make sure it never happened again.

"This is going to be short. I wanted to give you a heads up, you'll never be able to find me. But if you need anything, you know where to leave a message." I hung up, right as she started to scream down the line.

Whistling, I headed back to the house full of my family and a few unwanted guests. This was one of the last times at least two of them would know where we actually lived, so I didn't put up too much of a fuss.

It took an army to pack up a house.

VIENNA

THE DRIVE to the new house took some getting used to, especially after months of transitioning while construction was on going. We'd found the perfect location. Remote, but not so remote we couldn't get to town or go on supply runs.

It was on an island, but not a "true" island. Still, the ingress and egress points included bridges, ferries, and some backroads to follow the land back to where the peninsula jutted off from the mainland.

To be fair, we all loved the location and the house. Even more, we loved the "neighborhood" which in and of itself consisted of fixer uppers. Houses we'd purchased so we would own them all. In addition to the twenty-five acres that came with our house…it was our own little oasis.

Dae had offered to buy the land and the homes behind a series of shells, but it was Fletcher who negotiated every-thing. I had to admit, him handling financial matters, as well as burying all the paperwork, was just hot.

The disappointment expressed by Dae when he realized we did not *need* his assistance had been kind of sweet. While he'd been nothing but kind and direct with me, he'd been even kinder and more direct with Fletcher. I rather adored that, but then Fletcher was still calling Daddy, Daddy, and that left both Ratio *and* Dae in a little awe.

It was adorable. All Ratio requested was to be kept in the loop for the Network. This was a request I could honor, though his dinner invitation would wait until he and Cash had made some kind of peace.

As for the Network, I glanced over at the shopping bag on the passenger seat. It might take us years to clean out the Red Death stragglers. But we were making changes. The Network would be funneled through a central hub and that hub would be us—the jury.

I'd given the name some thought, it had been Cash's suggestion after a brainstorming session with Fletcher. While I'd been part of the Judge for so long, I was not the Judge. I was more a part of a jury. We would vet all our targets as we had been. Fletcher had mastered the files and he had so many targets, we'd be applying for retirement before we were done.

Daddy was more than happy to stay out of it unless I wanted his advice. He had his own work to do, and life to rebuild. Mart and I had taken to talking once a week on the phone. There was an ache where her friendship used to be. Rick said to give her time, and I agreed with him.

She said Daddy had come around to apologize. I didn't know if they would ever be more than they were, but a girl could hope. My lips curved higher, I really could hope.

Rick, Fletcher, and Cash had taught me to hope, to treasure, and to desire. That I could *want* more and I could *have* more.

The best part of our new house was the double-ovens in the kitchen. The house always smelled fantastic when I came home from a job. We'd have wine, sit down for a meal, catch up on the latest with each other before we moved to the movie room, where Fletcher would bring us up to speed on who was moving and shaking in the Network.

While no system was perfect, ours would no longer allow depravity to just slink into the corners and operate on the fringes. Criminal behavior was fine, people were going to lie, to cheat, and to steal. People might even be killed, the way the game was played.

But there was a difference between someone in the business and an innocent. No one in our network was allowed to harm, abuse, or use innocents. The bounties on outstanding members of the Red Death network brought us in a bit of work here and there, but for the most part... we were settled into this life and I couldn't love it more.

Didn't mean I didn't like to get my hands dirty, but if we could ensure the integrity of the Network, maybe we wouldn't have to deal with another Red Death tainting the well.

The door to the house opened as I pulled into the garage. There was a workout area right here, but another fuller gym, in the house next door. We'd added a fully padded room so that Cash and I could really work out our aggression when we needed it.

The padding had come in handy more than once. Rick smiled at me as I climbed out of the car. "I know," I said. "I told you I would be back at lunch, but I had drinks with Ratio to go over more of the bookkeeping. He refuses to pass anything to Fletcher without me seeing it all first."

"He likes the excuse for spending time with you," Rick said, brushing a kiss to my cheek as he took one of the shopping bags. "Did you find the wine you wanted?"

"I did," I said. "But we won't need it tonight. It should be chilled and Cash called me earlier, he said he has a new case for us to review tonight."

Rick grinned. "Good. It's been a couple of months since we had something to sink our teeth into."

Excitement threaded through me. "I'm glad that I'm not the only one jazzed for this."

He chuckled, leading me inside and pausing only to put the wine away and then motioned to the other bottle he already had out. "Do you want that first? Or are you taking Fletcher his shirt first?"

I hugged the second bag to me. "I got shirts for all of us."

"I approve. Give me mine and I'll wear it for dinner."

That was a stellar idea. I handed him his, stealing a kiss as I went, before I headed down the hall to Fletcher's executive man-cave. It was down a set of steps since our house was literally built into a hill.

I knocked on the open door and stuck my head in. Sometimes when Fletcher got too deep in the work, he forgot everything, but there was a display on the wall that was counting down the minutes.

Spinning away from the computer screen, Fletcher grinned at me. "You're early."

"Was that clock for me?" I nodded to the wall and he shook his head.

"Nope, that's when I have to shower because Rick won't let me eat at the table if I smell." He made a show of sniffing his armpits. "I don't think I'm that bad."

Chuckling, I crossed over to where he sat and straddled his lap. "I don't think you're bad at all, but I'm glad I got here *before* your shower. I got you a present."

"Oh, Drew, I have everything with you...I don't need presents." Then his eyes practically danced. "But I damn sure love getting them."

Amused, I passed him the bag and he opened it up without any coy show of modesty. When he dragged out the dark gray shirt stamped with two words on the front, his grin took my breath away.

"Hell yes, we're Team Drew." He wrapped a hand around my nape and tugged me forward for a kiss. "Want to take a shower with me?"

"We'll be late for dinner," I warned, but Fletcher was already rising and I locked my legs around his hips.

"Then we'll shower real quick like..."

"I've turned it down to stay warm," Rick called as Fletcher carried me up the stairs to the living room and then to the next set of stairs. "But Cash is running about thirty minutes behind, so you might get her all to yourself if you're efficient."

"I can be efficient, Big Guy. Give us fifteen and then come join us."

A swirl of desire had my stomach bottoming out. Desire and happiness. I cupped Fletcher's face and rained kisses down on him as he carried me up to our bedroom. It took up half the top floor and the bed was out of this world. Even better…they all shared it with me.

No one slept alone. No one was left behind.

When I started this journey, it had been with one goal and one goal only—find the man or men who'd murdered my father. It had been a twisted, winding path that took me to unexpected places inhabited by delightful men. They filled in every corner of my life with warmth, love, and passion.

Team Drew.

The Jury.

My family.

EPILOGUE

VIENNA

"I WOULD HAVE COME to the door, Sweet Girl," Daddy said as I hopped in the passenger's side of the old Prius.

"I was already outside," I leaned over and kissed his cheek. "And you should be thanking me. Rick is spring cleaning and he's got Fletcher and Cash both hard at work. If you step foot inside that door, he might put you to work."

He raised a brow.

Grinning, I snapped my seatbelt. "Rick wouldn't put you to work, but he might give you a disapproving stare to make you feel guilty."

"I doubt that," he said to the windshield as he pulled away. Tonight was our monthly father daughter dinner night. Now that we were each settled in our own lives, we didn't see each other very often. I suspected he stayed in the subdivision, even though he hadn't said. That had been his favorite of our properties.

To make sure we stayed in touch, he committed to flying out once a month to take me to dinner. For now, it would just be us. We had a lot of work to do on our relationship, but maybe sometime in the future, the guys could come every once in a while.

"You know, Fletcher said you haven't returned his calls lately."

A quirk of the lips appeared then disappeared just as fast. "I've been busy. Tell the boy to stop leaving me Daddy voice-mails. It's starting to get weird."

I laughed. "You love it, otherwise you would have stopped it the first time it slipped his lips. Admit it, Fletcher is like the son you never had."

When he only shrugged, I had to work to keep my mouth from dropping open. I expected him to say Ratio and Dae satisfied any urge he had for a son. But his lack of answer *was* answer enough with Daddy. He really liked Fletcher. He just didn't want to admit it out loud.

"You know, Rick said the next time you come over, he'll make the sticky toffee pudding you liked so much," I tossed out. The teasing smile made a brief appearance.

Ha! He liked Rick too. Biting the inside of my cheek, I racked my head for something to say about Cash, but nothing came to me. They really didn't like each other. Tolerated, yes, and maybe even respected.

It would happen. They had years to grow on each other.

"Have you spoken to Mart lately?" It was a complete change of subject, and one Daddy didn't appreciate.

"Sweet Girl," he warned.

"I was just curious," I defended, smiling out the passenger window.

Since Uncle David died, our relationship hadn't reverted to the way it had been before he was taken. Through the months, it settled into something altogether different. We still mostly talked about life lessons and jobs, sometimes some-thing frivolous, although very rare.

But now, I was truly an adult in Daddy's eyes. Standing on my own, in a committed relationship with men who loved me more than anything. It was different, but it made us closer because of the space he allowed me to be…me.

"Cash has a new method he'd like to try on the Waterton target. Have you ever heard of the Persian milk and honey technique?" The more things changed, the more they stayed the same.

***

RICK

"The mattress needs to be inspected for fluids, cleaned, and flipped. Who wants it?" They'd been good sports about helping with the spring cleaning all day. But with Vienna gone, their motivation had started to wane.

Fletcher, sprawled out on the floor in the living room, squinted at me. "Will you tell Drew I did it and was a good boy?"

I sighed as Cash stood up from the chair, stretching his arms over his head and emitting a long groan. "No worries. I'll take care of it, and I'll tell Vienna I did it myself."

"Like hell you will!" Fletcher rolled to his stomach, then hopped to his feet, but Cash was more than halfway to the door. In a last ditch effort to stop him, Fletcher tackled his legs and they both ended up on the ground.

"Why does it matter who does the chore?" I braced my hands on my hips.

"Because, Big Guy, Drew's preferred reward system is my wet dream come to life. You know this. You're always getting rewarded."

I pressed my lips together to keep the shit eating grin off my face. It wouldn't be nice to talk about Vienna that way, but at the same time, I did love getting my rewards.

"How about I find another chore, and then you each can have something to brag about?"

Cash pushed Fletcher off and stood up. "I have a better idea. Vienna has been stressing herself out about Mart's housewarming present. There's a weapon's master I met recently who creates wicked blades. Some are classy enough that Mart could disguise it in an evening gown. I'd already been thinking about commissioning something from him anyway." He brushed imaginary dirt off of his shirt. "This is a win. Vienna will love the versatility, Mart will appreciate the wealth behind it, and Thad will seethe in jealousy because he didn't think of it first." Then he walked out, pulling his phone out of his pocket.

"Ah man, that bastard. That's going to get a way better blowjob than mattress cleaning." Fletcher pouted and used the table as leverage to stand up.

"Both are important. Vienna won't favor one over the other."

It was true. Vienna never picked favorites, she never pitted us against each other. She did accept us for who we were, and supported our passions.

Our lover took care of us in all the ways we needed, and then some.

I thanked the stars every day that I found her in the alley and saved her. I still considered myself her guardian angel. And she was still the most beautiful woman I'd ever seen.

And all of us together? We just fit.

FLETCHER

"Yellow, this is Jell-O gelatin." I answered the call while spinning around in my chair. Drew stepped into my office with her brows raised. "Dae," I mouthed.

"Is this supposed to be your codename? Ratio told me you wanted one."

I frowned. His smooth, almost monotone voice killed all the fun for me. "No. I'd have a badass name. I just haven't thought of one yet." Except I was now part of Team Drew. We weren't telling people. Those kinds of names you didn't blurt out. You let them figure it out for themselves, and they'd quake in fear and maybe even piss their pants to not have realized how dangerous you were.

Although, Team Drew didn't exactly strike fear into the hearts of strangers.

In the Network though…

"I'm calling about the Network. Everything is running smoothly, except Ruben. He is an issue."

I held my arm out and Drew slid onto my lap, curling into me. Damn, it felt good to be here.

"What kind of issue? He's been vetted and never conducted any business for the Red Death network." When Drew gave me a questioning look, I mouthed 'Ruben' and put the call on speaker.

"The issue is that he has a gambling problem. He was free and clear when he was vetted, but now he's amassed a hefty debt with one of the cartel families. It's a security risk, and he needs to be off the roster."

"Dae, I'll take care of it and call you once we determine if he's staying in or not," Drew said.

Dae paused, then continued like he expected her to be able to hear him. He should, considering we were like one giant living organism. What one had, the others had, and that went for secrets too.

Drew started nibbling on my ear, and suddenly, listening to Dae wasn't so important.

"Like Drew said, we'll call you later." I hung up and leaned my head to the side to give her better access. "It's time for my reward, right? You're here because I cleaned our mattress like a good boy?"

Her husky laugh went straight to my happy man.

It was going to be a good day.

————

CASH

"Family meeting." I called through the house. I'd already told Rick and Fletcher what I was doing today. It was really only Vienna who would be surprised.

I stood by the large, open fireplace with my arms crossed as I waited for my family to come in.

One by one they appeared. Fletcher with a smirk, Rick with twinkling eyes. Vienna, my beautiful, dark saint, with a furrowed brow. She squeezed onto the couch between both men. Of course, they didn't miss the opportunity to have their hands on her in a subtle way.

"Today marks a very important day." I added gravity to my voice as I locked gazes with each of them. "Do you know what that day is?"

Fletcher and Rick stayed quiet, allowing Vienna to work this out on her own.

She glanced at each of their faces, looking for a clue, but they kept their attention on me.

"Dark Saint, no guesses?" This time, I let some of my desire for this beautiful creature seep into my tone. This wasn't a typical family meeting, after all.

"I'd like to think I'm fairly smart, but you've got me on this one." One side of her mouth curved down.

"I won't keep you in suspense then." I walked to the couch, stopping directly in front of her. Cupping her cheek, I silently groaned when she raised her gaze. Goddamn, she was so beautiful, it hurt to look at her. Those brilliant tawny eyes. They undid me every time.

"Today is the anniversary of our first job as a group. A

family. So, to celebrate, I've arranged a job for us. The Waterton target we've been watching." I let my words sink in.

After a beat of silence, her full lips split into the widest smile.

This was not a typical anniversary, but we weren't a typical family.

What we had was special, and what better way to celebrate than to do what brought us together?

Saving the innocent, and having fun while doing it.

———

You can stalk Blake in her closed reading group: Blake's Book Babes. In the BBB you can interact with her directly, find excerpts and information on upcoming releases, as well as play games and enter for giveaways.
To stalk Heather and keep up with all of her series, join her in Heather's Pack where you get all the perks of hanging out with her, play games, get sneak peeks, bonus scenes, and so much more!

AFTERWORD

Woo hoo! We did it! Confetti! Fireworks! Boom baby!

All jokes aside, thank you for reading. We love our readers and could not do what we do without you. Thank you for going on this journey with us. Thank you for loving Vienna, Rick, Fletcher, and Cash, but most of all, thank you for rooting for them.

While we're going to miss these characters.

We are so excited for what comes next.

xoxo

Heather & Blake

ABOUT HEATHER LONG

USA Today bestselling author, Heather Long, likes long walks in the park, science fiction, superheroes, Marines, and men who aren't douche bags. Her books are filled with heroes and heroines tangled in romance as hot as Texas summertime. From paranormal historical westerns to contemporary military romance, Heather might switch genres, but one thing is true in all of her stories—her characters drive the books. When she's not wrangling her menagerie of animals, she devotes her time to family and friends she considers family. She believes if you like your heroes so real you could lick the grit off their chest, and your heroines so likable, you're sure you've been friends with women just like them, you'll enjoy her worlds as much as she does.

Follow Heather & Sign up for her newsletter:
www.heatherlong.net
TikTok

ABOUT BLAKE BLESSING

Blake Blessing is no longer new on the Indie scene, but she's still ecstatic about this chapter in life. She is a mom, wife, art enthusiast, and author.

She attended ten different schools growing up, so books became her constant friend. Escaping into books of all different genres made life fun and exciting. Blake was also raised on music and still blasts it through the house and car at every opportunity.

She has a weird sense of humor and a penchant for chocolate milk. It only makes sense she would one day go on to write her own stories.

TikTok

ALSO BY HEATHER LONG

82nd Street Vandals

Savage Vandal

Vicious Rebel

Ruthless Traitor

Dirty Devil

Brutal Fighter

Dangerous Renegade

Merciless Spy

Always a Marine Series

Once Her Man, Always Her Man

Retreat Hell! She Just Got Here

Tell It to the Marine

Proud to Serve Her

Her Marine

No Regrets, No Surrender

The Marine Cowboy

The Two and the Proud

A Marine and a Gentleman

Combat Barbie

Whiskey Tango Foxtrot

What Part of Marine Don't You Understand?

A Marine Affair

Marine Ever After

Marine in the Wind

Marine with Benefits

A Marine of Plenty

A Candle for a Marine

Marine under the Mistletoe

Have Yourself a Marine Christmas

Lest Old Marines Be Forgot

Her Marine Bodyguard

Smoke & Marines

Bravo Team Wolf

When Danger Bites

Bitten Under Fire

Cardinal Sins

Kill Song

First Chorus

High Note

Last Word

Chance Monroe

Earth Witches Aren't Easy

Plan Witch from Out of Town

Bad Witch Rising

Her Elite Assets

Featuring:

Pure Copper

Target: Tungsten

Asset: Arsenic

Fevered Hearts

Marshal of Hel Dorado

Brave are the Lonely

Micah & Mrs. Miller

A Fistful of Dreams

Raising Kane

Wanted: Fevered or Alive

Wild and Fevered

The Quick & The Fevered

A Man Called Wyatt

Going Royal

Some Like It Royal

Some Like It Scandalous

Some Like It Deadly

Some Like it Secret

Some Like it Easy

Her Marine Prince

Blocked

Heart of the Nebula

Queenmaker

Deal Breaker

Throne Taker

Lone Star Leathernecks

Semper Fi Cowboy

As You Were, Cowboy

Magic & Mayhem

The Witch Singer

Bridget's Witch's Diary

The Witched Away Bride

Mongrels

Mongrels, Mischief & Mayhem

Shackled Souls

Succubus Chained

Succubus Unchained

Succubus Blessed

Shackled Souls (Omnibus)

Space Cowboy

Space Cowboy Survival Guide

Untouchable

Rules and Roses

Changes and Chocolates

Keys and Kisses

Whispers and Wishes

Hangovers and Holidays

Brazen and Breathless

Trials and Tiaras

Graduation and Gifts

Defiance and Dedication

Songs and Sweethearts

Legacy and Lovers

Farewells and Forever

Wolves of Willow Bend

Wolf at Law

Wolf Bite

Caged Wolf

Wolf Claim

Wolf Next Door

Rogue Wolf

Bayou Wolf

Untamed Wolf

Wolf with Benefits

River Wolf

Single Wicked Wolf

Desert Wolf

Snow Wolf

Wolf on Board

Holly Jolly Wolf

Shadow Wolf

His Moonstruck Wolf

Thunder Wolf

Ghost Wolf

Outlaw Wolves

Wolf Unleashed

ALSO BY BLAKE BLESSING

The Mazza Series

Marks of the Mazza

Bonds of the Mazza

Secrets of the Mazza

War of the Mazza

(Coming Late 2021)

Astrid Scott Series

Pretty Lies

Ugly Truths

Busted Dreams

Vivid Fears

Brittle Hope

Fragile Minds

Fractured

Altered

Contemporary Romance Standalone

Full Glasses and Burju Shoes

RH Standalone

Pin-up Girl